MURDER IN PASTEL

Ten years ago Cosmo Bari vanished, and with him, his legendary masterpiece, *Virgin in Pastel*. Since that day no one in the seaside art colony of Steeple Hill has heard from the eccentric painter.

Surrounded by an extended family of Cosmo's colorful compatriots, mystery writer Kyle Bari believes he has come to terms with being abandoned by his famous father, until the day Adam MacKinnon arrives with his new lover, the beautiful but poisonous, Brett.

Brett has an unerring instinct for other people's weak spots; soon the quiet colony is seething with hostility and suspicion as Brett hints he knows something about the missing artist.

Kyle doesn't take Brett seriously until the long lost *Virgin in Pastel* is discovered hidden in an antique dresser. A few days later the painting has vanished again—and Brett is dead. Murdered...

MURDER IN PASTEL
SEPTEMBER 2015
Originally published under the pen name Colin Dunne

Copyright (c) 2015 by Josh Lanyon
Cover by Johanna Ollila
Edited by Keren Reed
Book design by Kevin Burton Smith
All rights reserved

ISBN: 978-1-937909-81-9
Published in the United States of America

JustJoshin Publishing, Inc.
3053 Rancho Vista Blvd.
Suite 116
Palmdale, CA 93551
www.joshlanyon.com

This is a work of fiction. Any resemblance to persons living or dead is entirely coincidental.

MURDER IN PASTEL

JOSH LANYON

TABLE OF CONTENTS

CHAPTER ONE

Bad dreams.

Like your shadow, you never outgrow them. Waking in darkness, dry-mouthed and soaked in perspiration, heart banging away like a battered screen door…like the door to memory, blowing open then slamming back, no longer able to fasten tight…

That June morning was like all the other times. It took a moment to remember where I was: to realize that the tangle of sheets was all that held me prisoner; that the dreamed hand knocking on my window was in reality the clack of wooden blinds in the dawn breeze.

I lay there, watching the photographs on the dresser slowly materialize in the gray first light, like ghosts in the gloom. First my mother's face, then my grandfather's glowering disapproval, then my father's rare grin.

It's always the same dream. That's the one thing I do remember. The same dream which starts with a rap on the window, a soft insistent tapping—a sound that can't be ignored, like someone whispering in your ear. In my dream, I get out of bed and cross to the window.

The next thing I know, I am awake, drenched in sweat, with my heart thundering in my ears, the last terrifying images flickering through my brain: blood, a crescent moon, a woman's face painted blue.

The clock in the hall chimed once, six thirty. I threw off the quilt, found my Levi's, pulled them on.

It was cold for June. The salty bite of the damp air mingled with the perfume of flowers as I walked through the garden to the stairs leading down to the beach. I had the world to myself that gray morning, though we were past Memorial Day when the "summer folk" arrived. All down the coast highway, brightly hued umbrellas bloomed like giant flowers on decks; railings were draped with beach towels and swimsuits. Eventually the kids and dogs would find their way to our private beach. Then would follow a few weeks of the Sea and Ski crowd; of boom boxes and Frisbees and dune buggies, before our little corner of the universe was returned to us somewhat the worse for wear.

I didn't have to look across the meadow to Adam MacKinnon's cottage to know he was back; I knew, because I'd watched his headlights coming down the road last night for the first time in ten years. I'd waited to see the lights go on in his cottage and I'd watched them go off again. It had taken me a long time to fall asleep.

So it was a test of will not to look. I headed down the steps, as I had done nearly every morning of my life, bare feet scraping the sandy stone of the stairs built into the cliff.

I hit the beach and started toward the water, the pale sand squinching through my toes. I unbuttoned my jeans, *pop, pop, pop…*

A few feet from the tumbling green water, I stopped dead.

Rising out of the waves, and striding toward me, was a man. A stranger. A perfect stranger: tall, golden, godlike. All that was missing was the giant oyster shell and winged attendants—the red Speedos were a nice touch though.

"Hey," he called over the ocean's boom.

"Hey," I called back.

If there was a lack of enthusiasm on my part—and I'm sure there was, because I knew by then who he had to be—it didn't faze him.

He strode right up to me as the waves sucked the sand out from under our feet. I was pleased to see he was a couple of inches shorter, though built like one of those *International Male* models.

"Kyle, right?" he grinned whitely, and offered a hand. His skin was chilled from the surf, his grip of the manly-man variety. "Brett Hansen."

Mist rose like steam off the water. Goose bumps rose on my skin.

"Glad to meet you," I said, since I had to say something.

"I'm Adam's lover. Adam MacKinnon. You remember Adam?" He was still grinning, cat-green eyes sizing me up.

"Yeah, sure." It was kind of ridiculous. In maidenly modesty I clutched my Levi's to me with one hand; he still held my other.

"We're here for the summer."

"I heard."

"Adam's idea. Not mine. I'm just along for the ride." He laughed. "If you know what I mean."

I thought I knew. I pulled my hand free.

"I'd invite you up to breakfast but Adam doesn't like company before he has his daily dose of poison." His tongue touched his upper lip like he could taste the poison—or maybe it was my reaction that was so sweet.

"Thanks anyway." Wild horses, baby. I tossed my Levi's to a patch of dry sand, my self-consciousness over.

Hands on his hips, Hansen watched me retreat toward the surf.

The shock of cold water, the sting of salt on my skin, felt good. Bracing. *Thanks, I needed that!* stuff. As I forged the first wave he called out, "See you around, scout!"

I choked on a swallow of salt water.

Scout.

Striking out toward the point, I couldn't resist one glance back to the shore. Brett and his Speedos sashayed toward the stairs in the cliff. He didn't have to look back to know I was watching.

* * * * *

The path that leads from the back door of my cottage to Adam MacKinnon's, rambles through a meadow waist-high in summer with white poppies and lupine. Beyond Adam's cottage this same path disappears into the woods where Cosmo Bari, my father, vanished one soft summer's eve ten years ago.

My bedroom window offers a perfect view of Adam's bedroom window. Not that there's been anything to see for years. But that morning the blinds were up and the cottage windows glinted in the morning sun. A metallic-colored Acura NSX was parked in the front yard as though on display. These were the sole signs of life as I returned from my morning constitutional.

I thanked God I was no longer a self-absorbed adolescent believing all the world watched me behind inscrutable windows.

Someone was watching me however. Micky sat on my porch steps smoking a cigarette and tipping the ashes into my peonies.

"You shouldn't swim alone, kiddo," she greeted me as I joined her on the porch.

"Uh huh." The morning sun felt like a warm hand on my bare back. I stared out at the blue haze of ocean beyond the pastel clouds of flowers. The fog had dissipated like a magician's trick.

Micky took another drag on her cigarette. "So. What did you think of Brad?"

"Brett?"

"Is that his name? Yes, he looks like a Brett. So?"

"Young."

"How young? Younger than you?"

"I'd say. Twenty, twenty-one."

"And?"

I shrugged. "Like a Ralph Lauren ad. *Chaps.*"

She gave one of those smoky laughs. "Leave it to you to think in terms of saddle sores. He's a hustler. A New York City hustler."

I resisted the urge to echo *New York City!* like someone in a salsa commercial. "No way."

"Way," said Micky, who's fifty if she's a day. "Joel knows him. In the Biblical sense. Joel introduced them."

"How come I never heard this before?"

"It came out last night. Joel got drunk and spilled his guts. Literally and metaphorically." She shook her silver head and tipped more ash into my garden.

I studied Micky. She's still a lovely woman, her long blonde hair now paled to silver, her sea-green eyes crinkled at the corners with laugh lines, her body still slim and lithe thanks to the yoga she insists would be better for my heart than swimming and hiking. I used to wonder if Micky—Michaela

St. Martin to the art world—didn't bury herself here in Steeple Hill because of some unrequited thing for Joel.

I said finally, "They've been together a long time."

"Two years is a long time to you?"

"I only mean, Adam must know. He's not still hustling, right?"

"Adam?"

"Funny."

A humming bird darted in for a closer look, and then zipped away through the cigarette smoke. I expected to hear a tiny cough.

"I've never seen Joel like that," Micky commented.

"Like what? Don't tell me he's still got a hard—yen for the guy?"

"Is it so hard to believe?" She gave me a certain look, and I felt myself reddening. "Anyway, it sounded that way last night. It could have been the alcohol. He's a melancholy drunk."

"*In vino veritas?*"

"In six scotch and soda vomitus." She looked up at the burned-blue sky. "Did he say how long they were staying for?"

"The summer."

Silence while Micky puffed and brooded. "I've got a bad feeling about this," she said at last.

* * * * *

It seems like ever since I moved back to Steeple Hill, people—Micky for one, Joel, even Jen Berkowitz—have helpfully pointed out that I have no life.

My answer: Define "life." Okay, maybe they do have a point. I get up the same time every morning, take my morning swim, sit at the computer all day, take my evening walk, and fall asleep reading around eleven o'clock. No wonder I have nightmares.

I don't think it's really about the hours I keep. I've noticed that you can have your health, you can be successful in your career, you can be happy as the day is long, but if you're not married, engaged or seeing someone eligible, your friends are concerned. It's no different if you're gay.

Being gay in Steeple Hill is not easy. Sure, we're only about two hours from San Francisco, but it might as well be two light-years. Different solar system entirely. The only other homosexual in a hundred mile radius is Joel. As we both live in the "artists' colony," I guess it confirms what the townsfolk say about us: fags and liberals. And that's the nice stuff.

As artists' colonies go, ours is pretty tame. Yet we're still viewed skeptically by some of the town's old-timers, despite the fact that my father grew up here and, starting with my father, the income per capita has verged embarrassingly on the bourgeois. Very little suffering for art goes on these days. Very little suffering, period. That's okay. Fag though I am, I'm not into suffering much.

I'd been at the computer for a couple of hours when the phone rang. It was Joel.

"The Addison is holding an exhibition of Cosmo's work."

"I know."

"They've asked me to speak opening night."

"I heard."

Joel Shimada was my father's best friend. They started out together in the 1950s, doing the Greenwich Village Bohemian artist gig. Joel was the first one to earn the critics' attention, but in the end Cosmo's star eclipsed Joel's.

But Joel was gifted. He did a small oil of my father, age thirty, which hangs in the alcove in our dining room. It's brilliant; like I remember Cosmo—unless my memories stem from that painting.

Joel's later stuff is in the style of Peter Samuelson; lush homoerotic studies. He was painting for himself; why not? Then he quit painting altogether and started writing, beginning with *Greenwich Time*, a colorful memoir about my father and their reckless youth. Thus Joel became the accepted expert on Cosmo. Cosmo. No last name. Like Rembrandt. All the world was on a first name basis with my father, thanks to Joel. A couple of years later Joel wrote a critical treatise on Cosmo's work. Who better?

The latest project was not going so well. He wanted my story. Son of Cosmo. I had declined. I kept declining. It made for some strained moments.

"I think you should go," Joel said.

"I think not."

"They've invited you. You should go. When are you going to forgive him?"

The psychological angle. That was new. Usually it's all about my filial duty to keep the flame burning.

"*Forgive* him? What the hell are you talking about, Joel? What is there to forgive? He went his own way from the time I was a kid. It's all I knew. It's all I expected—and don't quote me either."

"If you don't resent the way he walked out on you, then I really don't understand why you continue to refuse to participate. It's what Cosmo would want."

I guess Joel had been making stuff up about my father for so long he was starting to believe his own bullshit. I said, as mildly as I could, "Joel, I don't want to argue with you."

"What did you say? I can hardly hear you."

"I don't want to fight with you."

Silence followed my terse words.

"Kyle, don't get upset. Just consider it, all right?"

"No."

"Oh. Then don't."

Another silence. I opened my mouth to say I had to get back to work. Joel rushed in nervously, "Have you spoken to Adam yet?"

"No." I was dismayed at the way my gut knotted at the unexpected mention of Adam's name. I was over this, right? Surely this wasn't going to be a problem? "Not yet."

"But he *is* back?"

"Yeah."

"Micky says you met…Brett."

It was that naked pause before the name "Brett" that threw me. Was I supposed to know that Joel had history with Brett, or not?

"I met him."

"I didn't think Adam would bring him here. I would have thought some sensitivity…what do you think?"

"About?"

"Brett. How did he seem? Did he say why they were here?"

"I only met him for a moment. Micky thinks Adam's putting the house on the market."

"He wouldn't have to come here for that."

"Maybe he wanted to see the place one last time."

"Maybe. Do you realize we're all here together for the first time since Cosmo—since your father—"

"Went out for a pack of cigarettes?"

Joel ignored my flippancy. "Are you going to the Berkowitzes' *soirée* tomorrow?"

"It depends on if I get any work done today."

"I suppose that's a hint," he huffed. "Well, fine." He banged down the receiver.

I sighed, considered ringing him back. But I decided I didn't have energy for Joel's emotional crisis—or even time for my own. I returned to my computer.

I was thirteen when Adam MacKinnon moved into the cottage across the meadow. Originally the cottage belonged to Drake Trent who had been a silver screen heart throb in the 1940s, but was a paraplegic alcoholic by the '70s when he rolled his wheelchair down the seventy-five narrow steps leading to the beach.

Authorities listed Trent's death as an accident, but everyone knew—even I knew—that he'd killed himself. Adam picked up the cottage and most of the furnishings in a state auction. Very practical. Cosmo's friends and students weren't known for their practicality.

At the time Adam joined our merry band, he was twenty. He had a mane of curly black hair, a mustache and a Vandyke beard that gave him the look of a cavalier out of a Romantic painting by Gericault or Delacroix. He was tall and spare and beautiful. He wore a gold earring. He was the first openly gay man I had ever known, my "uncle" Joel not counting. No wonder I fell in love; I saw him every day for the next four years.

Adam was cool about the puppy love. Maybe because I was Cosmo's kid. Adam was one of my father's students. The best. The brightest. Which was saying something, because my father didn't suffer fools. He didn't suffer anyone for long. Including me.

After Cosmo split the last time, and I'd been packed off to Stanford, I lost touch with Adam. I didn't lose track, because you can't live in an artists' colony where everyone eats, sleeps and drinks oil paint, and not hear about Adam MacKinnon from time to time.

I wasn't a painter. I didn't inherit my father's gift. But I kept the cottage in the colony. After I graduated I moved to Oakland and lived for about a year in a closet—the closet being of the mind as well as of real estate—but I ended up moving back to Steeple Hill. Despite the isolation and the shortage of eligible males, it suited me.

Lunchtime came and went. About one thirty I stopped long enough to throw a banana, some frozen blackberries in the blender with some cranberry juice and the last of the Häagen-Dazs frozen yogurt. I measured in a scoop of lecithin and bee pollen and swigged it down while I re-read the last pages I had typed.

Another hour of trying to find words—another hour of struggling to keep my thoughts from straying to the cottage across the meadow.

The doorbell rang, ripping me out of my creative cocoon.

"Who the hell now?" I exclaimed peevishly, pushing away from the monitor and pulling my glasses off.

Who now wished to be regaled with the details of my two-minute encounter with Adam's hunk lover? The Berkowitzes? The Nashes? Had it spread to the village? Maybe the mayor himself?

As I padded into the living room I could see a familiar outline through the screen door. My heart sped up.

He was smiling at me through the mesh.

"Hello, Kyle."

The door wasn't hooked. I pushed it open.

"Hello, Adam."

CHAPTER TWO

I stood aside. Adam stepped past me, close enough that I picked up the scent of almond soap.

He stared about the room. "My God, it hasn't changed a bit."

Adam had though. The long curls were cropped short and wavy, the beard, mustache and golden earring were all gone. He was still startlingly handsome: tall, lean, but older. Maybe harder around the edges.

"I expect to see Cosmo come striding through that door any minute." His eyes, blue as the faded denims he wore, homed in on my face.

"How are you, Kyle?"

"Good."

"You look good." He still studied me; it was not a rhetorical question. "Actually, you look great." His eyes tilted up at the corners when he smiled. I'd forgotten that.

He lifted his hands and then dropped them. I think he wanted to hug me, but didn't quite know how to bridge the years. I was a big boy now. A big, self-conscious boy, and I couldn't have made a move toward him if my life had depended on it. Not after Brett's "scout" crack.

Instead Adam turned to the fireplace where *Virgin in Pastel* used to hang. In its place was mounted a gilt-framed mirror I'd picked up at an auction for twelve dollars. It reflected the two of us appraising each other.

"The *Virgin* never turned up?"

"No," I answered.

He was making conversation; if it had shown up, he would have known. *Virgin in Pastel* is theoretically considered Cosmo Bari's masterpiece. I say theoretically, because the painting went missing the same time as my father. The cartoon, or rough draft, hangs in the Getty, and a series of preliminary sketches are in the Addison Gallery of American Art in Andover. Although the prelims and the rough draft were done in pastels, which Cosmo was experimenting with at the time, the completed work was painted in oils. It was called *Virgin in Pastel* for the delicate coloration he achieved.

Adam gave a funny laugh and said, "I'm trying not to say something idiotic like, Gee, you're all grown up!"

"Is it such a shock?"

He didn't answer directly. "I read your books. Both of them. Funny as hell." His cheek creased in a faint smile. "The 'Gay Donald Westlake,' huh?"

"They have to put something on the book jacket."

He continued to smile at me in the old affectionate way. It bugged me.

"I met Brett," I said.

"He told me. In fact, that's why I'm here. We want you to come to dinner tonight."

I threw myself into emotional reverse, stripping gears in my panic. "No. Uh—that is, I'll let you get settled in first. Let Brett get used to—"

"We're not newlyweds," Adam interrupted. "It was Brett's idea."

"Great." That's what I was afraid of.

Adam headed for the door. Hand on the screen, he paused. "You never heard from him? Not a word?"

I knew whom he meant.

"No. Never. Not a postcard." After a moment I said, "I think I would have, if he'd lived."

"What?" His blue-blue eyes narrowed.

"I think he's dead. I'm almost sure of it. Otherwise, I think he'd have come back—if only for a day. He liked to see the finished product."

I never could read Adam's face.

He smiled after a moment. "See you about seven?"

"I'll be there." If my prayers for divine intervention in the form of earth-quake or tidal wave went unanswered.

* * * * *

My grandfather has the only existing picture of my mother. Mine is a copy of her high school graduation photo; she's younger in it than I am now. All the other photos, all the paintings he did of her, were destroyed by my father after her death.

Judging by her high school photo, Kyria Lipez was pretty, but not exactly the type to inspire lifelong devotion. She was my father's high school sweetheart. There's no graduation pic of Cosmo, because by then he'd booked for parts unknown. After a number of years and unexpected artistic success, Cosmo Bari, former resident-black sheep came home to Steeple Hill, and against the fierce opposition of her father, married Kyria. This house was their wedding gift, my grandfather being of the opinion that my father could never provide my mother with stability or security.

Who knows? They were married for two years when I came along. Three years later my mother took an ambulance ride and never came home. I don't remember her except as a gentle voice, the cool scent of Wind Song, and the bleakness in my father's eyes.

The house is hers though. The garden was hers. She planted the purple-blue wisteria that winds along the porch overhang. The tangle of peonies and roses that grows as high as the front steps. The William Morris patterned rugs, the "Osbourne" china—everything in the house was hers and her mother's before her and *her* mother's before her. I know my mother through the furnishings of the house I grew up in—and a spiral notebook of sweet but sophomoric poems she wrote in high school, which my father spared for reasons known only to him.

This is to say I know her a lot better than I ever knew my father, with whom I shared this house for sixteen years. I don't know that anyone ever knew Cosmo. I read Joel's books, and frankly, I don't think Joel knew him either.

But maybe it's easier for me to think so than face the fact that I never knew my father because he wasn't interested in knowing me. After my mother died he used to disappear for weeks, even months, at a time. No one knows where he went, though Joel speculated plenty in print. I know he traveled abroad because he once brought me back a poster of an air show in France— the only time I remember him bringing me a souvenir, or giving indication that I was ever anything but out of sight, out of mind.

Anyway, I take after my mother in looks: tall and slim and ordinary. And I suppose in temperament too, being quiet and something of a homebody. My father looked like Stewart Granger, and carried on like Stew in his more dramatic roles. It's that artistic temperament thing, I guess.

* * * * *

I brought peonies from my garden and a bottle of Merlot to dinner.

The lights from Adam's place twinkled through the trees as I walked across the meadow. The still-warm earth released a pungent scent of sage and wild flowers into the dusk. As I drew nearer I could hear Stan Getz on the breeze, the sultry voice of Astrud Gilberto murmuring *"Corcovado,"* recalling long summer evenings spent listening to Adam and my father talk Art on our front porch.

It's bullshit, Adam. Modern painting is significant in one way only: it's new. You've got these young punks focused on nothing but trying to top each other; switching styles and manners, feverishly seeking new thrills, new chills, new giggles for a jaded bourgeois audience.

I don't agree, Cos. I think—

Kyle, are you still awake? Bring us a couple more beers.

Adam met me at the door and slipped a cordial arm around my shoulders.

"I'm glad you came, Kyle," he said, as though he knew how much I hadn't wanted to.

"Thanks for inviting me."

He looked good enough to eat, in charcoal drawstring pants and an indigo blue collarless shirt; soft flowing clothes that somehow emphasized rather than detracted from his masculinity.

"Brett's cooking," Adam added, and by his wry smile I understood that Brett's cooking indicated An Occasion.

Right on cue Brett stepped out of the kitchen. He looked too gorgeous to cook or do anything more practical than lie on a beach in Cannes or swat a tennis ball around a Malibu court. His hair was slicked back and shining in the light from the candles; he wore no shirt, and his burnished skin gleamed like pirate's gold. He wore white denims with a multicolored serpent and dagger design on one leg. Even his bare feet were beautiful.

"Kyle." He smiled. "At last we meet. Officially."

He smelled of cigarettes and musky aftershave, sexily gliding up and taking the flowers from me. "From your own garden?"

"Yes."

"Lovely."

The peonies looked especially lovely against his taut abdomen; their white silky petals flushed pink and coral against his brown skin. I thought it was no wonder Adam loved him. He was the embodiment of masculine beauty. It was hard to take my eyes off him. When I did, Adam was smiling quizzically in my direction.

"We need a bowl for these, Adam," Brett said, handing the flowers over. Adam took the wine and the flowers and vanished into the kitchen from whence savory scents issued.

"I hope you like curry," he called over his shoulder.

Brett drew me over to a chintz-covered sofa that I remembered from my sickly adolescence. I had a flashback of what it used to feel like drowsing in this room, with the drone of bees floating through the open window and the soft brushing of Adam painting at his easel.

"Is it like you remember?" Brett inquired, sitting next to me. He exuded a kind of animal energy and warmth. I eased over a few inches. He offered me a cigarette which I declined. "Is Adam like you remember?"

"It's been ten years. Nothing's the same."

"You can't go home again," mused Brett. "Though Adam keeps trying."

Actually Adam's cottage did seem unchanged—almost identical to the way it had been in Drake Trent's day: bronze-nymph lamps, glass doorknobs, and numerous prints of fox hunting and dead game birds.

Brett's steady green stare made me uncomfortable. "Do you paint?" I asked at random.

He bit off a laugh, blew a stream of blue smoke through his nostrils and called, "Adam, we need wine in here."

"Yo." Adam's voice floated back.

The turntable dropped the next record. Instant mood change: Sonny Stitt's fast, flirty alto-sax pursued by quietly smiling keyboards.

"So you're a writer?"

"Yeah." At least I'd got past the "uh—yeah" stage.

"Do you have any copies of your books I could read?"

"Sure. If you like."

"I want to know what makes you tick."

Why do people assume you are what you write? That every character is you or someone you know? That if you've written it, you've either done it or want to? Whatever happened to imagination and research?

I gave him an uncomfortable smile, but was saved from answering by Adam's return with wine glasses and the open bottle of Merlot. He settled in the chair across from us and poured the wine.

"What's Kyle's best book?" Brett asked, reaching for a glass.

"They're both good."

"What one would I like?"

Adam rose and turned down the stereo. "Records," he said, glancing up and catching my eye. "Remember LPs?"

I remembered all Adam's LPs. Mostly jazz. Jazz was forever equated in my mind with the smell of oil paint, the scratch of old records, the warmth of a man's hand against my own sensitized bare skin.

I felt Brett's stare. "That's a good color on you," he remarked. "What is it? Burnt orange?" He plucked at my T-shirt.

"Bittersweet," Adam supplied. "That's what Crayola used to call it anyway."

"Kyle hasn't played with crayons in years, Adam," Brett chided.

There was a strange pause. Brett drained half his glass in one swallow. "So...what was Kyle like in the good old days of records and Clearasil?"

Adam shrugged. His smile made my stomach do an unexpected flip flop. "I remember you used to read Louis L'Amour Westerns. In fact, I found one tucked between the sofa cushions today. *Mustang Man*."

"I always wondered how that turned out."

"Did you know you were gay?" interrupted Brett.

"When?"

"When you had a boner for Adam."

I managed not to spill my wine. "Yeah, I knew." I took a sip and avoided looking at Adam. I'd known this evening was a mistake.

Brett looked from me to Adam. "Come on, Kyle, open up. Did you have a dog and a bike and a baseball mitt?"

What the hell was his fascination? "Yeah, sure." And an eccentric genius for a father who didn't care if I was alive or dead. "It was pretty average. How about you?"

"Let's see…" He leaned back, stretching out his long legs. "Foster homes till I was fourteen. A year on the street. A year modeling. A year in rehab. A year—"

"Brett," Adam murmured.

"Shit," Brett exclaimed, leaping to his feet. "The curry!" He disappeared into the kitchen.

Adam's eyes followed him. I wondered if all the tension in this room was mine or if they had been quarreling before I arrived. Adam looked back at me.

"How are you Kyle? Really."

"Good. Really." I set my glass on the table, my attention caught by the music. Something teasing and sexy and familiar; something I hadn't heard in ten years. "Bebop in Pastel?" I guessed.

Adam didn't reply; his expression was odd.

"What is it?" I asked, puzzled.

He said slowly, "You know, until this second I never realized just how much Brett reminds me of you."

"You've got to be kidding." That came out wrong. I was sure he meant it as a compliment. I tried, "It must be the light."

"Not so much your looks." He reached out and turned my chin toward the lamp. It was automatic on his part, merely positioning a model, but I stiffened. He let me go at once. I still felt the warm imprint of his fingers on my face.

After a moment he said, "You do have similar bone structure. Similar coloring. You both have that trick of tilting your head when you're listening. I'm not exactly sure what it is."

"Coincidence," Brett said lightly, dropping practically into my lap. I scooted over. "You like your boys slender and fair and—are you tanned *everywhere*, Kyle?" He ran his hand down my arm. My skin prickled as though from heat rash.

"Give him a break, Brett."

Brett laughed and emptied his glass. "Shall we eat on the verandah, gents?"

We ate on the verandah in white wrought-iron chairs that were less comfortable than I remembered. There were citronella candles in stone lanterns to keep off the bugs, and their smell combined with the garden scents and the curry. The curry was good if you like curry, which I don't. This one was made of tiger prawns simmered in ginger, cilantro, coconut milk, and served over rice. We polished off the Merlot I'd brought, and Adam decanted a couple of bottles of Napa Valley white, which we also drank.

Adam grew quieter as Brett grew more confidential, tossing out phrases like, "Since I feel like I already know, Kyle..." By the time we got to the espresso, the feeling was mutual. I believed I already knew more about Brett than I'd ever need to know—which shows how wrong you can be.

It was after nine o'clock when a slow moving pair of headlights turned off the main highway and wound down through the trees toward us. The music had gone quiet, moody, slow. Astrud Gilberto was singing "Once Upon a Summertime" in that slurred, slightly-off way, like she was tipsy too. I was listening to her rather than Brett's theories on outing closeted politicians, but I did notice when he trailed into silence.

We watched as the headlights turned into a 1967 Chevy convertible.

"What's that supposed to be?"

"The welcome wagon," I answered.

"Not the Cobbs?" Adam said, sounding ready to laugh.

"That's Mayor Cobb and the Honorable Miss Irene to you," I said.

"*Mayor* Cobb?"

"Mayor of what?" Brett wanted to know.

"Of Steeple Hill. By formal election. We're a township now."

We watched as Mayor Cobb unfolded himself from the navy blue Chevy. He turned to help his sister, precariously balancing a pie, disembark. Irene's foot caught in the hem of her long cotton skirt, and for a second it looked like all three of them would end up on the gravel.

"Spinster" is no longer politically correct, but if ever a woman fit the bill, it was Irene Cobb. Micky told me Irene had been attractive in an *au naturel* way back in the days of frosted lipstick, but by the time she was teaching my ninth grade biology class she wasn't fueling any adolescent fantasies. She fixed her mouse-colored hair in place with plastic barrettes, and wore granny glasses that perpetually slid down her small, bony nose. A rumor circulated the freshman class that she was actually the mother of her nephew Jack, whom she and her brother Norman had raised from infancy. But then there were also rumors that Mitzie Stevens had made it with the entire Varsity Squad—and it turned out Mitzie was studying to be a nun.

Brett laughed and poured himself more wine. Adam pushed his chair back and went to greet the Cobbs. A warm, callused foot rubbed over mine insinuatingly. I moved my foot away. Brett laughed again.

"Glad to have you back, Adam," Norman Cobb said, pumping Adam's arm in best politician style.

Norman is round and soft like the Pillsbury Doughboy, with the same inane giggle. Still, a man who drinks Guinness can't be all bad.

"Good to be back," said Adam.

"You'll hardly recognize the place, I imagine. You've been by the McDonald's of course?"

"The—?" Even in the dark I could see Adam racking his brains for yet another faceless name from his past.

"Fast food franchise," I supplied.

"Oh."

"And the new Albertsons." The mayor stood aside while Irene offered her pie with the air of one sacrificing to the gods. Adam received it automatically.

"We read about you in *Newsweek*, Adam," she said, referring to an article published six years earlier chronicling the Who's Who of the art world.

"Is that you there, Kyle?" the mayor asked, peering through the gloom at the table. "I thought I recognized your voice. And who's that with you?"

Brett rose and sauntered over to the mayor and his sister. He offered a hand. "I'm Brett. Adam's lover."

"Adam's brother?" Irene repeated, pleased and shaking hands.

The last record ended and in the silence Brett pronounced loudly, "Lover. L-o-v-e-r."

Following the shocked pause, Irene began fluttering and clucking. "Oh that's—that's—well, this is to welcome you home, Adam. It's pecan. Chocolate pecan."

Norman was stiff all the way to his lips which barely managed to form the words, "Nice to meet you," as Brett wound himself around Adam like a cat in heat.

Seven minutes later they departed in a cloud of dust turning red in the Chevy's tail lights. Brett guffawed. "You forgot to mention Steeple Hill was one gigantic closet."

Adam freed himself rather pointedly. "That was unnecessary."

"Was it?"

"Yes. You don't have to shove it in their faces."

"Shove *it?* Now you're ashamed of being queer? Or just ashamed of me?"

"Neither. I don't see the point of embarrassing and offending a pair of sixty-year-old—"

"Homophobes?"

"They're not homophobes. For Christ's sake, they know what I am. They're a different generation. They don't talk about sex, period. Let alone something considered perverse in their day."

"Don't ask, don't tell? Is that it? You are such a goddamn hypocrite!"

"How about don't tell until you're asked?" Adam retorted.

This was clearly well-trod ground. I got up from the table. "Thanks for dinner. I'm going to head off."

"Stay, Kyle," Brett said quickly. "It's early. Have some more wine. Have some of this goddamned pie."

"No, I've got to get back."

He grabbed at my arm as I walked past. I eluded him and he nearly toppled over. Adam caught his shoulders, steadying him, and said grimly over Brett's head, "Good night, Kyle."

Brett yanked away, shoving clumsily at Adam. "Keep your fucking paws to yourself!"

I walked back across the meadow, spears of lamplight and the angry echo of voices falling behind me.

CHAPTER THREE

The next morning I woke determined to steer clear of Adam's happy household. To that end I waited until I'd seen Brett return to his cottage before I ventured down to the beach.

I had a leisurely peaceful swim and was back at my computer by ten, but not long after, a knock on the door jolted me out of my beta rhythm. Jen Berkowitz fidgeted on the front porch.

Jenny is cute. She's small and slight with silky red-brown hair and freckles: the quintessential kid sister. She can be just as big a pain.

"Can we borrow your wok?" she asked. "We're having a dinner party tonight. Joel, Micky, Adam MacKinnon and his lover—and you too, Kyle."

Shoot me.

"I can't make it, but you can borrow the wok."

"Why can't you make it?" One thing about Jen: she's direct.

"I've got plans."

She trailed me into the kitchen and helped herself to the cookie jar. "Since when?"

I retrieved the wok and handed it over. "Since last week. I'm having dinner with friends."

"Well, what are we?" She wrinkled her nose. "These cookies are stale." She set the jar aside and took the wok from me. "Anyway, cancel. This is more important."

"I don't want to cancel."

"Don't you want to meet Adam MacKinnon and his boyfriend?"

"I've met them."

"Seriously? When? What happened?"

"Jen—" I put my hands on her shoulders, guiding her out through the kitchen and toward the front door. "I'm working."

"You're always working. I want to hear details!"

"Later."

"Kyle!"

I closed the door and went back to my research.

It was a couple of hours before I looked up again, this time starting at the sight of Brett standing in the study doorway.

"Jeez-us!"

He chuckled. "I did knock."

"Most people wait till they get an answer."

"Sorry. I wanted to apologize while I still had the nerve."

Nerve didn't seem like something he lacked. "Apologize for what?"

"For last night. Adam says I was drunk and disorderly, *SIR!*" He clicked his heels and mock saluted on the "sir."

Against my better judgment I found myself smiling at him. "S'all right," I said like Bubba Louie. Seeing this, Brett slinked in and looked about the room as though he were thinking of renting it. Today he wore a mint-green muscle-T and denim cut-offs that proved his time at *Blackie's Gym* had not been wasted.

"So this is the home of the famous Cosmo." He wandered into the dining room. For a moment he considered the portrait Joel had done of my father back when they were sowing their wild oats in Greenwich. "That's him, right? He sort of looks like Stewart Granger. Ever hear of him?"

I sighed and readjusted my specs. "*King Solomon's Mines, Beau Brummell...Sodom and Gomorrah.*"

"One of *my* favorites." He padded back into the study, leaning over my shoulder. I felt the hair at the nape of my neck prickle at his nearness. "What are you reading?"

"I'm researching explosives."

"Ah, I have that effect on people." He smiled, treating me to a close-up of his perfect set of choppers. "Horn rims. Very sexy. You should wear them all the time."

"Only for reading and driving at night."

"Speaking of night driving, where's the nearest club?"

"Clubs? Gay clubs? In Steeple Hill?" He looked at me like I was an idiot. I guess I did sound a little "Here *on Plymouth Rock!*" "There isn't one."

"Where do you go?"

"I don't."

His expression was priceless. "You're telling Auntie Brett you never get horny?"

"Sure. But I haven't found the answer to that in a bar."

"You must be going to the wrong bars. Where do you think I met Adam?"

"I thought you met Adam at an exhibition. I thought Joel introduced you."

"That's Adam's version." He eyed me speculatively. He was probably right. Like a lot of writers, I lived too much in my head. I was lonely. And horny. "So what is there to do around here?"

I shrugged. "You could drive up the coast toward Frisco. Or down the coast toward Monterey. There are plenty of stops in between. But why, when—" I bit the rest of it off too late.

"When I've got Adam?" He laughed. "Don't tell me you're still in love with Adam?"

I felt myself flush. "Look, it was a teenage crush, okay? I was in love with Richard Gere too."

"Yeah?" Brett snickered. "Are you sure you don't write Harlequin Romances?"

I took my glasses off, wiped them on my T-shirt and put them back on. "Now you know my secret. And I don't mean to be rude, but I've got a deadline." Okay, so it was six months away.

"Oh. I've offended you." He continued to laugh at me with his eyes. "If your thing for Adam isn't a problem for me, why would it be a problem for you?"

"Don't you have to be someplace?" I couldn't help the edge that crept into my voice.

Brett tilted his head. "Have it your way. I guess I'll check with Joel. When it comes to gay nightlife, dial 1-900-OUR-JOEL."

I reached for my book. When I checked over the top again, he was gone.

* * * * *

The next days passed without incident. I didn't see Adam except to wave to him across the sea of grass and wild flowers. Once I spotted him fishing down on the dock. By himself. Most mornings I could look up from my computer to see Brett pounding down the dirt road in a variety of skimpy "onion-skin" shorts, plugged into a Walkman, his muscled body glistening bronze in the sun. If he caught me spying he would wave jauntily, not losing stride.

From Micky I learned that the evening at the Berkowitzes' had been a huge success. Everybody played *Pictionary* and ate *Chow Mein* cooked in my wok. Micky said she had to admit that Brett was charming and amusing, and she had never seen two people more in love than Adam and his child bride. Brett made a hit with the Berkowitzes too. I noticed that usually he stopped by there as a part of his a.m. routine.

My work was going well, the stack of typed pages beside my computer mounted daily. And no wonder. I sought the immersion of writing the way an ostrich looks for soft sand.

The summer grew hotter and the hills dried to gold.

At night I gazed across the meadow to the lights twinkling cozily from Adam's cottage, and I was both comforted by Adam's nearness and depressed by the knowledge that he could as easily live on the moon. He was that far out of my reach.

A couple of evenings I saw Brett zip off in the Acura by himself, and one morning I caught him stumbling home as I was heading out for my swim. He was a sight to behold in black leather jeans and a cobalt silk shirt in a brown baroque print right out of *GQ*.

Spotting me, he waved and blew a kiss before disappearing inside the sleeping cottage.

For Adam's sake I hoped Brett was taking the normal precautions. He didn't seem like a cautious kind of guy.

Two weeks after Brett's visit my garden suffered the yearly infestation of aphids. I seized the opportunity to mend bridges with the Cobbs, and drove into Steeple Hill.

After some initial awkwardness, Irene invited me into the "parlor" where she served lemonade so cold and sweet I could feel my teeth shivering.

"Norman's bird-watching this afternoon," Irene excused the mayor's absence. "Poor dear, these days he has so little time for his hobby, what with all his civic duties."

I made commiserating noises. I knew full well that, lifetime member of the National Audubon Society or not, the only birds that Norman was likely to be watching on a day this hot were the ones who hung out at the Class Room pool hall. I thought Irene probably knew too, though she never let on.

"That's a peculiar young man staying with Adam MacKinnon," Miss Irene said a little stiffly after I'd drunk two glasses of lemonade and described my battles with black spot fungus to the last skirmish.

"Brett? Well, he's from New York."

Actually she did consider this a sort of explanation. "He seems familiar to me. Is he an actor by any chance?"

"He's done some modeling."

"I expect that's it." She held up the pitcher. "More lemonade?"

"No, thank you, Miss Irene. I should be going."

Miss Irene led me out back to her own splendid rose garden which looked like a commercial for Miracle-Gro, and handed over an obscene-looking contraption with a thin rubber hose which her nephew Jack had made for her own war on garden pests. Along with the insecticide I got numerous strictures on standing upwind and avoiding breezes.

"It contains a good jigger of cyanide," she informed me, making it sound like a refreshing cocktail.

"I'll be careful," I promised.

As I started the jeep I considered stopping by my grandfather's house. I hadn't seen him in weeks. But then sometimes months passed between our meetings. I don't think my grandfather's bitterness toward my father extended toward me, but I was a product of my unorthodox upbringing, and that didn't leave us much in common. Micky said once that she thought I looked enough like my mother to stir painful memories. If I'd been a girl, it might have been different—and no use dwelling on the irony of the situation.

In the end I decided to give the family reunion a miss, and drove straight on toward the colony. Twenty miles from Steeple Hill, the "colony" consisted of six cottages straggling down the shoreline. This was the original town site, which is why there is an abandoned chapel, complete with graveyard, in the woods. No one remembers why this site was discarded in favor of the inland location of modern day Steeple Hill, but its loss was our gain.

Passing Vince and Jen's, I decided to stop in and grab my wok. Anything left longer than a week at the Berkowitzes' tended to be considered a donation.

Before Vince gave up a lucrative career as a commercial artist in favor of the challenge and frustration of Real Art, he used to bring down a tidy six-figure income. It was no secret he had trouble adjusting to a restricted budget, and he and Jen mostly managed on her salary from the Cobb House Historical Society.

Vince was tall, bearded, with hazel eyes and an irritating laugh. Maybe I found it so because he was frequently laughing at me, usually when I wasn't trying to be funny. As for Vince's artistic standing, the colony's ruthless verdict was that Jen had all the talent in the family, and Vince should have stuck to designing smiling dogs and dancing blueberries to encourage mass market consumption of dog biscuits and cereal.

Jen's stuff is startling: bold primary colors and aggressive brush strokes. She won't exhibit. She says she paints for her own pleasure. I think she's afraid of showing Vince up.

I turned in at the wooden gate of the Berkowitzes' cottage. Wind chimes hung motionless in the hot air. The lawn was overgrown with sea grasses; wild flowers overran the garden. The cottage's paint was gone and the wood had worn to satiny gray. Still, the place had a rustic appeal.

Not so appealing were the sounds issuing forth from an open window.

"What do you want?" Vince was yelling. "Do you want me to lie? Do you want me to live a lie?"

I couldn't hear Jen's reply, only the emotion throbbing in her low tones.

"That's right," Vince overrode her. "It's my fault. Every goddamn thing that happens is my fault. You can't have kids and that's my fault too—or no, I'm just supposed to make it up to you by spending the rest of my life—"

His voice grew louder still as he headed toward the door. By now I was backing up, hoping to sneak off before I was spotted through the window.

No such luck. The front door flew open and Vince stomped out. He checked a moment at the sight of my discomfited retreat and said, still loud and mostly for Jen's benefit, "Don't run away, Kyle. You can take my place in the guilt pageant. I figure she's good for another thirty minutes."

"This is a bad time," I began.

"We don't have any *good* times," Vince informed me. "Not anymore." He walked around me and banged out the garden gate, leaving it swinging gently on its off-kilter hinges.

I turned back to the cottage. Jen stood crying in the doorway. "Come in, Kyle," she sobbed.

"Jeez, Jen, I'm sorry." I was still trying to escape down the path myself. She grabbed my arm with surprising strength and drew me into the house.

She looked like hell, her face blotchy and swollen from crying, her eyes red. "I can't go on like this," she told me.

"Do you have to?"

She stared at me as though I were speaking a foreign language, and blinked her spiky lashes. "Do you want some ice tea?" she inquired on an apparent tangent.

"No, thanks."

She turned away, walking into the kitchen. Unwillingly I followed, watching her pour two glasses of tea from the jug in the fridge. I try to steer clear of caffeine. Today it seemed easier to shut up and drink it.

We went out on the porch and I set my paraphernalia on the railing. Jen eyed it gloomily. "What is that, a hookah?"

"Some kind of bug-killing apparatus Jack Cobb manufactured for Miss Irene. For my peonies." I was afraid that if I left it heating in the sun it might blow up the jeep.

"Oh."

The silence stretched. I gulped my tea as fast as politely possible. Jen stared off at the ocean, pushing the old-fashioned glide swing we sat on in desultory fashion.

"Vince thinks he's gay," she said at last.

I choked on my tea. When I finished spluttering, Jen continued in that too calm voice, "It's all because of that little—little *cocksucker* Adam brought home."

"Brett?" Like there was any other little cocksucker in question. "This is kind of sudden, isn't it?"

"Vince says no. He says he's always been curious. That he's always had certain feelings. He said he ignored them."

"Uh…" I stopped, not knowing what I could say that wouldn't make it worse.

"It's bullshit," Jen said wildly, rocking the swing harder so that I had to steady my glass. "I'd know if he was gay. I'd be the first one. He's not. It's that little—"

I interjected, "Are you sure this is about Brett?"

"Isn't it obvious? He's a hustler. A male whore. Adam must be insane bringing him here. He's come on to everyone. Everyone! Joel, Vince. He came on to me. *Me.*"

"You?" I was shocked. Why, I'm not sure; Brett appeared to be a liberal kind of guy.

"Maybe we can get a group rate," Jen said wildly. "He can screw the entire colony, physically and figuratively, for one low, low price."

I set my glass on the wooden floor.

"Vince thinks he has feelings for Brett. Feelings! My God, I could *spew.*"

I hoped she wouldn't. She did look ill.

"What you and Vince have is real," I said at last, not knowing if it was true or not. What does anybody ever know really about someone else's private life? "This thing with Brett, whatever it is, it's just…infatuation. Or something. Besides, Brett has Adam."

"So?"

"So? He's not going to jeopardize that."

"Oh, Kyle." Jen looked at me with pity.

I felt myself changing color. Was it so fucking obvious to everyone how I felt about Adam? Was it obvious to Adam?

"I'm only saying that Brett's onto a good thing with Adam. He's not going to jeopardize that."

"Brett isn't you. Brett doesn't value anyone or anything. Not even himself."

We brooded for a moment.

"Well, he'll get his," Jen said. "He'll probably die of AIDS."

"Jesus, Jen. Don't say that. What a thing to wish on anybody."

"I guess I'm learning some things about myself this summer. I guess I'm not a good sport about having my life ruined. Mine and Vince's."

"I'm sorry, Jen," I said at last.

She started to cry again.

* * * * *

I almost skipped the annual beach party. Every year the colony kicks off summer with a barbecue in the cove. When I was a kid I looked forward to s'mores and ghost stories by the sea, but I would have given it a miss this year if Adam and Brett hadn't walked over to fetch me.

"You're not ready?" Adam asked as I opened the door.

"No, I—"

"Shake a leg, scout," Brett said exuberantly. He raised his hands over his head, snapping his fingers and shaking his hips. "Time to par-tay!"

I finished polishing my glasses and slid them back on. Adam was frowning at me. In black denims and black turtleneck he looked like a French film star. A stern French film star. Though he had been Brett's age when he moved to Steeple Hill, he had never seemed as young or free as Brett. Despite his sense of humor, Adam was a serious person. Serious and self-contained. I wondered what, besides sex, he and Brett had in common. Something had to hold them together for two years.

"I think he's in a stupor," Brett observed. "He definitely needs some fresh air."

Brett wore artfully torn jeans and a baby-blue cashmere pullover that seemed a trifle overdone for beach blankets and weenies.

"I lost track of time," I lied, rubbing my prickly jaw. "Go on ahead and I'll meet you there."

"We'll wait," Adam said.

"And don't bother shaving," Brett ordered. "Five o'clock shadow is sexy on *you*."

Adam shot him a look. "Grab a jacket, Kyle," he said to me. "It's cold by the water."

I wished to hell he would stop thinking of me as a sickly child. Neither he nor Brett wore jackets. I opened my mouth. They waited expectantly. I tried to think of a good excuse, but nothing came readily to mind. With a not very gracious mutter I ducked back inside, dragged a sweatshirt over my T-shirt, flicked a comb through my hair, splashed on some cologne and shoved my feet into tennis shoes.

Adam leaned against the porch post, staring out at the meadow as I rejoined them. Brett perched on the railing, twirling a red rose. Something in their silence struck me.

There's a painting by Jacob Van Ruisdael called *The Jewish Graveyard*. Beautiful and somber, it captures the same ominous mood that I felt that evening observing them in the dying light.

"Ready?" Adam asked me brusquely as Brett got to his feet.

"As I'll ever be."

Brett slipped his arm around my waist and hugged me. "Mmm. You smell delicious. What is that?"

"Soap."

"No. It's sandalwood. It's fabulous."

Adam turned on heel, leaving Brett and me to trail along behind him. I watched him though I tried not to: his carriage erect and graceful, shoulders broad, back leanly muscled. He disappeared down the stairs leading to the beach.

Brett nipped my ear playfully—then chuckled at my scowling recoil. I pulled away from him, speeding up after Adam.

Down in the cove a bonfire shot red embers into the last cadmium ribbons of the sunset. We were the last of our crowd to arrive; I was surprised to see Jen and Vince already settled around the fire. They were never on time for anything. Vince was drinking a Dos Equis. At a glance it wasn't his first. Jen and Micky wrapped cobs of corn in foil, talking quietly to each other.

"There you are," Micky greeted us. "We were about to send out Search and Rescue."

Vince raised his bottle in a toast and then completed the gesture, chugging down beer. As he lowered his arm, Brett moved over to him and took a swig from the bottle. Joel, sitting next to Vince, stared at his feet.

"We heard some terrible news," Jen piped up. "The Nashes aren't coming down this year. Mrs. Nash has had a stroke."

"The last of the Old Guard," Adam commented quietly.

The Nashes were our oldest residents, contemporaries of Drake Trent. Their passing would indeed signal the end of a chapter.

Micky said, "It's the only summer I can remember that they haven't come down. Not since…"

Not since Cosmo walked off into the sunset.

"So this is everybody who was there that summer?" Brett inquired. He planted himself between Joel and Vince on the fallen log. Joel rose and came over to join Adam and me. Again Brett took Vince's beer bottle, this time draining it.

"When are you flying to Massachusetts?" I questioned Joel. "When is the exhibit?"

"What exhibit?" Adam inquired.

Joel replied, "The Addison is showing Cosmo's work next month. I'm supposed to make a speech." He shrugged as though this weren't the kind of thing he lived for.

It was odd how everyone referred to Cosmo formally, impersonally. Even to me. Almost no one ever said "your father." It was always "Cosmo."

"Have you changed your mind about going?" Joel pressed me.

"I'm considering it." That wasn't exactly true, but I was increasingly aware that I could do with time away from our soap opera by the sea.

"Let me know what you decide," Joel said. "We could travel together. I can make all the arrangements."

I nodded noncommittally.

Adam rummaged in the metal tub of ice, uncapped a beer and handed it to me. Our fingers brushed. Yeah, I could definitely use time away when the touch of Adam's hand had my nerves twitching as though magnetized.

"Hey, Kyle, what do you think about this rumor that Aaron Lipez is hiding a bunch of Cosmo's paintings?" Jen inquired, apparently continuing an on-going discussion. "Could he have *Virgin in Pastel*?"

"Not much," I answered. Not that I had any more insight into my grandfather's actions than anyone else. "I don't think he put a lot of value on Cosmo's work."

"Philistine," Vince muttered. "They're all philistines around here. The only good thing about the local yokels is they're too cheap to toss anything. Look at old man Cruz finding that painting at the bottom of his chicken coop."

Cruz's chicken-coop coup was a local legend. Before my father had gone off to set the world on fire, he had spent years filling canvases with pictures nobody thought were suitable for anything but chicken coop flooring or white elephant sales. After he became famous, and art collectors started showing up, my father's former neighbors started pillaging local thrift stores and attics in hopes of discovering a cache. Several found original Cosmos, which had immediately been snapped up for mucho bucks by East Coast buyers.

"What a find," Micky agreed. "What did he get for it? A cool ten grand? And that was way back then."

In the envious silence that followed, Jen said, "Suppose *Virgin in Pastel* is lying at the bottom of somebody's chicken coop?"

"Why not?" said Brett. "It's never turned up, has it?"

"There's no proof it still existed at the time Cosmo disappeared," Joel said. "Cos could have painted over it."

"No way!" exclaimed Vince.

Joel laughed. "Oh, it's possible all right. It's just the kind of self-destructive thing Cosmo would do."

I shivered. Adam glanced at me and put a companionable arm about my shoulders. "Warm enough?"

"Yep, fine," I replied and moved away, hard though it was. I took a place on the log and said to Joel, "The *Virgin* is still around somewhere. I remember seeing it a few days before Cosmo disappeared."

There was an astounded silence.

"You never said so before," Joel said.

"You never questioned the painting's existence before." I glanced up. They were all staring at me.

"Kyle, you had been pretty ill. Maybe you're confusing—"

"I'm not confusing anything. Cosmo had taken it down for the exhibition at the MOMA. It was propped in the dining room. I remember wondering about that because he had never shown it before."

"I'd give anything to find that painting," Vince said, breaking the moment. "I'd be set for life."

Brett retorted, "Who cares about one missing painting? Where's the painter? That's what I want to know!"

Following this there was another of those uncanny silences.

Enjoying himself, Brett rose, a lithe shadow in the firelight. "Maybe it was Professor Plum in the conservatory with the wrench. Or maybe a wench! What do you think, Kyle?"

Joel said finally, "That's not exactly in the best of taste, is it?"

"No?" Brett laughed. "Well, let's talk about something else."

"What would you like to talk about, Brett?" Micky asked dryly. "Yourself?"

Vince gazed up enraptured. "God, I'd love to paint you, just like that. The embodiment of the pagan spirit."

Joel's breath sucked in sharply. My eyes caught Jen's. If looks could kill...

Brett laughed. A carefree kid's laugh. "Bare ass naked? What do you think, Jenny Wren? You want me to model for you too?"

Deliberately Jen took a frankfurter and jabbed the end of a wire hanger into it. Brett laughed again.

"Brett," Adam said quietly. That was all, but the air seemed to go out of Brett's balloon. He made a face and headed for the space on the log between Joel and me.

"Adam thinks I'm a bad boy, Joel." Then to me he confided, "Joel knows how bad a boy I can be. Joel used to get off on spanking me."

Vince inhaled beer and began coughing.

Joel's face turned livid in the firelight. He rose and stalked away on the pretext of gathering more driftwood.

"Jesus," I muttered.

I thought that Joel's pain didn't stem from the embarrassment of having known Brett in his trade days, so much as the fact that he still cared for him—was eaten alive with lust and jealousy.

"You're a little shit," Micky informed Brett pleasantly.

Brett swung his sights her way. He chanted softly, "Oh Micky you're so fine. You're so fine, you blow my mind. Oh Micky!"

Micky smiled a smile I didn't trust.

I drank my beer and wondered how soon I could decently leave.

CHAPTER FOUR

After this everyone seemed very much preoccupied with handing out picnic plates and flatware. The discussion was restricted to Jell-O salad and how everyone wanted their hotdogs cooked.

"Come on, Kyle," Brett said, openly bored. "Shall we see sea shells down by the seashore?" He linked his arm in mine and drew me to my feet. I glanced around the faces circling the fire. Only Adam watched us.

Brett tugged on my hand. I decided I'd do everyone a favor and I let him drag me off.

The water creamed inches from our feet as we walked along the shore-line. Brett didn't seem to feel the cold. He nattered on cheerfully, maliciously, about Vince, about Joel, about everyone except the one person I would have liked to hear about.

We walked a ways till we rounded Smuggler's Point, the rocks cutting us off from view of the others. Brett headed for the lichen-crusted boulders; I followed. We sat down and he took out a pack of cigarettes, offering them. I shook my head. He tapped one and lit it. He inhaled and blew a smoke ring. It floated delicately away on the night air.

"Smoke bother you?" he asked after a time.

"No."

He blew another smoke ring. "You're okay, Kylie," he said at last. "I was prepared to hate your guts, but actually you're the only one of these assholes that's remotely human."

"Wow. Thanks."

He gave an odd laugh. Took another puff. "How bad's your heart anyway?"

After an astonished moment I said, "Well, I washed out of NASA. I'm okay for normal living."

"Whatever that is. Are you okay for normal fucking?" And he reached across and planted his hand on my crotch.

My own response to that warm insinuating weight took me by surprise—and I felt myself go rigid like a Victorian heroine. I grabbed his wrist. "I appreciate the gesture, but—"

He twisted his hand, and now it was his fingers grabbing my wrist. "Who are you kidding? You're so tight I'm surprised you can walk." He tugged me forward and I half sprawled into his lap. His free hand resumed massaging my swelling crotch through the stiff material of my Levi's. He was stronger than he looked. And he knew what he was doing.

I closed my eyes for a moment. Gave in to the idea that this painful throbbing want could be satisfied quickly and secretly. No harm, no foul. We were both adults and this was just sex.

"Knock it off, Brett," I said coldly—if belatedly. I pushed his hand off my aching crotch. With my free hand I felt for the crusty surface of the rock, bracing myself up and away. Hard to be dignified and defend your honor at the same time, but I tried.

"Why? We can both feel how bad you want this." Brett tried to kiss me. I turned my face and he kissed the corner of my jaw.

It was kind of funny really, except for how it would look to Adam if he came walking up. The thought of Adam was terrifying and—unnervingly—even more arousing.

"Relax, Kylie," Brett whispered, his hand sliding up under my sweatshirt. His cool fingers slid across my chest and found my nipple. Even to my own ears my protest didn't sound nearly fierce enough. "Let go. I know what you want. Better than you do yourself." We tussled some more, breathlessly; Brett was laughing softly, his hands everywhere, like Kali making her move.

"Don't..." I caught a ragged breath as he pinched my nipple. "Brett, don't."

He said throatily, "It's too late..." His nails scraped across the hard flat planes of my chest, found my other nipple. Scratched lightly, maddeningly across the tingling nub.

I felt a wave of relief. Too late. It was going to happen. All I had to do was lie back and let this wave take me out.

And that would make it pretty much unanimous. Brett would have fucked every guy in the colony—including me. And I didn't even like him.

Finally I was mad. I pushed upright and shoved him so hard he fell off his perch.

"Shit." He clambered back to his feet. Feeling his forehead, he brought fingers away bloody. "Shit, Kyle. I wasn't going to rape you."

I stared at his red fingers; at the scrape on his forehead. My mouth opened.

"I'm…sorry," I managed at last. I couldn't remember ever drawing blood from anyone before. No schoolyard rumbles for me. No siblings to battle with. A nonviolent childhood. Maybe that was why I took to writing mysteries. A passive-aggressive thing.

Brett laughed at my expression, leaned in and kissed me again. This time I didn't object. He tasted smoky-sweet. "Don't look so scared. It's not the first time I've been beaten up. Adam has a mean left hook."

My eyes jerked up to his. "Yeah, right."

His expression was enigmatic. "There's a lot about Adam you don't know, Kyle."

I shrugged.

He reached out to lightly stroke my face. I turned my head. "You don't like me much, do you?"

"I don't know you."

"We can change that anytime you like."

The knee-jerk seduction routine was getting old fast. I said irritably, "What, is it like an issue with you? Do you have to make it with every guy you meet?"

To my surprise he chuckled. "You underestimate yourself, Kylie."

There didn't seem to be a lot to say as we walked back to the bonfire. I could see the beach blanket party had livened up in our absence. Vince and Jen were laughing together at Joel and one of his involved ghost stories. Micky was eating a hot dog. As we shuffled up through the sand, Adam set down his beer bottle.

"What happened to you?" he asked Brett.

Brett dabbed at his temple again. "I fell. On the rocks."

"Poetic justice," someone commented. I couldn't be sure, but I thought it was Joel.

We settled down by the fire. Someone passed me a hot dog and a plate of potato salad and baked beans. I could feel Adam's eyes on me but when I looked up, he was staring at Brett.

Studying the circle of fire-lit faces, I remembered that these were people I'd known for years, all my life in the case of Joel and Micky. Tonight I felt that they were strangers. And it was Brett's presence that had triggered this transformation.

I don't recall who suggested a moonlight swim. It might even have been Brett. He was certainly the one who pushed for it, egging everyone on, and at last turning to me. Tugging my hands, he tried to pull me up out of the sand.

"Come on, Kylie. Let's go skinny dipping."

"Maybe later."

He was beautiful in the moonlight, bringing to mind those Hermann Liemann neoclassic photographs of sandaled young men brandishing swords. I didn't know where to look. Not everyone was as beautiful naked—in fact, no one was. But a lot of drinks helped them get over it.

"Fuck. You're an old man!"

Brett gave up on me, and darted ahead, plunging into the waves. The others were right behind him in various stages of undress.

I stood, tugged my sweatshirt over my head. Put my hands on my belt buckle. With sudden clarity I wondered what I was trying to prove. I'd just eaten. It was cold. My bare skin was breaking out in goose bumps as the wind off the water hit it. The blue-black water was rough, sweeping in on the incoming tide. Who was I trying to impress? And how impressive would it look keeling over in cardiac arrest?

Reaching down, I shook the sand out of my sweatshirt and pulled it back on. Adam still sat on the log drinking beer.

"You're not going in?" I asked, dropping down beside him.

"No." Curt.

Was Adam always the designated driver?

Silently, we sat watching the others scream and frolic in the inky waves, their bodies alabaster in the moonlight, reminding me of those stark black-and-white woodblocks Gauguin did in Tahiti.

Adam smelled like almond soap and sunscreen. He smelled warm and familiar, although at the edge of my vision his outline—lean, hard, smooth-shaven and close-cropped—was suddenly alien.

His shoulder brushed mine as he leaned forward toward the tub of ice. "Want another beer?" he asked.

"No. Thanks."

For the first time in my life I had nothing to say to him. It was weird and a little sad.

"Everything okay, Kyle?" Adam's abrupt voice cut into my thoughts.

"Yeah, why?"

I flicked a look his way. He was staring into the fire, half his face in shadow. "You seem…distant. Have I done something to offend you?"

"Of course not."

Hesitation. Then he said colorlessly, "Has Brett done something?"

"Huh? No." I heard the nervousness in my voice. Adam stared at me. I said, "I just—I'm preoccupied, that's all. The book I'm working on."

"Because if I've done anything or said anything that…hurt you…"

"No." I jumped up, pacing. "No, Adam. I said no. Let it go."

Kyle, Ace of Spies.

"Okay," Adam said evenly, after a pause.

After that there really was nothing to say. I walked out a way from the fire, my shadow exaggeratedly long and sinister across the bleached sand. Adam continued to drink, gazing out at the ocean.

"Do you see Brett?" he questioned suddenly.

I scanned the waves. "No."

He rose, striding toward the water's edge. At the same time there was a yell for help, half-strangled.

The swimmers closest in, Micky and Vince, turned. A wave knocked Micky to her knees and Vince splashed back to drag her up.

I couldn't see who was further out, only pale bobbing shapes cresting the rolling black peaks.

"Adam, *help!*" That ghostly cry was Brett, his voice choked off as he went under a second time. By then Adam had kicked his shoes off and was running for the water.

I ran after, stopping only to remove my own shoes. The others were calling out "What's happening? Who is it? Is it Brett?"

Adam plunged into the water and disappeared.

Wading out to my waist, I stood beside Vince who said grimly, "I told him not to swim so far out."

"Where are they? Can you see them?" Micky demanded from the other side of Vince. "It's as black as pitch out there."

"Where the hell's Jenny?" Vince questioned suddenly. He waded out hollering for Jenny.

She answered distantly. I saw her white face materialize a few yards down.

"Do you see them?" Micky asked me, moving in. Her teeth were chattering.

"No." My eyes strained to see. The surf was deafening, the moonlight deceptive. A piece of wood looked like a body tumbling over and over in the surf.

"There!" Micky grabbed my arm.

"No, look!" I pointed the other direction.

"Oh, thank God. Is it both of them?"

"I can't tell." I could discern Adam. It looked like he had his arm locked around Brett's shoulders as he struck out toward the shore. "Yes, he's got him."

Lunging through the water to meet Adam halfway, I draped Brett's other arm over my shoulders. Between us we half dragged, half carried him up to the beach and dropped him in the sand.

Adam rolled Brett onto his side and proceeded to empty water out of him like an old-fashioned pump. I knelt at Brett's feet as the others grouped round, hushed. I was conscious of my soaked, stiff Levi's and the wind biting through my clammy T-shirt. My hair dripped down my nose, an annoying distraction to the drama before me.

Brett started to come around, choking and coughing even before Adam eased him onto his back. His eyes flew open and he gazed up at the circle around him.

"Brett, are you okay?" Adam urged.

Brett stared blankly and suddenly jack-knifed up, clutching Adam who locked his arms around him.

I didn't hear what he said, distracted by the pain of watching them, but I felt the shock wave that rippled through the ring around us.

"What?" Adam demanded.

Brett pushed back in his arms. "I said, someone tried to kill me! Someone grabbed my feet and pulled me under. Someone tried to drown me!"

There were assorted gasps and gurgles before Micky said harshly, "He's in shock. He doesn't know what he's saying."

"You must have caught your foot in some rocks," Adam said.

Brett scrubbed his wet face. "There aren't any rocks that far out. You think I don't know the difference between rocks and hands!"

"What's going on?" Joel inquired, coming up behind us.

"Brett swam out too far," Jen said. "Now he claims someone tried to kill him."

Everyone began to talk at once. Brett clutched at Adam and spoke tensely, his profile pale and saint-like in the moonlight. I couldn't hear what he said, but Adam was frowning.

"Okay, lover, calm down," he said finally. "Let's get you home and warm."

He helped Brett stand. Hastily everyone gathered their belongings. Joel dumped the ice from the metal tub into the fire and kicked sand over it. There was a strange hush as we packed up. I think we all tried not to watch the lumbering two-headed figure of Adam guiding Brett up the cliff.

"He's lying," Jen said finally.

No one replied.

When I got back to my cottage, I followed a scalding shower with a cup of chamomile tea, and wrapped myself in the heavy terry robe I usually saved for cold winter mornings.

The light on my answering machine was blinking. I pressed Play. Brett's hoarse voice filled the room.

"You and Adam screwed up your big chance to be together." Raspy laughter. "Meet me tomorrow for breakfast. I've got something to show you."

* * * * *

That morning I could hear the music clear across the meadow as I started over to meet Brett: Sonny Stitt playing "Bebop in Pastel."

He was kicked back on the verandah, wearing side-split denim short-shorts and a pink polo. The guy didn't have an ugly bone in his body: elbows, knees, ankles—every inch of him was brown and smooth and polished.

"Adam drove into town, so we won't be interrupted." He poured juice out of a jug and shoved a basket of croissants my way.

I took a sip of juice and felt my eyebrows shoot up. "What is this?"

"Mimosa." He rolled his eyes at my ignorance. "Orange juice and champagne."

"Three parts champagne. I have to work today."

"Oh, lighten up. You sound like Adam. Look." He set one bare brown foot on the tabletop, clattering the gleaming porcelain dishes.

There were ugly purple bruises around his ankle.

"Someone did try to drown you last night."

"No shit, Sherlock. Did you think I was making it up? I'm not talking about the damn bruises. Notice anything else?"

He was wearing an anklet, gold links intertwined with pink-gold grape leaves. It was pretty and unusual, but hardly worth getting together over breakfast. "The ankle bracelet?" I asked doubtfully.

"Recognize it?"

"Should I?"

Brett stared at me with eyes as hard and green as jade. He seemed intent on my reaction.

"Sure you don't recognize it?"

I shrugged. "No. Did Adam give it to you?"

"Adam?" He snickered. "You think Adam's an ankle bracelet kind of guy?" He swung his leg off the table and leaned back in his chair. He lit a cigarette. "So...since you don't want to get it on with me, how about a three-way? You, me and Adam? Adam digs that."

I tore open a croissant, and slathered it with the butter melting in the sun. "No, thanks."

"'No thanks!'" Brett mocked. "Talk about Virgin in Pastel. No wonder you never got anywhere with Adam. I was thirteen my first time. One of my dear old foster dads obliged." He laughed at my face. "Sorry. Ancient history."

I made an effort and swallowed the wad of dough and butter.

He propped his chin on his hand and said slyly, "I bet you would have offered your ass up without a murmur if it had been Adam last night. Wouldn't you?"

"You've got a one-track mind."

"You're only kidding yourself, Kyle." He poured me more spiked OJ, ignoring my feeble protests.

"Sit tight. I want to show you something else."

Oh goody.

He was back in a moment carrying a book. He opened the book and a folded square of thin drawing paper glided to a stop on the table. I picked up the yellowed paper, unfolded it. Two pieces of paper, actually. I studied them, my throat knotting.

The first showed a boy of sixteen sleeping in the grass; a graceful sprawl of long limbs, angular features, tumbled hair. There was a good deal of tenderness in the portrayal of a too-thin, too-sensitive face relaxed and dreaming.

The second sketch was a head study. Same youth: wide eyes and childish mouth; the hollows and delicate bone structure of a child who had been ill a long time and was still fragile. Moreover, it was the face of someone in love as only an adolescent can be, intensely and vulnerably.

Brett chuckled at whatever he read in my face. I refolded the sketches and tucked them back in the book, which I handed to Brett. He tossed it aside onto one of the faded flowered cushions.

"You were a cute kid," he remarked.

"That was the summer I got sick. Rheumatic fever."

"Which left you with a weak heart."

"It was the summer my father disappeared."

"What I Did on My Summer Vacation," quipped Brett. "So how come they didn't stick you in some juvey facility?"

"No one realized Cosmo was gone for good till about eighteen months had passed. By then I was packing for college, so no one bothered. It's different in a small community. I had plenty of surrogate parents: Micky, Joel—my grandfather, if I'd needed him, I suppose."

"I'd prefer juvey."

I believed him. "You really hate this place, don't you?"

"The scenery's nice. It's the people I loathe." He granted me one of those blinding smiles. "Present company excepted."

"Gee, thanks."

"Still, the place has its amusements."

"Such as pulling the wings off Vince Berkowitz?"

Another grin.

"Do you care about Adam at all?" I really needed to know.

He shrugged. "More than I've ever cared for anyone else."

What did that mean? In the bright sunlight he looked haggard. A foreshadowing of what he'd look like in ten years when the drinking, the one-night stands and the rest of it caught up.

"Don't worry about Adam," he advised. "He knows exactly who I am. Adam needs to be needed. It's his frustrated maternal instinct."

Jack Cobb's sky-blue antique pickup pulled into the yard and Jack got out wearing tight jeans and no shirt.

"Boy howdy," murmured Brett. "Enter the handyman. What's his name? Seth? Jude?"

"Jack Cobb," I answered. "He's the mayor's nephew, and he's straight—as a yardstick."

Brett laughed. "Why that metaphor?"

I played dumb. "You mean analogy?"

"Whatever." He stood up, waved to Jack who was tussling with the ladder in the truck bed. "Yeah, I'd say things are looking up."

"Brett—" I wasn't sure what I wanted to tell him. Vaguely, I remembered Jack from high school; very macho and not too bright. I knew he was well able to take care of himself, so maybe it was Brett I was thinking of—or maybe Adam.

As I spoke, Brett paused, his expression tightening. "Back off, Kyle," he said. "You blew your chance. Get in my way and you won't know what hit you."

* * * * *

One evening, not long after, Adam caught me up on my walk.

I always took the same route, the path through the woods past the old cemetery. The same path my father had walked the night he left Steeple Hill forever. What had been in his mind that night? I used to imagine him stopping at the graveyard, perhaps seeing himself buried alive, trapped by responsibilities and obligations he had never asked for. I pictured him turning on heel, heading down the trail away from the colony, walking faster and faster until he was running, running through the woods as though running for his life until he came out on the highway.

In my mind's eye I could see him hiking along the deserted stretch of road until he flagged down a truck, hitched a ride, watching the lights of Steeple Hill grow smaller and smaller in the truck's side mirror before he vanished into the night.

A writer's imagination?

But I wasn't thinking about Cosmo that evening; my thoughts were preoccupied by an unforeseen problem in my manuscript. When Adam called my name I stopped dead, as startled as though one of the graveyard's tenants had addressed me.

Adam stepped out of the shadows of the old church, sketch pad under his arm. For a moment I wondered if he was a ghost. The ghost of himself ten years earlier.

"Hi," I said.

Maybe he heard the wariness in my voice. He wasn't smiling.

"I wanted to ask a favor, Kyle," he said. "I wanted to ask if you would try to be a friend to Brett."

Has Adam ever showed you his tattoo? Brett had inquired a day or so earlier. Brett had a knack for suggesting things that got under your skin like fire-ant bites. Now I couldn't help studying Adam and wondering what his tall, thinly muscled body looked like under the paint-daubed Levi's and old T-shirt that bore the Chinese character *hé* for harmony.

I said neutrally, "What does being a friend to Brett entail?"

It seemed Adam didn't know exactly because he didn't answer right away. Then he said, "He doesn't have a lot of friends. He doesn't have any here."

"Go figure."

I watched Adam's lean cheek crease in a wry smile. "You're going by what other people have said, Kyle. You haven't made any effort to get to know Brett yourself."

"Give me a break. I've seen him in action."

Adam didn't question what I meant by that. Maybe by now he had learned not to ask the questions he didn't want to hear answered.

"He likes you," Adam said. "He thinks you're funny."

At the face I made, Adam added shortly, "He thinks you're honest, and that counts with Brett. He hasn't had a very happy life. He didn't grow up sheltered and loved."

I opened my mouth for rebuttal, but then I had to shut it again. The truth was, I did have a happy life, as lives go. And my childhood had certainly been happy. Maybe my father hadn't been an active participant, but I had been loved and sheltered by the other adults around me—and Adam had been one of them. So I guess it was payback time.

Not that I was gracious in defeat.

"What are you hoping for, Adam?" I inquired. "The traditional exchange of Hot Wheels? Or do we slice our fingertips and pledge eternal sisterhood by the sea?"

Adam snorted. "How about not avoiding us like the plague? In the old days you used to be over at the cottage all the time."

I watched the harmony character rise and fall with his chest. *That was Zen, this is Tao.* "Yeah, well…" I shoved my hands in my pockets and gazed at the graveyard, at the trees standing in black silhouette like barbed wire against the sky. Sunset flushed the headstones and statuary red; the angel poised over Drake Trent's grave looked apoplectic. "I'll try, okay?"

It seemed neither one of us had anything more to add, but we continued to stand there, side by side.

I thought, *If the Fates were kind you would have a paunch by now. You would be losing your hair. At the very least you'd have bad breath.*

I thought that Brett was right. If Adam had laid hands on me on the beach, I would have given him whatever he asked—and probably more than he wanted.

Adam sighed and said regretfully, "You used to be easy to read."

I had to laugh.

But I wasn't laughing as I lay awake in the warm night, listening to the crickets and the distant sound of "Moonglow" drifting on the breeze. I pictured Adam and Brett dancing on the terrace in the light of the stone lanterns, or lying in each other's arms in Drake Trent's huge sleigh bed, whispering to each other the words lovers do.

CHAPTER FIVE

"**W**hat was Cosmo like?" Brett asked idly one afternoon in July.

We were sprawled on the sofa watching *Mystery Science Theatre 3000* on the new television set Brett had finally talked Adam into buying. Brett was drinking Miller Lite and eating microwave popcorn.

I pondered his question and shrugged. "He was a genius."

"What's that mean?"

"I don't know. Geniuses are hard to get along with."

"He was hard to get along with?"

I scratched my chest, preferring the movie to Brett's favorite game of Twenty Questions. "Yes and no. He was an artist. You know what it's like living with someone who has a—a vocation."

"A *what*?" Brett was laughing at me now. "If you mean he was a bore on the subject, I got you. What was he like as a father?"

This was something I hadn't thought about in years. It was something I had never thoroughly explored.

"He was okay," I said slowly. "He made sure I had a home and security. Those things weren't important to him. It couldn't have been easy for him to remain here, especially when he and my grandfather didn't get on."

"What if he walked through that door today?"

"Why Adam's door and not his own?"

"You know what I mean."

Grabbing a handful of popcorn, I munched reflectively. "I guess I'd wonder where the hell he'd been all these years."

"No," said Brett. "No, you'd be thrilled to pieces."

"If you say so."

"I do. Yeah, it would be a shock, but you'd be happy. Mostly."

He had my attention.

"Now Joel...think about it. Here's old Joel making a living on the legend of Cosmo. What happens if the legend pops up with a different version? What happens to the Cosmo franchise?"

I shrugged. "If Cosmo was alive, he'd be painting. No new paintings have ever shown up. *Ipso facto*: he's dead."

"Everyone seems to think so. What really happened that last day?"

"I don't remember," I said. "I didn't realize he was leaving, so I wasn't paying attention."

"Adam remembers. He says he spent the day with you. Or you spent the day with him. He painted and you napped. You shared a picnic lunch and then you napped and he painted. You sound every bit as stimulating company then as you are now."

I signed him in his native tongue and turned back to the TV.

One thing Brett could not stand was to be ignored. "So you and Adam provide each other with alibis. Sort of."

"Alibis for what?" Now I was irritated. "You know, Brett, has it ever dawned on you that maybe one reason somebody might want you dead is your habit of sticking your nose into other people's business?"

Brett scraped at the label of his beer bottle, scowling. "If Cosmo was still alive, do you think the market value of his paintings would fall?"

"I doubt it."

"Suppose he has been painting all these years and has a truckload of canvases ready to flood the market?"

"I'm no expert on the art market."

"Come on, Poindexter, an educated guess?"

"Would it ruin the market value of Rembrandt if a cache of Rembrandts were discovered?"

"Rembrandt's a special case though. One, he really is dead. Two, lots of the Rembrandts we have are doubtfuls, things finished by students or apprentices."

I was surprised he knew that.

"I think it's a moot point," I said. "Cosmo is dead."

"There is that," agreed Brett.

At the time I believed that Brett's fascination with Cosmo's disappearance was due to the fact that he was an inveterate mystery buff. I'd never known anyone who read as many mysteries as Brett, especially "gay" mysteries. He'd read everything from *The Butterscotch Prince* through *Fatal Shadows*. He'd read Jack Ricardo, Stephen Lewis and Steve Johnson. He'd read everyone who'd ever written a gay mystery, and naturally, being Brett, he had an opinion on everything he'd read, and everyone who'd written.

"I read your second book," he informed me another evening over pepperoni, sausage and black-olive pizza. "I didn't like it."

"For Christ's sake, Brett," Adam snapped with unaccustomed annoyance. This was one of the rare times Adam joined us. When he had asked me to be a friend to Brett, Adam had apparently meant exactly that. I don't think he was avoiding me exactly—why should he after all? He had a show coming up in the fall, his first in several years. I think he was anxious. He was sharper with Brett, edgier in general.

"No, it's okay," I said. "What didn't you like about it, Brett?"

"It was silly. I hate silly."

"It's supposed to be a comic caper."

"Yeah. I hate that."

We were drinking beer out of tall pilsner glasses. When Adam was around we bothered with things like glasses and utensils. We bothered with "please" and "thank you." Adam was a civilized kind of guy. Now he pushed back in his chair and drained the pilsner to its foamy dregs. He was drinking a lot for Adam.

"Who do you like?" I asked Brett.

"Michael Nava. He's not afraid to be gay."

"I'm not afraid to be gay."

"Yes, you are." Brett's lip curled. "You're very careful not to offend Grandpa Aaron or Miss Irene or the Honorable Mayor."

"That's not true—well, it's true that I try not to offend people, but I still say what I need to say."

"You don't get it, Kyle," Adam said. "Subtlety is lost on Brett. You have to shove his nose in it."

"Have another beer, Adam," Brett drawled.

"Thanks, I will. Kyle?"

"No. Thanks."

Adam got up and walked steadily inside, apparently none the worse for a six pack.

"I'll tell you what I didn't like in Nava's books," I told Brett. "I didn't like the way he handled the break-up between Josh and Henry."

"Hey, I cried at the end of *The Hidden Law.*"

"I cried too. So what? If the point is that marriage for us is the same as marriage for straights, then I think their relationship should have illustrated commitment and responsibility and compromise."

"It's a story, Brain Guy."

"It's a story that confirms stereotypes about gays."

He yawned hugely. Adam, who had paused in the doorway, came out and joined us once more.

"How would you know?" Brett asked me. "You're not married. Hell, you haven't had a real fuck in over a decade."

I was careful not to look at Adam. "I know what I'd expect if I was. I know what I'd want. And I know what I'd be willing to give to make it work."

Brett giggled. "Do you sometimes smell orange blossom when those around you do not? Are you always a bridesmaid and never a bride?"

Stupid to let him get to me, but I felt my face growing hot. I reached for my glass.

"You're never going to meet Mr. Right holed up in this backwater, mooning over What Might Have Been with Adam."

"You are an asshole, Brett," Adam said in a low voice.

"But I'm your asshole," Brett reminded him. He turned his gaze toward me, bright and challenging.

* * * * *

Joel came to see me the day after he returned from Andover.

"I don't know how much longer I can put up with this." He looked like hell. There were dark circles under his almond eyes. His skin looked sallow, his face drawn. He'd lost weight over the past weeks, I could see now.

"Put up with what?" I asked, bringing him a glass of lime-flavored mineral water and sitting down across from him.

Joel gulped the mineral water down. He was flushed and sweating as though he had a fever. "With this situation. It's intolerable!"

"Which situation?" It wasn't like Joel to be incoherent.

"This situation between Brett and myself."

I said carefully, "I didn't know there was one."

"Of course there is!" Joel drank more water and pressed the cool glass to his forehead. "He was waiting for me last night when I got home from the airport. He—he deliberately let me think he would stay with me, that he wanted to spend the night. Then when I—when I had revealed myself to him, he left. He simply walked out. He was testing me. Making sure I still wanted him."

There were tears in Joel's eyes, I realized with a jolt. It was like watching a parent cry. I felt horrified and helpless.

I felt anger at Brett for doing this to Joel—and anger at Adam for letting Brett do it.

I couldn't think of anything I could say that would comfort Joel. The clock on the mantle chimed softly. It was late. *It's later than you think.* Finally I queried, "You know what he's like. How can you still care for him?"

"I don't know!" Joel cried. "I simply do." He wiped his eyes. Took out an immaculate hanky, unfolded it, and blew his nose. "I simply do," he repeated muffledly.

I said at last, "I don't think he has any intention of leaving Adam."

"I know that."

"Then why do you—"

"Adam might leave him."

That went through my system like a jump-start on a dead battery. Even my fingers tingled. "Why do you say that?"

Joel shook his head. "Because I hope it's true."

I hoped it was true too. Not because I believed Adam would turn to me; Adam kept a friendly but cautious distance between us. I knew he would never be able to stop thinking of me as that sickly adolescent "mooning" over him. And I knew it wasn't anything to do with our ages because at twenty-one, Brett was six years younger than me.

I told myself it was for Adam's sake that I hoped he unloaded Brett. Brett was not good for Adam. He was not good for anyone, as evidenced by the effect on our colony in little more than a month. Like a cat among the pigeons, he had set a snowstorm of feathers flying.

Which isn't to say that I didn't like Brett, because strangely enough I sort of did. I appreciated his malicious sense of humor (when it wasn't aimed at me), and he had certainly livened things up. But he was dangerous. Dangerous in the way of beautiful wild things. You could admire his beauty, but you couldn't trust him.

Unless you were Adam.

I assumed Adam trusted Brett, but maybe he just loved him unconditionally.

My other problem with Brett was the periodic assault on my chastity—such as it was.

"Haven't you ever been with anyone?"

"Of course!" I closed my mind to the memory of awkward and fumbling collegiate encounters, more painful than pleasurable, and just plain embarrassing after the fact.

Brett was disconcertingly serious. "I mean—"

"I know what you mean."

His smile was unkind. "Are you saving yourself for Adam?"

"Bite me."

"I'm trying to!" He chuckled. "Hey, you get a boner at the mere mention of his name. I could ask him to do you once as a favor. He'd do it for me. He'll do anything for me."

"Well, that is sweet of you. I'll think about it," I drawled, which seemed to amuse the hell out of Brett. He actually dropped the subject.

The best thing was not to give him a reaction. Easier said than done.

"What is it with Adam and the graveyard?" I inquired, politely batting off Brett's groping hands one day when I was paying one of my obligatory visits.

"He's painting the chapel. Maybe he's getting religion. Or hoping I will. Shit, you are so *shy*—"

"I'm not shy. I'm not interested."

"Yes, you are."

"No, I'm not—*hey!*" As his hand shot out to twist my nipple.

"You're hard again."

"I am not!"

"Made you look."

"You are such a juvenile, Brett."

These impromptu wrestling matches usually ended with Brett collapsing in laughter. The funny thing is, I often ended up laughing too. I'm not sure why.

Once, though, I came up for air to find Jack Cobb standing at the screen door, silently watching us.

Brett was unfazed. He hopped up and went out on the verandah, paid Jack for mowing the lawns and cutting the hedges, and came back inside whistling.

As we sat there listening to the eight-cylinder roar of Jack's pickup fading away, Brett slid his eyes my way, slapped his forehead and said slyly, "Hey, I could have had a V8!"

* * * * *

Then, on a hot July night when the full moon hung ripe and golden above the ocean, and the fireflies darted about the woods like fairy lights, something truly extraordinary happened.

The way the story was retold to me, Jen was stripping the varnish off a dresser Vince had purchased at a local yard sale. It was an ordinary dresser, not an antique, but real cherry wood beneath the white enamel. Each drawer had a lion head handle with a brass ring through its mouth. Jen removed all the drawers and was waxing the runners when she noticed that the back wall of the dresser appeared to be canvas not wood.

She pulled at it gently. The canvas was nailed to the wooden backing. She tugged harder, working it free. One by one she pried the nails out.

When the last nail was out she slid the canvas up, easing it out through the slats, inch by inch. At last she pulled it free. Immediately it rolled up into a tight scroll.

Jenny carried the rolled canvas into the kitchen and spread it out on the wooden table, using jam jars on the ragged corners to hold it flat.

What she saw there in the lamplight had her gasping for breath. She ran outside, shrieking for Vince.

Vince spilled out of his hammock. He grabbed a hoe and raced in ready to do battle with snakes, mice or spiders.

Jenny dragged him into the kitchen and pointed to what lay on the table. Vince gaped and goggled, and then they phoned Joel.

I heard the tale many times after that, in particular, I heard it from Vince who eventually claimed the find as his own, but it was Joel who called first to tell me that *Virgin in Pastel* had been found.

CHAPTER SIX

Brett and Adam threw a party for Vince and Jenny to celebrate their good fortune. Later I heard from Micky that Vince had tactfully suggested that it might be awkward having me there. Apparently he was afraid I might lay claim to the painting. Adam had told Vince that if I wasn't on the guest list, there was no party, so Vince had to put up with my awkward presence.

Though the night of the party turned out to be of the dark and stormy variety, everyone came, even several folks from Steeple Hill, including the mayor, Miss Irene and Jack Cobb. I suspected Brett must have invited them to get Jack there.

The wind kicked up off the ocean and set the leaves whispering like a thousand gossiping tongues. Now and then the lights flickered, and a boom of thunder rolled across the music. Joel acted as bartender, mixing up alcoholic concoctions he called Gypsy Queens which were four parts vodka, one part Benedictine and a dash of orange bitters blended into a foamy freeze. They made your forehead numb, but we swilled them like water from opalescent green cocktail glasses that had belonged to Drake Trent.

Everyone contributed. There was enough food for a funeral. Joel brought marinated green olives and prosciutto-wrapped melon. Micky fixed her specialty: endive with herb cheese. The Cobbs donated a variety of tarts and cookies. Irene could cook like an angel with an eating disorder. It hadn't affected Jack's waistline yet, but the mayor wasn't likely to squeeze into his old army uniform anytime soon. I made the bachelor special: nachos—and ended up eating half the plate before I left the house.

Adam's cottage was already crowded by the time I arrived.

Greeting me at the door with a sympathetic grin, Adam steered me over to the bar where Joel was working his magic. Adam was immediately called away.

"Well, what do you think?" Joel said, and he nodded over his shoulder. I stared at the canvas tacked up on the wall behind the bar. Vince, apparently afraid to let it out of his sight, had brought *Virgin in Pastel* to the party. "Is it the real thing?"

For a moment I felt light-headed. The painting was shockingly familiar, though the last time I'd seen it had been the night Cosmo left. Now it was like I couldn't quite focus. I had a hazy impression of cream and ochre and pink, like the heart of a rose or the lining of a cloud or summer moonlight...

"Kyle? Are you all right?" Joel's voice was sharp. "You're sheet white."

"I'm fine." I gave him a quick shaky grin and avoided looking at the canvas.

"Here, have a drink."

He watched narrow-eyed as I drank.

"Really, I'm okay," I said, embarrassed at my reaction. Joel looked unconvinced, but his bartending skills were being loudly sought, and he had to let it go.

I was fine by then, a little puzzled by my freakish response. I hoped no one else had noticed, and no one seemed to have. I downed two Gypsy Queens in quick succession, and chatted with a few people, but it was an effort. I've never been much of a party animal. Crowds make me want to bite my fingernails.

"I so admire people who can write fiction," said a woman from the local paper. "It must be so rewarding."

"Sometimes."

"You're Cosmo Bari's son, aren't you? I wonder if you would consider giving an interview..."

I spotted Irene Cobb; she looked more miserable than me. I remembered that I hadn't been able to find the bug killer apparatus she had loaned me. My garden now purged of the dreaded aphids, I'd meant to return it that night.

I excused myself from the lady journalist and got myself another drink, but Brett swooped down upon me and snatched it away as I raised it to my lips. When I opened my mouth to object, he kissed me; a wet smooch that effectively shut me up.

He flitted away.

I talked to more people and checked the grandfather clock in the corner, trying to decide if it would be rude to leave before midnight. I was conscious every moment of where Adam was in the room. It was like I could see him even when I wasn't looking at him. I glanced across and, yep, there he was, handsome and at ease as he chatted with his guests. His skin was very brown against the white of his shirt; his black hair gleamed in the mellow light. It was getting longer again, starting to curl.

"Stranger on the Shore" came on the stereo, and I realized how badly I wanted to dance with Adam, to be held tight in his arms, to be held close against his hard, spare body. Brett was right. I had it bad.

Instead, Jen asked me to dance. We swayed dreamily to the music, each of us pretending we were with somebody else. We moved past the bar and I glimpsed the painting—and felt that unnerving shift in my head.

"Stranger on the Shore" ended. Joel asked Jenny to dance. I sat down on the settee, rubbed my forehead. The room seemed hot and noisy.

Someone sat down beside me. I opened my eyes.

"What's wrong, Kyle?" Adam was inspecting me, his blue eyes kind.

"Who me? Nothing."

"Bullshit."

A lot of things were wrong, so I picked the one I thought was safest to talk about. "I guess…all these years I took it for granted that when the *Virgin* showed up, I'd finally know what happened to him."

Adam put his hand on my shoulder. It took everything I had not to turn to him for comfort. His touch seemed coded into every cell of my body. How could a casual gesture affect anyone this way?

"I know I've been saying it all along, but I guess it finally hit me that he really is dead. That we never are going to—" I couldn't put it into words because I didn't know myself what I felt.

"Reach an understanding?"

"I guess that's it." I laughed shortly. "Sad, huh?"

"It is sad. He would have wanted that too."

"Oh come on, Adam. Cosmo? You don't have to sugarcoat it for me."

"No, listen, Kyle." He seemed dead serious. "He cared about you."

"In his own way?"

"Yeah, in his own way. Like he did everything. He said to me that summer…when it looked like you might not make it…that the worst part was that you were just getting interesting." Adam's eyes tilted, and I had to laugh because that was so much my father.

"What's so funny?" Micky joined us on the other side of the settee. She was wearing a black lace vintage dress, the kind of thing she found at thrift shops and turned into high fashion.

Adam gave my shoulder another of those casual squeezes, and departed.

"I was telling Adam that it doesn't make sense to me. If Cosmo didn't take the painting with him, who did take it? And why would someone nail it in the back of an old dresser?"

"To hide it?"

Hide it from what, I wondered? "You couldn't sell it on the open market. It's too well known. It would have to go to a private collector."

We were both silent; I was remembering allegations that Sotheby's Auction House had been selling stolen masterpieces to collectors overseas. Such things did happen.

Except the *Virgin* hadn't been sold in private auction. It had been sold for $10.00 with a chipped dresser at a local yard sale.

I wondered if anyone had tried to track the history of the dresser.

"Could it be a fake?" Micky wondered aloud.

I studied the painting from across the room. Even at this distance the nude girl in the painting seemed warm and breathing, touchable, from the pink soles of her small feet to the glint of gold around her neck.

I shook my head. "Gut feeling? No. I grew up staring at that painting. It looks real to me." Of course, that was the point of a good forgery, wasn't it?

Micky's face was sympathetic. "You know, legally you have a pretty strong claim on that painting."

I reached for my drink. "I'm not going to court with Vince."

"'You're a better man than I am, Gunga Din.' It's an awful lot of money."

Unbidden, the question sprang into my mind: how much was enough to kill for?

"Did you know my grandfather has one of my father's paintings?"

"You're joking."

I shook my head. "My mother gave it to him, which is the only reason he hung on to it. It used to hang in his workshop. Probably still does. Sunrise in the old cemetery; Drake Trent's angel bathed in fiery light."

"I don't remember that one."

"It's probably worth a small fortune—and a lot easier to steal. A lot easier to market too."

I'm not sure what I was trying to say; I can't claim that I was beginning to put two and two together. Hell, I didn't even recognize the equation.

"When the Cobbs had their painting appraised, it was worth close to a hundred thousand dollars." Micky scratched her nose meditatively. "I bet a lot of people in Steeple Hill are kicking themselves now that they didn't hang on to their own works by Cosmo."

"I always sort of assumed Cosmo took the *Virgin* with him." I wiped the dampness from my forehead with the heel of my hand. "It's weird to think I'll never know what happened to him."

Micky started to answer but broke off as "Bebop in Pastel" dropped onto the turntable. In the center of the room Brett began to dance. He danced by himself, completely absorbed in his own perfect body and its response to the rhythm of the music.

He wore tight white jeans and a crimson silk shirt that was unbuttoned to reveal a sculpted chest and washboard stomach sprinkled with golden down. Irene Cobb watched in a kind of titillated shock. Jack Cobb stood with his back to the room but I could see him watching Brett in the mirror over the bar.

Everyone watched. For those few minutes Brett was the focus of the entire room, and how he loved it. The expression on his face was that of someone having a mind-blowing masturbatory experience—which was not far from what he was doing.

I rose and walked out onto the verandah. The air was moist with the hint of rain. Brett and Adam had strung Chinese lanterns down its length. The lanterns bobbed in the wind, and in the trembling light I could see Jenny at the far end. She was staring out at the black velvet night, watching the lightning crackle over the ocean.

"Hey," I said, leaning next to her on the railing.

"Hey." She rubbed her cheek against my shoulder like a friendly kitten.

There were shouts from inside the house. Cat calls.

"The storm's moving closer," I commented.

"Mmhmm." We watched the lightning flash and fade. "Kyle, have you ever been with a woman?"

I peered at her in surprise. "No."

"Never? Then how do you know—?"

What I was missing? That I was really gay? What? "I'm not sexually attracted to women," I said patiently.

"But you've never been with one."

"Jen, that's as silly as suggesting a heterosexual woman would have to sleep with another woman to know for sure that she's really heterosexual."

"It's not the same thing."

"Because one's 'normal' and one isn't?"

"I wasn't going to say that."

I knew this was really about Vince. Vince and his newly-confused sexual identity. I wished I had an answer for Jenny Wren, pat or otherwise.

She said softly, "Maybe you're subconsciously afraid of women."

"What? Like if I stick my penis inside a vagina it might fall off?"

"Kyle!"

"You started this conversation, Jen."

"Well, it would be a subconscious fear, not a rational thing." She gestured broadly, just missing my nose, and I wondered how much she'd had to drink. Since I was answering her, I'd probably had enough myself. "Maybe because of your heart condition. You're anxious about being the dominant sexual partner."

I wasn't about to get into my sexual practices with Jen, but I said, still trying to be polite, "I didn't have a heart condition until I was sixteen. I always knew I was different. I wasn't sure how or why; I didn't think about it a lot. But in high school I finally noticed what was different about me."

I hadn't had a chance to do anything about it, assuming I'd had the nerve or opportunity to act on my inclination.

She didn't say anything. I couldn't offer her any insight because I'd no idea what was going on in Vince's head. They had always seemed happy to me, but I hadn't experience at long-term relationships, homosexual or otherwise. Jenny continued to gaze up at me, her skin pale in the glow of the Chinese lanterns, her eyes huge and black as though she were on opium.

"Kiss me, Kyle," she whispered.

I kissed her. Somehow it seemed easier than explaining why it wouldn't solve anything. Jenny's lips were soft and cool. She tasted like orange bitters and she smelled of rain and flowers. It was nice.

"You son of a bitch! I thought you were supposed to be gay!" Vince's indignant voice behind us broke the spell.

I let go of Jen. She didn't let go of me. "I am gay." I tried to untangle my hands from Jenny's. She clung.

Brett, standing behind Vince in the French doors, exclaimed, "Adam, Kyle's making out with Jenny Wren on the verandah!"

The verandah spots came on like the lights in a police raid.

"How could you do this to me!" Vince yelled at Jenny, starting toward her.

She dived behind me. "You should talk!" she shot back from around my shoulder. "You're fucking him!" She pointed to Brett.

"Jenny!" gasped Vince. I think it was her language more than anything that struck him speechless. He glared at me, his hands clenching and unclenching.

By now the verandah was full of people. The entire party seemed to have moved outdoors. A pitchfork of lightning flashed above the black ocean like old Poseidon himself waking up. It started to sprinkle.

Adam maneuvered between the deliciously horror-stricken Cobbs, and put a hand on Vince's arm speaking under-voiced.

Vince shook him off and lunged at me. But now Joel had his other arm. Vince wriggled to get free. Jenny made alarmed squeaking noises, clutching me.

"Fisticuffs! I love it!" Brett was laughing so hard he had to hang on to the doorframe to keep upright. "Kyle, you slut."

"Shut up, Brett," Adam snapped, struggling with Vince.

That wiped the smile off Brett's face. He let go of the doorframe and charged at Adam. Adam stood his ground, but had to let go of Vince who shoved Joel with all his strength. Joel was not cut out for the bouncer gig. He and Vince shuffled a few feet in an awkward foxtrot.

"Now boys. Boys!" Norman Cobb expostulated, detaching himself from the other spectators. His leather dress shoes slid on the wet deck.

Brett swung at Adam.

It was at this point that the power went off.

CHAPTER SEVEN

Immediate chaos.

It was like a scene in one of John Wayne's early Republic flicks when someone throws a punch and then chairs start flying. Somebody slammed into me, and I staggered back knocking Jenny down. Jenny, her nerves raw, screamed. Loudly. There was scuffling and grunting over to my left. Adam and Brett?

Someone else started forward and crashed into the patio furniture. The table scraped forward a couple of feet and Jenny screamed again. Someone inside the house, Irene, I think, screamed too. Possibly out of sympathy, I felt like screaming myself.

"Jenny, would you shut up?" I requested, trying to get her back on her feet. She had decided to go in for the vapors or something and was a dead weight.

"Folks, would everyone stay where they are?" Adam called out exasperatedly. "Brett, get some candles."

"Get them yourself," Brett's muffled voice reached us from inside the house where he had retreated.

The heat of battle was over, but Vince was still seething.

"Get your goddamned hands off her!" He bore down on us, nearly falling over Jenny as I stepped aside with unheroic haste.

From inside the cottage came a crash and the sound of glass breaking. Irene quavered an inquiry as to whether Brett was all right. He snarled something back.

Adam, standing near me, swore. "What the hell is the problem? Brett?"

Micky appeared in the French windows holding a candelabrum. The candlelight wavered over our faces. "Adam, the power's off. And Brett's sick."

"I'm not surprised, the way he's been hammering down drinks," Adam retorted with uncharacteristic lack of sympathy.

"I hate you!" Jenny told Vince on a sob as he helped her to her feet.

"Jenny!" Vince was all injured innocence.

She shook him off and stumbled toward the stairs at the far end of the verandah. Vince followed in a kind of sleepwalking shuffle. Like Mrs. Danvers' sexy sister, Micky joined the parade, guiding them by the light of her candelabrum. The three of them squelched across the lawn to where several cars were parked. Other guests straggled behind. The party was over.

Inside the house, points of light flared in the darkness as Joel went about lighting the hurricane lanterns and candles.

"I think we should be going as well," Norman Cobb told Adam. "The power's probably gone for the night. What do you say, Irene?"

"Once it's out, it's generally out for the duration," Miss Irene agreed.

"No, Sister." The mayor strove for patience. "Are you and Jack ready to leave?"

"Jack has gone, Norman. He left before the power went."

Nonplused, the mayor turned to Adam. "Well, an interest—*enjoyable* evening, Adam." They shook hands.

Adam walked the Cobbs out across the wet grass, and I found myself alone on the verandah. I picked up the knocked-over chairs and went back inside.

"Another drink?" Joel offered, holding up one of the opalescent green glasses.

"No thanks. I'm buzzed now."

Micky joined us. "Brett is as sick as a dog," she announced. "How much did he have to drink?"

"A lot," I replied. "He finished off my third drink, and I know he'd had a few before that."

"Not that many," Joel defended. "I only fixed him four. He's got a pretty high tolerance."

"Adam says he was knocking them back."

Joel shook his head. "No."

Adam came back from seeing his guests off. He raked a hand through his damp hair. "It's pouring out there."

"Rain?" Micky sounded as alarmed as the Wicked Witch of the West caught without her umbrella. "Adam, I hate to leave you with this mess, but that road!"

"Don't worry about it," Adam said. "Joel and Kyle will pitch in."

Joel and I tried to sound keen.

Adam walked Micky, still apologizing for her defection, out to her car. Joel went to check on Brett. He came back a few moments later.

"He's got the bathroom door locked."

I thought this over. "Did he answer you?"

"If you call groans and retching an answer."

"I call it a good reason to keep the door locked."

Joel looked unconvinced.

"Adam," he said as soon as Adam reappeared. "I think you should check on Brett."

Adam nodded, looking vastly weary. Joel began screwing caps on the bottles of vodka and gin and orange bitters. I went into the kitchen and ran water into the sink. Adam came in and started rattling through the drawers.

"I need a screwdriver," he said.

I handed him a glass. He said impatiently, "A screwdriver, Kyle. A tool, not a drink. Brett's not answering me."

I helped him hunt. He settled for a steak knife, and I followed him back to the bathroom, watching as he swiftly undid the screws in the ornate bronze plate. He removed the glass doorknob and pulled open the door.

Brett lay face down on the floor. He was alive because I could see his shoulders heaving. The smell of vomit, urine and worse bounced off the aqua-and-indigo tiles.

Adam turned to me. "Tell Joel to phone for the doctor."

I nodded, only too happy to depart.

But when Joel tried to dial out, the line was dead. "The storm must have knocked the cable out again," he muttered. It was a common problem in the winter along the coast. We frequently lost electricity, cable or phones for hours at a time. "I'll drive into Steeple Hill and bring him back with me." He thrust a flashlight into my hand. "Tell Adam."

Joel disappeared into the night and I returned to Adam. I knew he wouldn't ask for my help, and I knew he needed it.

Adam pulled off his shirt and tossed it aside. I propped the flashlight on the sink and together we got Brett stripped and into the shower, tiles edged with delicate shells and seaweed painted by Adam many years before.

He turned the tap on full and I stepped back. I was impressed by his patience. And dismayed by the lack of my own.

Brett came to under the warm spray, sobbing and hanging on to Adam, soaking him also.

"Forgive me, Adam."

"I forgive you."

"Don't hate me. Don't…"

"I don't hate you."

"I love you so much."

"I know. I love you too." There was more forbearance than love in Adam's voice.

I was glad we were in the dark. Glad my face couldn't reveal my thoughts. The flashlight ray caught the glitter of shower spray and the glint of Adam's eyes—watching me—over Brett's bent head.

The lights came back on as we hauled Brett out of the shower. We toweled him off, and Adam got Brett into his bed. He flopped back into the pillows, dead to the world.

"I don't understand why you put up with this."

I hadn't meant to say it aloud, but there the words hung.

The skin tightened over the fine bones in Adam's face. "Don't you?" His eyes looked black in the washed light. "No clue at all?"

I couldn't hold his gaze and I couldn't seem to look away. "Sorry," I said. "That was stupid."

To my relief, the harshness left his face. In another minute I'd have been like Brett, begging him to forgive me. "It was honest," he said wearily. "Either way, this isn't your problem."

Dismissal, no doubt about it.

I nodded. But on my way past the bathroom I bundled Brett's filthy clothes and the soiled towels, dumping them into the washing machine. I turned the washer on and returned to the bedroom.

Soft light filtered through the pink-silk lampshade. Adam had changed out of his wet things. He sat beside Brett who appeared to have fallen into an uncomfortable doze. Perspiration sheened the tanned planes of Brett's chest and chiseled face. With the white sheet draped across his waist he looked like a fallen gladiator or something equally poetic and preposterous. Adam held his hand, but stared out the window at the lightning flitting across the black night. He looked drained, emptied of all feeling.

As though he felt my gaze, he raised his head. Our eyes locked.

I ducked back out of the room and began clearing away the dirty glasses and empty plates from the party. After several trips the rooms looked almost normal. There was no sound from the bedroom and no sign of Joel and the doctor.

I wandered over to the window overlooking the beach; the dock shone silver in the moonlight. I stood there wondering about Adam and Brett. Wondering about what binds people together.

I felt rather than heard Adam come up behind me. My skin prickled with awareness, like old bones aching at winter's approach.

He stood behind me and I could see his image in the window glass, overlapping my own. We looked like two ghosts, pale, half-vanished. Raindrops glistened in our reflections.

"It was a mistake to come back here." His breath was warm on the back of my neck. I shivered and he slipped his arms around me. I stood very still though I'm sure he could feel the betraying thud of my heart against my breast bone.

I understood my reaction to Brett. It was about sex, pure and simple. Or maybe not so pure, but definitely simple. My reaction to Adam was so much more complicated. I wanted him, yes—badly. But this yearning was more than physical. I couldn't define it and I knew there wasn't a hope in hell of satisfying it. And yet, after a moment, I relaxed and leaned against him. We stood there for what felt like a long time.

"Why was it a mistake?" I asked finally. I was thinking that in a moment he would let me go and I would feel colder than I had ever felt in my life.

But under the circumstances I guess it was a silly question. Adam didn't bother answering, resting his cheek against my head.

"For so long I thought of you as a kid." He turned his face to my hair, breathing in. "Jesus, you still even have that little boy scent."

"I think it's the…uh…baby shampoo." My voice sounded odd.

So did Adam's laugh as he turned me to face him. His hands were gentle, almost tentative as he drew me against him. I could feel his body taut and powerful down the length of my own. And I could feel the erection straining his jeans. I pressed closer, hoping he couldn't tell I was shaking. It's a little frightening when a dream comes true. For an instant we stood there, eye to eye, cock to cock. His breathing was even but fast, like he was holding himself in check.

"Adam," I whispered and fastened my arms around his neck. We kissed. Not gently, not tentatively, but hard and hungry. As though we had both been waiting for this from the day he returned.

"Oh, God, Kyle," he muttered into my mouth. I made a soft inarticulate sound of encouragement. His kiss deepened and I opened to it.

Instead he withdrew, kissing the corner of my mouth and then the sensitive hollow beneath my ear. I turned my mouth, seeking his. He kissed my eyebrow, and then—tenderly—my lips.

My heart pounded heavily in my chest, but it wasn't with happiness or excitement; it was anxiety. There was no joy in that kiss: it felt like good-bye. I opened my eyes.

"This isn't fair to you," he said unsteadily.

A car door slammed.

We pulled apart like boxers at the sound of a bell. There was a crunch of feet on shale, and then the front door opened and Joel and the doctor came in.

I've known Dr. Hicks all my life. I guess his was the first face I ever saw, if a newborn can see. He hasn't changed much over the years: iron-gray hair, iron-gray eyes which now met mine in stern disapproval. Hicks is small and spry for his age, which I always took to be advanced until it occurred to me recently that at the beginning of our acquaintance he must have been a young man.

I read Hick's disapprobation as the result of my having skipped my last check-up. However, when Adam and the doctor had disappeared into the bedroom, Joel hissed at me, "I give it two thumbs-up, dear boy, but if you're planning on a return engagement, keep in mind that this room is like a stage when the blinds are drawn. Steeple Hill is watching."

I viewed the room ablaze with candles and lanterns, and recognized the truth of that. Anyone happening to look out his window would have been treated to a cliché straight out of the *Late Show*.

About an hour of sick-making sounds later, I was on the sofa starting to doze when Adam and Dr. Hicks came out of the bedroom.

"Call me if there's any change," Dr. Hicks was saying.

"Yes. Thanks for coming out this time of night," Adam replied.

Dr. Hicks paused to glower at me. "You should be home in bed, young man."

"I'm just going," I said.

"And I want you to call this week to set up another appointment."

"Uh, sure. Yes."

Joel made the naughty-naughty sign before following the man of medicine into the night. I wasn't sure which "naughty-naughty" he was referring to.

Adam and I stood on opposite sides of the room. Adam said, "Go home, Kyle. You look dead."

"I'm going. If you're sure you're all right?"

Adam nodded. "Terrific. Brett told the doctor he thought he had been poisoned."

"What?"

"Hicks took some—samples to get them analyzed."

"Food poisoning? Is that what Brett meant?"

"Brett told Hicks he thought someone was trying to kill him. He didn't mean Jen's guacamole."

"Why would he say that?"

"Presumably because he believes it." Adam pinched the bridge of his nose. "Who the hell knows why Brett does anything? I gave up trying to figure him out a long time ago."

Which wasn't to say that he had stopped loving him.

* * * * *

The rain had passed and the moon shone. I stood out on my front porch, too restless to sleep, though I was beat. The lights were off in the cottage across the meadow. I could still feel Adam's arms around me and the taste of his mouth on mine. On impulse I decided to walk out to the old church and watch the sunrise.

When I was younger I used to walk out to Steeple Hill often. I think it started as a kind of proof to myself that I wasn't actually in the graveyard if I could walk to it. Too, I guess the silence and peace appealed to me. My imagination was stirred by the graves with their ornate headstones and flowery epitaphs. Lest I appear some fey creature of the woodland, I didn't wander that way much anymore, but I still could trace the path in the dark.

The church stood lightless and silent, windows boarded, the doors padlocked. The bell in the steeple hung motionless, its tongue stilled for many years.

I'm not sure how long I had been sitting on the steps watching the marble angel frozen in its dance when I heard a rustling sound behind me.

Warning prickled down my spine. I half turned and something slammed down on my shoulder. I was in motion so it was a glancing blow, but it hurt unbelievably and it scared the shit out of me.

I think I yelled, "What are you *doing*?" Which should have been obvious already. I scuttled over the broken stones in the walk, dodging a kick aimed at my midsection.

It happened so fast. It didn't occur to me to fight back. I'd never been in a fight. I wouldn't have known where to begin. My focus was on escaping in one piece, and for that I was well equipped, being limber, relatively fast, and familiar with the churchyard.

I dived, rolled across the wet leaves and grass, and scrambled to my feet as my assailant slammed the board into a stone urn, showering bits of cement flowers over my face and hair.

"Don't like it rough, *honey*? Don't want to play anymore?"

It was too dark to see more than a bulky outline. His voice was hoarse, rasping, unfamiliar.

"Fucking faggot!"

I scrambled up and bolted for the break in the fence. He was right behind me. I wriggled through, tearing my sweatshirt, managed to get to my feet and raced for the shelter of the woods.

Once inside the muffled darkness I slowed. Stopped. Listened.

He was coming up fast.

Slipping off the path, I moved carefully, cautiously, while nerves clamored to break and run. Quietly, quietly… Creeping through the tangle of vines and underbrush, the humid smell of earth and mold assailed my nostrils.

Something moved nearby. I froze. Leaves crackled. I sank down on my haunches behind a tree trunk. My heart was clamoring like an eight-bell fire alarm. *Steady, steady*, I warned my faulty pump.

Silence.

I was afraid to breathe. He was not gone. He was listening for me, as I was listening for him.

I thought of my father vanishing in these same woods ten years ago.

The crack of a tree branch beside me was like a gunshot. I jumped up, thrusting through the mass of thorns and brush. My face and hands stung as I plowed on.

There was crashing in the undergrowth behind me.

And then, at last, I was out from under the canopy of trees and into the wide-open space of the meadow. The white flowers glimmered like fallen stars. My lungs burned as my feet pounded the dirt.

Like an arrow I flew down the path straight onto my porch and through my front door, which I slammed and locked—for the first time in four years—behind me.

I staggered over to the window. Nothing moved along the woodline. The moon shone down colorlessly, the high grass rippled in the breeze. I stared and stared, shaking with exertion and adrenaline, still trying to catch my breath. Nothing moved in the night.

It was unbelievable. I stumbled around checking the side door, the windows; locking, bolting, securing myself against siege. I even threw open closets, to reassure myself. After checking the back bedroom, my old room, I turned out the light. The ceiling glowed fuzzily. I regarded it in surprise.

Far, far away in a distant galaxy...

I hadn't given this a thought in years; when I came home from the hospital my father had stuck tiny glow-in-the-dark stars, moons and meteors all across my bedroom ceiling. When the lights were off, I had my own private galaxy.

Gazing upwards now, this memory comforted me.

I circled back to the front room. There was still no sign of pursuit. Across the meadow, Adam's cottage was dark and silent. I picked up the phone, listened to the dial tone. I hesitated.

Fag bashing in Steeple Hill?

Ridiculous. Had I heard correctly? *Fucking faggot?* No one could have known I would be at the old church tonight. I hadn't known myself. So someone had followed me.

Or had waited for someone else.

* * * * *

The next morning dawned hot and clear; the sky was achingly blue, the water glittered with what my father used to call "sun dazzle." Sail boats dotted the waves in perfect composition like one of Frank Benson's painted summer idylls.

Walking over to Adam's, I found Brett holding court on the terrace. True, Vince was the only courtier, but he seemed sufficient. They had been deep in conversation but shut up at my approach. Neither looked particularly thrilled to see me.

"How are you feeling today?" I asked Brett. His face looked pinched and jaundiced. There were circles like bruises under his eyes. Still, he looked hunky in a white gauze caftan that didn't cover his spread knees.

"Okay." Was it my imagination or was there hostility in the eyes meeting mine?

"Someone tried to kill Brett last night," Vince announced.

"You're kidding," I said. "Someone tried to kill me too."

I couldn't have asked for a better reaction. They both gawked. Brett finally sputtered, "*You? Why would anyone want to kill you?*" Like murder was reserved for the select few.

"Maybe they thought I was someone else."

Brett's eyes narrowed. Vince was asking all the normal questions: when, where, how, why? Brett said nothing, but by the time I finished relating my adventure he had a peculiar look on his face.

"You have no idea who attacked you?" he asked.

"No. Do you?"

"Me?"

Vince said slyly, following his own line of thought, "But what exactly were you doing in the churchyard at two o'clock in the morning? Hmmm?" He exchanged a knowing glance with Brett who merely looked pissed.

"That's right," I said, "my social life is so dead I meet my dates in the graveyard."

"Kinky," laughed Vince.

"Shut your goddamn mouth," Brett bit out.

Vince looked wounded.

"You're obviously feeling better," I remarked. "See you later." I turned to leave.

Brett sniped, "Are you going without seeing Adam?"

So that was it. I stared at Vince who avoided my eyes.

"I didn't come to see Adam."

"I really should be getting back," Vince said hastily, rising from the iron chair. "Tell Adam to bring my painting over when he gets home."

Brett and I ignored him. Brett patted the chair next to himself invitingly. I stood where I was.

"Don't frown, Kylie, you'll make wrinkles."

"Do you mind not calling me 'Kylie'?"

"Do you prefer 'scout'?"

"I prefer 'Kyle,' which is my name."

His lips formed a sneer, but he let it pass. "Don't stand over me, Kyle. You're blocking my sun."

My sun. That about summed it up. I sat down in a chair across from him and said, "Brett, do you really think someone is trying to kill you, or are you doing this for attention?"

"I don't need to get my stomach pumped for attention, okay? I get all the attention I need."

"How much did you have to drink last night?"

"Alcohol poisoning?" he hooted. "You've never seen me seriously drunk."

I had a feeling I wouldn't want to. "I guess the real wonder is nobody's tried to kill you before."

He chuckled. "I'm hurt. I thought we were buds. It's what Adam wants, you know. He worries about me." He studied my face to see how I responded to that.

I had no response to that. Brett continued to eye me and then said thoughtfully, "You've got scratches on your hands and face. Your lover plays rough. I guess that lets Adam out." He got to his feet. The sunlight shone through the gauzy nightshirt. He stretched hugely and his dick bowed to the audience. Me. "Let's fuck."

I sighed and rose. Brett grabbed my arm as I started to walk away. "Don't get snotty, Kyle. You're my only friend. You're the only person here I trust."

The survival instincts of a lemming.

"Don't you trust Adam?"

His expression went blank. "Sure. But that's different."

Something was glittering on the stair. I picked up Brett's anklet. He snatched it out of my hand. "Shit! The clasp must be broken."

I remembered he had been wearing it the night before. Irene's gaze had fixed on it as though she had never seen a man wearing jewelry. Maybe she never had.

Brett chuckled, and dangled the anklet in front of me. "401K."

"Huh?"

"Get it? Instead of 14 karat—never mind. It's my retirement fund."

"What are you retiring from?"

"You'll see. Then we'll find out how good a friend you are."

"I have my limits."

"Where Adam is concerned?"

Something about the way he said that made me uneasy. "What the hell are you talking about, Brett? Spit it out, would you?"

With all the cunning of a ten-year-old he taunted, "You'll soon find out."

CHAPTER EIGHT

Adam sketched me and Brett together a number of times that summer. He seemed fascinated by some fancied likeness between us—or maybe it was the differences. In pencil, the fact that my eyes were hazel and Brett's green, that his hair was blonde and mine brown, wasn't noticeable; there was only the similarity of our bone structure, the shape of our eyes, the line of our noses.

Having grown up with artists, I barely noticed when Adam would grab a napkin or the back of the TV Guide and start penciling, but it irked Brett. If he found one of those impromptu portraits of the two of us, he would crumple it up.

A lot of things irked Brett. He ragged on Adam about his painting, about working in his "comfort zone." Ten years ago Adam had found his niche. He was doing well financially which permitted Brett to live in his comfort zone. But Brett sneered at Adam's stuff, called him the Painter of Graveyards, in mockery of Thomas Kincaid's success.

Me, I thought Adam's work was lovely. Accessible. But as Brett pointed out, what did I know? According to Brett, Cosmo was the real thing, and Adam was a cheap imitation. Per Brett, Adam had sold out. He was going to end up a footnote on commercialism in the annals of Art History. *You'll be right there with Tommy Kincaid and the Marty Bell cottages.*

I don't know if Brett's barbs worked their way into Adam's psyche, but they worked into mine. It was hard to keep my mouth shut sometimes.

The evening after the party I was sitting on the verandah stairs beside Adam. Adam was idly pitching pebbles across the lawn at the sundial.

"Did you read Joel's book?" I asked.

Adam grimaced. The next pebble pinged off the point of the sundial's arrow.

"He implies that he and my father…"

After a moment Adam said, "I wasn't there. I don't know. Straight guys do experiment occasionally."

"But Cosmo *was* straight?"

"As the shortest distance between two points." There was something rueful in his smile that made me wonder if Adam had had a thing for Cosmo. Not a comfortable thought.

"Did he know I was gay?"

For a minute I didn't think Adam would answer. Then he took a deep breath, expelling it slowly. "Your father only said one thing to me on the subject. He said, 'let him make up his own mind.'"

I mulled this over. The way Adam repeated it, it sounded vaguely like a warning. Why would my father have felt it necessary to warn Adam off? I studied Adam's profile. His lashes were down, veiling his eyes as he reached for another pebble.

"Why did you come back, Adam? Why now?"

"Brett wanted to. It was his idea."

Brett shoved open the porch door, which banged against the wall of the house. "Do you know there is no one in this entire goddamn county who delivers Chinese?"

Adam glanced around. "You want me to go get take-out?"

"I want to go out to dinner," Brett said. "I'm sick of this dump!"

"Don't turn into Betty Davis," Adam said mildly. "We'll go out. Kyle?"

"How about you and me for a change, Adam?" Brett gave me a stare as green as broken glass. "I'm sure Kyle understands."

"Sure," I said hastily. I stood up.

"See ya," said Brett.

The next morning I woke to sunlight on the floorboards and the smell of newly-mown grass on the breeze, but the chill on my heart felt as though it were the dead of winter. The star-crossed lovers thing was getting old fast.

My "friendship" with Brett wasn't helping Brett and Adam, and it was bad for me.

Watching the shadows on the ceiling, I reasoned that it would be best for everyone if I finished the summer someplace else. New scenery. New faces. I remembered the air show poster my father had brought me so many years ago. I'd never been to France. The City of Lights? Gay Paree? Hell, I'd never been anywhere. I tried to work up some enthusiasm. The more I dreaded the idea of leaving, the more I knew I had to go.

After lunch I drove into the village to pick up supplies. When I walked into the grocers I could tell by the way the old biddies clammed-up that rumors about "goings on" at the colony were rampant.

"Storm's coming," Mrs. Hammett informed me as I paid for my salmon steaks and low fat milk.

There wasn't a cloud in the sky, but Mrs. Hammett's rheumatism is as reliable as a ship's barometer. "We could use the rain," I said.

"Your grandfather was in here, Kyle."

"Yeah? How is he?"

I've known Mrs. Hammett since I was tall enough to push my three pennies across the counter for her homemade taffy. She replied tartly, "Lonely. I'd say he could use some company."

Probably some company he *liked* would be a better idea, but I only said, "Maybe I'll stop by there on the way home."

Mrs. Hammett gave a mollified sniff and handed over my change.

* * * * *

Aaron Lipez lived in one of those white two-story Victorian jobs with a red roof, gingerbread trim and lots of geometrically shaped windows. I have vague memories of playing under the spreading shade trees when I was very small. As I recall, I buried a whole platoon of WWI tin soldiers under that leafy roof. I also recall my grandfather telling me he would bury me with them if I didn't exhume each and every one. An idle threat since here I was, walking onto his front porch and knocking.

And knocking.

There was no answer.

I wandered around back. My grandfather's pickup was gone. Relieved, I climbed back in the jeep and headed for the colony.

Once home, I unloaded my groceries and gave the nearest travel agency a call to price out tickets to France. That done, I felt better. I changed into swim trunks and trucked down to the beach.

On the way down to the cove I spotted the weed killer apparatus Irene had loaned me sitting in a rose bed. I picked it up, examined it. It was empty. Had I left it outdoors so long that the liquid evaporated? I didn't think so. I carried the weed killer back to the porch and continued down to the beach.

I was hoping to have the cove to myself, but I noticed Brett lurking under the dock a few yards away. Seeing me, he ducked back behind the piles. That suited me. I didn't want to talk to Brett. I started for the water. But Brett stepped out and beckoned me over imperiously.

"What are you doing here?" he asked accusingly when I was within earshot.

"Swimming."

"You never swim this time of day."

"Sometimes I do. What's it to you?"

"Are you spying on me?"

"Are you nuts?"

Seeing that I was pissed, he said quickly, "I'm kidding, Kyle." He looked at his watch. As I turned away, he said, "Where are you going?"

"I'm going to swim."

"Can't you swim some other time?"

"Who are you waiting for?"

"No one."

I snorted and turned away.

"Wait."

I waited none too patiently.

"You may as well keep me company."

"I'm not in the mood."

"What did I do?" He sounded genuinely hurt. I ran a hand through my hair, feeling the wind ruffle it up.

"Nothing. I came to swim."

Brett wasn't listening. He looked at his watch again. His expression changed; I couldn't tell if it was irritation or disappointment. He seemed to relax though. He questioned suddenly, as if the thought had only occurred, "Did Cosmo keep a journal?"

"No."

"What about letters?"

"He wasn't sentimental. He didn't hang on to things."

Brett looked like he didn't believe me, but it was the truth. Cosmo had kept nothing that didn't relate to current business transactions. He had an excellent memory. Perhaps he relied on that.

"Did it ever occur to you that maybe Cosmo never left Steeple Hill?"

"Huh?" I said intelligently.

"If he left, why wouldn't he come back? He always came back, right?"

"Maybe he will some day," I said, not believing it. "If he's still alive. Maybe he planned to, but..." I shrugged.

"You told me you thought he was dead."

I said reluctantly, "I do."

"You think he died after he split. Suppose he died before he could leave?"

"What? But that's..." I gestured confusedly. The thought had honestly never occurred, and I didn't like it now. "His body," I expostulated. "What about his body? It would have been found if he'd drowned or fell or..."

"I'm not talking about an accident."

"What *are* you talking about?"

"Shit, use your brain, Kyle. What kind of mystery writer are you? Why would he leave right then? Didn't you ever ask yourself?"

I put into words for Brett what no one had put into words for me, but what I knew everyone believed. "I think my getting sick was the last straw," I said. "He wasn't cut out for fatherhood. I think he cared for me but it was too much responsibility. And then my getting sick—it was obvious right away there was a problem with my heart. It was just too much for him, I think."

"You think he'd walk out without a word? Without a note? Without a change of clothes?"

"Who says he didn't have a change of clothes?"

"Did he?"

I shrugged. "I don't know. I wasn't in noticing shape. He never took much when he split. He was used to roughing it. Living off the land. Living off his friends."

Brett leaned back against one of the thick posts supporting the dock and lit a cigarette. "It doesn't make sense. If—"

The post gave way behind him. As Brett staggered back, the dock seemed to collapse in slow motion, crashing down upon him. I jumped to the side, tumbling out of the way, and came up staring in disbelief.

The center portion of the dock lay on the sand; Brett pinned beneath. He was alive, because he was yelling his head off, but he was as shocked and scared as I was—and in a lot more pain. The old planks were heavy, and besides the splinters and jagged pieces of wood, there were thick nails suitable for crucifixion jutting out everywhere.

I dragged off one plank as thick as a railway tie, and Brett screamed, "God, watch what you're doing! You'll cut me in half!"

I dropped to my knees and cleared the debris away from around his head.

"What happened?" Brett was crying. "What the fuck happened?" He made an effort to raise himself and fell back. "Kyle, the tide!"

"The tide's not coming in, Brett," I reassured. "Not for hours." Which wasn't exactly true. We probably had under an hour before the waves rushed the beach.

"You've got to get me out of here."

I was trying; I scooped sand out from under him, thinking I could extricate him that way. But shoveling sand with my hands was slow going and inefficient; the sand burned as I scraped my hands in and out of its deceptive softness.

"Can you get your arm free?"

"It's broken, I think. I can't move it."

"Shit." I jumped up, ran around to the other side and tried once more to lift off one of the posts. It was no use. "Brett," I said, kneeling beside his head. "I'm going for help."

"No!" he cried. "No, don't leave me."

"I can't free you on my own."

"Yes, you can. Don't leave me, Kyle."

"Brett." I touched his face. Tears and blood mingled with the sand. I wiped them away. "Listen, I can't do it on my own. Let me get help."

He stared up at me, his green eyes drowned. He nodded jerkily. "Hurry. Please."

I hopped to my feet and raced for the cliff.

Seventy-five stairs. Midway up I felt something slip in my chest and my heart began to batter itself against my rib cage. I couldn't get my breath, the blood sang in my ears, my vision darkened. I tried to push past it.

Big mistake.

I dropped onto one knee, sucking air into my lungs.

I couldn't hear Brett anymore. I couldn't hear anything over the thunder in my ears. I reached for the railing, hauled myself up another step. Then another.

"Kyle." Strong arms closed around me. Adam's voice was in my ear. "What is it? What's wrong?"

I could feel myself slipping through his hands like water, pouring onto the rock at his feet. I huddled there. Colored stars shot through the blackness of my vision. "It's Brett," I gasped. "The dock—he's pinned—I couldn't—"

"Brett!" Adam's hands bit into my shoulders. "Jesus. Can you hold on, Kyle?"

I nodded, hands to my chest, still fighting to get my breath. My vision cleared a little.

Adam crouched down, trying to see my face. "I don't want to leave you like this."

"Go."

Still he hesitated, his eyes dark with concern and doubt.

"Go," I wheezed. "Be fine—go!"

"Sit tight," Adam ordered. "I'll be back in a minute. Stay still."

I assented and Adam was gone.

Leaning back against the steps, I closed my eyes, willed my heart to stop the insanity. I was as afraid for myself as Brett by this point. Was I having a full-blown coronary? Was I dying?

I massaged my chest, took another shallow breath; bit my lip at the pain. Probably not indigestion. Angina maybe? No way. Maybe I'd pulled a muscle lifting the plank off Brett. It didn't have to be anything really serious. I'd been fine for ages. It could be some kind of panic attack, right? I tried to fill my lungs and winced.

Fuck.

I blinked back the sting in my eyes. How stupid was this?

After what felt like eons my pulse eased, slowed. I could breathe again; the tightness in my chest relaxed. I debated continuing up the stairs to get Adam help. I was so tired. I only needed a minute, I promised myself.

A shadow fell across my face. I heard the heavy whoosh of wings as a gull swooped down. The sound alarmed me in some indefinable way. I opened my eyes, and Adam stood over me, his back to the sun, his face unreadable.

His silence, his stillness, scared me. I whimpered; made some small sound of pain and fear. Adam knelt so that our eyes were level. There was still something I didn't understand in his expression, but I recognized concern for me in his gaze.

"Put your arm around my neck, Kyle," he instructed, putting his own arm around me.

I obeyed, weak and fumbling. "Where's Brett?" I whispered. "Did you get him free? Is he okay?"

Adam's other arm slipped beneath my knees. Giving a grunt, he lifted me up as though I were still a kid. I clutched his neck, feeling muscles move beneath his damp T-shirt, feeling his warm, sun-browned skin under my hands. I breathed in his scent: almond soap, clean sweat, and faintly, turpentine. A fragrance straight out of my childhood; instantly reassuring.

"Hang on, Kyle," Adam muttered. "I'll get you out of this."

I let my head drop on his shoulder. "Sorry. Feel so…stupid."

"Quiet."

His exhalations fanned lightly against my face. It was a relief to let go, to leave it to Adam. My heart had slowed but it was still irregular, kicking twice, pausing too long, thudding against my side in a dizzy tattoo.

"Here we go, baby," Adam reassured breathlessly as he climbed. "Almost there."

Only another twenty steps to go. I wanted to apologize again for being such a wuss. Instead I closed my eyes.

The next thing clear was Adam lowering me onto the sofa in his cottage. He spread the black crocheted afghan over me. I could hear him moving around, then the sound of a drawer opening and closing. I heard him dialing the Sheriff's Department.

"Steeple Hill. The colony. That's right. There's been an accident." Adam requested paramedics, an ambulance. He spoke in a low, calm voice as though he was used to making 911 calls. Childishly comforted, I drifted.

"Kyle, don't you have some pills or something?"

I opened my eyes. Adam was frowning down on me. "At the house."

"Jesus, Kyle!"

"Adam, what about Brett? How badly is he hurt? You shouldn't leave him so long."

Adam didn't say anything. His eyes avoided mine. Something in his silence…

I shifted against the cushions, tried to sit up. "What is it?"

Adam pushed me flat again. "Simmer down, scout."

The cold sickness pooling in my gut had nothing to do with my own physical frailty. "What aren't you telling me?"

Adam said slowly, "Brett is dead."

"Dead?" Adam said nothing. "He can't be dead!" I started to shake. I couldn't believe it. "He can't be dead," I repeated.

"Take it easy, Kyle."

"He can't be dead. Are you sure?"

"I'm sure," Adam said grimly.

I wiped at the wet spilling over my cheeks. "He can't be," I repeated.

Adam said, "Where are these pills of yours kept?"

"Kitchen cupboard." At his expression, I added defensively, "I haven't needed them in ages, Adam."

"Okay, okay. I know. Try and rest. I'll run next door."

I nodded, dragged the back of my arm across my leaking eyes.

By the time Adam got back I had myself under control, although he was so kind, so concerned, I nearly lost it again.

"Come on, baby. Let's get these down." He helped me sit up, his fingertips brushing my mouth as he slipped the pills between my lips. He held the glass for me and I took a couple of sips of water. "Thatta, boy. Lie back. I'm going to put these cushions under your legs."

I could have managed on my own, but I gave myself up to the unmanly pleasure of being cosseted.

*　*　*　*　*

The paramedics and the cops arrived at the same time. Adam took the cops down to the beach and the paramedics got to work on me, despite my protests that I was fine after all.

By the time Adam returned with Sheriff Rankin and his deputy in tow, I was sitting up feeling almost back to normal. Almost.

The paramedics informed Adam I had refused to go to the hospital and Adam insisted that they take me anyway. While they debated the legalities, the sheriff sat down across from me.

Rankin was a big man with a handlebar mustache and cowboy boots like a lawman out of a Zane Grey western. I remembered him from when I had my first bike stolen. My father had decreed filing a police report would be a good experience. Perhaps he had anticipated a lifetime of police involvement.

"Howdy, Kyle."

I nodded hello. The deputy took her notebook and pencil out.

Spotting our tableau, Adam tried to intercept. "You can't question him. He's on his way to the hospital."

"No, I'm not."

"Yes, you are."

I informed the paramedics I wouldn't be taking an ambulance ride, that my health insurance wouldn't cover it. These were the magic words and they began to pack up.

The sheriff inquired, "Some reason you don't want Kyle to talk to us, Mr. MacKinnon?"

Adam's face changed. "What the hell is that supposed to mean?"

"Just wondering." Sheriff Rankin turned to me. "You feel up to talking to us, Kyle?"

"Sure." I gave Adam a look which meant "power down," but which he didn't seem to recognize. He continued to hover.

"Sure," Sheriff Rankin agreed. "Kyle and I are old friends, right?"

"Right." If he said so.

"Right. Let's start at the beginning. You and the deceased, Mr. Hansen that was, were down in the cove. You were swimming? Or what?"

"We were talking."

"Talking? On a beautiful hot day like today? What were you talking about?"

I shrugged. "Just…talk."

His eyes were brown and unexpectedly shrewd—like a savvy old hound dog's. "Uh huh. So you were standing where in relation to the dock?"

"We were standing in the shade. Brett was right beneath. I was a little to the side."

"What happened then?"

"It…collapsed."

"Like that? No warning?"

I tried to remember. "There was a kind of cracking sound and then one of the pillars gave way, and it came down. Fast."

"But not so fast you didn't have time to get out of the way?"

I stared at him dumbly.

"Then what happened?"

"Brett was pinned underneath. There was a section of logs—planks across his chest and thighs. He was yelling and crying. There were nails, jagged pieces of wood. I tried to lift off the planks but I couldn't, so I tried to dig the sand out from under him. I thought I could drag him free that way." I turned to Adam. "He—Brett—was begging me not to leave him, to help him. I didn't think straight."

"Was there anyone else in the cove besides yourself and Hansen?" the sheriff questioned.

"No." I hesitated, remembering Brett checking and rechecking his watch. Had he been waiting for someone?

Observing me the sheriff said, "You sure about that?"

"I didn't see anyone." Someone could have waited a few yards down behind the rocks or hid on the hillside, but Rankin could figure that much out for himself.

"Uh huh. Then what happened?"

"I was afraid it would take too long to get Brett free on my own. He was worried about the tide. I was too. I told him I was going for help. He—" I stopped and rubbed my chest.

Adam bit out, "If you're going to question him you should have a doctor present. He's already had some kind of seizure."

"I'm fine," I said quickly.

The sheriff didn't say anything for a minute but clearly the more Adam intervened the worse it looked. "I appreciate that, Mr. MacKinnon. That's why I'm permitting you to stay while I question Mr. Bari."

"I'm not a doctor."

"I'm all right, Adam," I repeated.

Adam folded his arms and clenched his jaw, as though physically restraining himself.

"What were you and Mr. Hansen talking about on the beach for so long?"

"My father. And it wasn't for long. Maybe five minutes."

"Your father? What about him?"

"Brett was curious about his disappearance. He had this theory Cosmo was murdered."

"What?" Adam ejaculated.

The sheriff and deputy exchanged looks but all Rankin said was, "So you left Hansen and came running up the stairs for help and bumped into Mr. MacKinnon?"

"Yes."

"MacKinnon was coming *down* the stairs?"

I nodded.

"But you, as Mr. MacKinnon says, had some kind of heart seizure about then, isn't that right?"

"I came up the stairs too fast."

"Uh huh. So you explained to MacKinnon that the dock had collapsed and was crushing Mr. Hansen, and he ran down to see if he could help. About how long before Mr. MacKinnon rejoined you?"

"I'm not sure."

"Sure, sure. You weren't feeling too swift yourself. Do you have any recollection of time? Thirty minutes? Five minutes?"

"I don't know. It didn't feel long." I turned to Adam for help. He didn't respond. He looked pale and somber.

"I'm sorry, Adam," I faltered. "I know it's my fault."

"How's that?" The sheriff raised a brow.

"I wasted too much time trying to dig him out. I should have gone for help straight off. But he begged me not to leave him. I didn't realize—was it shock? Was he hemorrhaging internally? It *can't* have been the tide." I looked from one to the other. Their matching expressions dried the words in my throat. "What is it?"

Sheriff Rankin said slowly, "You don't know, do you?" He turned to Adam. "You didn't tell him?"

"No."

"Know what? What are you talking about?"

"Your friend Hansen didn't die of shock or internal injuries. Not from any dock falling on him anyway." The sheriff said slowly, as though savoring the words, "He was murdered. Someone stove his head in with a rock."

CHAPTER NINE

"**A**re you sure you're all right?" Adam asked for the twentieth time.

"It was mostly the shock, I think."

"You look like hell," he said roughly.

"Yeah, well," I tried to joke, "I'm having a bad heart day."

Brett's body had been removed. The sheriff and company had resumed combing the beach after the tide had retreated once more. They had questioned Adam for nearly two hours. Now there was nothing left for him to do, so he insisted on driving me the few yards to my cottage.

Pulling up on the shell circle outside the garden gate, he turned off the engine. I didn't know what to say to him. I stared at the dashboard. Brett's Ray-Bans lay there. I felt a burning in my sinuses like I was going to sneeze. Or cry.

"I can't face that cottage tonight," Adam said. "Can I crash here?"

I swallowed dryly. Nodded.

The phone calls began as soon as we closed the door. First Micky. Then Joel. Then the local paper. Adam took the calls, explained I was still recovering and fielded the expressions of sympathy and curiosity about Brett.

From the leather sofa in the study I listened and wondered at how calm he sounded. Not sounded, *was*. Because he had something to focus on: me. Taking care of me. Not exactly flattering to be used as a grief substitute, but what are friends for?

After a time Adam took the phone off the hook and poked his head in the study.

"Are you hungry? You should eat something."

"I can't right now, but you need to eat, Adam."

"I could use a drink."

I joined him in the kitchen. Adam had a drink while he heated a can of tomato soup. Sitting at the table, I watched him butter a stack of saltines as meticulously as though he was applying oils in short paint technique.

The old refrigerator hummed noisily, the clock on the wall ticked slowly. Neither of us spoke.

Adam ladled out the soup and we both made a pretense of eating, in hopes of encouraging the other.

The evening had turned cold, mist rolling in from the sea and swallowing the cottages and gardens of the colony in gloom. It seemed very still. Ominously still. As though the entire world were hushed and waiting.

Following our meal, Adam laid a fire in the study. I had another dose of medication and stretched out on the sofa; Adam took the chair by the fireplace. He was drinking Courvoisier, his glass winking in the firelight. He began to talk about Brett. He said Joel had introduced them two years earlier at an exhibition in Soho. Instant simpatico. They had left the Guggenheim and walked till they found a café with a small garden in back. They sat in the garden all night, talking and drinking cheap champagne. Brett had moved into Adam's loft before the week was out. They had never spent a night apart in two years.

I rested on the couch and listened. That was all that was required of me fortunately; I didn't have energy for more. The meds left me feeling dull and depressed. I watched Adam's face in the flickering shadows, watched his strong, beautiful hands, listened to his voice. A million times growing up I had pictured him like this, sitting across from me, sharing his heart. Now he was here, even spending the night, but I could have been anyone. Or no one. I could have been Adam's own shadow moving against the wall as he lifted his glass once more. It wasn't me he wanted, it was Brett, stiffening up in a drawer in the county morgue.

Outside the window the fog pressed against the glass, turning the night white.

"He wasn't like that," Adam repeated. I realized I was nearly asleep. I repositioned myself against the arm of the sofa. "Not really. He had been hurt. Some of the things that happened to him in foster homes…physical and sexual abuse…like something out of the frigging dark ages." He wiped the heel of his hand to the corner of his eyes. I saw the wet glittering there. My heart clenched and unclenched.

Adam went on talking about Brett, not noticing when tears slipped past and trickled down his cheeks. I watched him through my lashes, losing the battle to keep my eyes open. He seemed to be getting smaller and smaller, receding into some untouchable distance…

* * * * *

When I opened my eyes again, Adam had fallen asleep in the chair. He was frowning at his dreams, his mouth slightly open. The cognac bottle was empty at his elbow. The fire had died down to gray ash. Cautiously I sat up. At some point he had thrown the Irish chain-stitch quilt over me. I stood up, wrapping it Indian style around me, and tip-toed upstairs.

But once in bed, comfortable and alone, my brain kicked into gear. I lay there running everything over in my mind. On the bureau, my father's photographed grin reappeared Cheshire Cat style as the room grew lighter and lighter. I mused over Brett's suggestion that Cosmo had never left Steeple Hill. Murder. That's what Brett had been talking about. And now Brett was dead. Murdered.

It still didn't seem real. I tried to feel something. There was nothing there beyond a dull shock. A sense that it had to be a mistake.

Why would anyone kill Brett? Maybe that was a rhetorical question. There were probably a number of people who might want Brett out of the way, but murder? Murder was such a drastic step to take. So risky. And so unnecessary, surely? Unless…Brett had been right, and Cosmo had not died a natural death. Suppose Brett had discovered something about that unnatural death? Wouldn't that knowledge give someone who had murdered once, a reason to risk murder again?

The problem was, how would Brett know anything about a ten-year-old murder? And if Cosmo had been murdered, wouldn't there have been some suspicion of it in all these years? There had never been a hint.

Another thought: if Brett was right, if my father had been murdered ten years ago, then he had likely been killed by someone I had known all my life.

On this comforting thought I dozed off.

When I opened my eyes again I was confused to hear someone tapping on my bedroom door. I was trying to work this out when the door opened. Adam stuck his head in and I remembered Brett was dead.

"Morning," I said, trying to focus.

Adam came in and, to my surprise, sat down on the edge of the mattress. Cozy bedside chats had never been part of the big brother scenario.

"How are you this morning? The truth."

"I'm fine," I said truthfully. "How are you holding up?"

He looked tired. His blue eyes were rimmed with red, and his head had to be throbbing, but he said, "I'm okay. Thanks for putting up with me last night."

I nodded.

"You'll call the doctor today, right?"

"Sure."

"Take it easy, okay? Rest. If you're not up to answering more questions—"

"I'm fine."

"You don't have to prove anything."

I pushed up on my elbows. "Adam, don't treat me like an invalid. I can't live that way."

His face tightened. He nodded. There was something going on here that I didn't understand. Maybe Adam didn't know how to relate to me as a healthy adult. Maybe he didn't *want* to relate to me man to man.

To distract myself from this idea I asked, watching his face, "Adam, suppose I *had* known how Brett died?"

He didn't answer.

"Was it some kind of test?"

I thought that he wouldn't answer that either, but he said finally, bleakly, "I had to know."

"You thought I could have killed Brett?" For some reason this shocked me more than anything that had happened thus far.

"I didn't know."

"You didn't?" I bunched a pillow under my head and considered this. It blew me away, because I was so sure Adam couldn't have killed Brett, yet for all I knew he *could* have been just ahead of me on the stairs, and not coming down at all. "Do you know now?" I inquired.

"Yes."

I didn't know if I believed him or not. "Suppose I had killed Brett?" I was curious.

Adam patted my knee beneath the blankets and rose. I guess there are some questions it's better not to ask.

Adam left after unsuccessfully trying to get me to eat breakfast. I tried to break it gently that I don't eat breakfast. He argued that it was the most important meal of the day. I wasn't sure if he was kidding or not.

I decided to forgo my morning swim, and logged on to my computer, but it was only after nine that my front door resounded beneath a peremptory knock. Sheriff Rankin nodded a genial good morning, asked how I was feeling, and invited me to accompany him down to the beach.

On the way down he casually mentioned that he'd interviewed the paramedics who had examined me the day before. Until that moment I don't think I really appreciated that I was a suspect in Brett's death. There's naiveté for you.

"You were over the worst of it then, of course, so they couldn't tell a lot."

I nearly missed a step. I said, "You can talk to Dr. Hicks, he's been my doctor all my life."

"I spoke to Doc Hicks," Sheriff Rankin assured me. "He was willing to confirm that you do have an arrhythmia of the heart, and that given the circumstances you described yesterday it could in theory have triggered an attack."

"In theory?"

"In theory."

We reached the bottom of the stairs. The beach was pristine, except for the soggy yellow crime scene tape posted around the wrecked dock, which still lay crunched in the sand. Sky and sea and shoreline looked as vivid as though freshly painted, all the colors intensely dark in the unreal witchlight of the impending storm. Sandpipers left tracks across the silken dunes. The borough where Brett's body had lain was washed smooth and flat by the tide.

I showed the sheriff where Brett and I had stood talking.

"Run me through it one more time, Kyle," Sheriff Rankin invited. "You heard a sound like—?"

"Groaning wood. Like something was tearing apart."

We ran through it one more time. From the moment Brett had hailed me on the beach to the moment when I collapsed on the steps.

"Can I ask you something?" I asked.

"Ask away," the sheriff said laconically.

"You must have examined the dock. Was it tampered with? How could it collapse like that?"

"It was an old structure, Kyle. That dock was put in by Drake Trent. He was a big star back in the Forties. Used to own MacKinnon's place."

"I know who Drake Trent was."

"I guess you would, at that." He spat out a dark stream of tobacco juice. "But to answer your question, yep, that dock was tampered with all right. The post was sawn right through. All that had to happen was someone lean against it, and over she went. Like Lincoln logs. Tell me again what happened once Hansen was pinned down?"

We went through that again.

"How come neither you nor MacKinnon mentioned yesterday that Hansen claimed someone was trying to kill him?"

I thought instantly of the missing weed killer.

"I—because I guess we didn't believe it."

"Might interest you to know the lab results Doc Hicks got from the night Hansen collapsed. Hansen was suffering from digitalis poisoning."

I stared at him, struck dumb in every sense of the word.

"Digitalis; that's what you take for your heart condition, isn't it?"

"Digitalis and Quinidine. Derivatives."

"Yeah. That's what Doc Hicks said."

"You think *I* poisoned Brett?"

"Did you?"

"Of course not." I probably sounded more scared than convincing. "It would be stupid to use my own pills, wouldn't it?"

Rankin shrugged. "Murderers aren't the brightest folks, contrary to those books you write."

"Look, I didn't kill Brett. I didn't bash his head in. I didn't give him my heart meds."

"Didn't you notice you had half a bottle of pills missing?"

"Who says I do?" I tried to explain. "Even if the stuff was mine, I don't take digitalis daily. Only when I have an attack. I haven't needed it for quite a while."

"Where do you keep these pills?"

"In the kitchen cabinet. What does it matter? Brett didn't die from taking my heart medication."

"He didn't take digitalis by accident, did he? Was there any way he could have accidentally got hold of your pills?"

"No."

"So someone fed it to him. Probably slipped it in his drink the night of that party MacKinnon held for the Berkowitzes."

"That doesn't make sense."

"No? Who knows where you keep your heart pills?"

"I don't know. It's not a secret."

"Adam MacKinnon know?"

"He does now. He got them for me yesterday. He had to ask though." The memory of that reassured me.

"Who else knows?"

"It's not a secret," I repeated tersely.

"Anybody have a key to your place?"

"I don't think so. Well, my grandfather probably does. Joel may."

"Joel Shimada?"

I nodded. "He and Cosmo were pals from way back."

"You and Brett pretty tight?"

"What?"

"You and Brett," he explained painstakingly, as to one a bubble or two off plumb, "you get to be pretty good friends?"

"I guess so."

"You don't sound sure."

"He was Adam's friend and Adam's my friend, so yeah, I made an effort."

"How much of an effort?"

"What does that mean?"

"Hansen told Vince Berkowitz that you and him were lovers."

"That's a lie!"

Rankin studied me thoughtfully. "Well, maybe what he said was he believed you and him would be lovers before the summer was out."

Now I was mad. Sheriff Rankin had lied about Brett claiming we were lovers; he could be lying about this as well. Or Vince could be lying.

"Bullshit," I said. "Did you get that from Vince?"

He wiped his face as though I had spit at him. I felt moisture on my skin. It was starting to rain.

"You don't think Berkowitz is a reliable source?"

"I think Vince—" I caught myself. "I think I'd have known if Brett and I were going to be lovers."

The warm summer rain freckled the sand, turning it dark.

"Berkowitz says Hansen told him fucking you was the only way of keeping you and MacKinnon apart."

His tone was deliberately offensive, his words crude. I could feel the blood draining out of my face. "I don't believe that."

"What is it that you don't believe? That Hansen told Berkowitz? Or that he knew you and MacKinnon would be hump buddies before the autumn leaves were falling?"

My lips were stiff. I had to work to get the words out. "Any of it. I don't believe any of it."

"It's true though, sonny boy." He tucked a wad of tobacco in his mouth, worked it and added, "You don't seem too broken up over your pal Brett getting his head cracked open."

It took me a second to recover. I said sarcastically, "We all handle grief in our own way, Sheriff."

He eyed me beneath his bristling brows. "I don't remember you being such a smart-ass kid."

"I don't remember you ever finding my bike for me."

To my surprise he laughed. "No, I guess not. That was what you might call the perfect crime. This one ain't."

When I got back to my cottage I called Joel.

He was taking Brett's death more calmly than I had expected. Or maybe he was still numb. We talked for a while and then I asked, "Do you have a key to my house?"

There was silence on the other end of the line.

"Probably. Somewhere. Why?" Joel responded at last.

"The sheriff was asking."

"We all have keys. Or did."

"Who all?"

"Me. Micky. Adam."

It was my turn to digest silently. "Why would you all have keys to my house?"

"To your father's house." Joel cleared his throat. "It wasn't an official arrangement, but we used to take turns checking up on you. You were recuperating. You were still underage, and who knew when the hell Cos would be back. Hell, we'd been keeping an eye on you for the past sixteen years."

I knew that. When my father was there the doors were generally unlocked anyway. I was used to Cosmo's students and friends coming and going, but it gave me an eerie feeling to know anyone could have walked in on me at any time over the past four years. And it flat creeped me out to know someone could have come in and swiped those pills.

"Why?" Joel asked for the third time. "Why is that redneck so interested?"

I explained about Brett being poisoned with my heart pills. When I finished, Joel commented, "If you ask me, it's the kind of thing Brett would do to himself for attention. He faked that drowning attempt, you know."

"What are you talking about?"

"The night of the beach bonfire when someone allegedly dragged him under the water? It was a total hoax. He faked it. He told Vince. He wanted to see how everyone reacted."

"But his foot was bruised."

"My dear boy! And you call yourself a mystery writer?"

I couldn't believe it. I sat there trying to put two and two together and kept coming up with sixty-nine.

Joel said, "I believe he swiped some of your meds and took them himself. You'll notice he didn't die."

This seemed rather cool for someone who had been weeping over Brett a few weeks before. But maybe Joel had worked through his feelings for Brett.

"Eventually he did. Eventually someone smashed his head in."

Joel considered this and returned to my original question. "To be honest, Kyle, I haven't seen that key of yours in years. I guess someone could have taken it, but more likely it's in the back of a drawer full of junk."

That was probably true. Joel wasn't the most organized guy in the world. He said, changing the subject, "Adam wants Brett buried in the old cemetery. Did he tell you?"

"No."

"No one's been buried there since Drake Trent. I don't know what he's thinking."

I wasn't sure why this idea seemed to agitate Joel.

"Probably that it's a peaceful place. Peaceful and private. And beautiful, I think. Does he want me to ask my grandfather?"

"I think he plans on doing it himself. Asking, I mean." Joel's voice shook. "I think it's disgraceful."

"Why?"

"Shoving Brett off in a corner like, like a poor relation. Like a guilty secret."

So much for thinking Joel had come to terms with his feelings for Brett.

"Joel," I said, "Adam has been painting the cemetery all summer. Maybe he's comforted by the thought of Brett being so near."

Joel made a sound that could have been a sob or a snort, and hung up.

* * * * *

Adam had been in town seeing to the funeral arrangements. When he got home he called and asked if I could help him pack up Brett's things. It didn't seem tactful to point out the sheriff might plan on searching through them again. I said I'd be glad to help and headed across the field.

Adam sent me to clear out the bathroom. I opened the shower doors and figured out why. "Eternity for Men," proclaimed the shampoo and shave gel. The shower smelled unnervingly like Brett. I tossed the bottles in the plastic trash bag.

Rice bran cleansing scrub, a "voluminizing" hair dryer, a pair of red Aussie rower shorts crumpled in the corner: it wasn't hard to tell Brett's stuff from Adam's. Adam was using the same Caswell-Massey brand soaps and talc he had used when I was a kid in high school.

He came in while I was emptying a drawer which contained among other things Pearl White tooth gel, a tube of Astroglide lubricant and a bottle of Natural Sex for Men which, due to the magical ingredient of green oats, guaranteed a boost in sex drive and frequency of orgasms.

In the very back of the drawer was a scrap of paper. I smoothed out the crinkles. *Meet me in the graveyard after*, read the cramped but neat script. After what? I wondered. The handwriting was obscurely familiar.

"What have you got?" Adam queried from behind me.

"Nothing. Trash." I balled it up, not knowing why I lied.

Adam didn't question this. "Did you want a drink, Kyle? I could use one."

"I'll have a beer."

He turned away and I scrunched the note in my pocket.

"Hey," I said, following him out to the kitchen. "Do you have a key to my house?"

To my surprise Adam colored. "Yeah. I do." He seemed so uncomfortable I didn't know what to say. He handed me a beer. After a moment he elaborated, "Your father gave it to me the year before he left. He was going to Los Angeles, and he asked me to look in on you."

"Oh."

He said awkwardly, "After you were sick, after Cosmo took off, I used to come over sometimes and make sure you had food in the fridge and were taking your medication. You were seventeen, a kid. We used to take turns. Micky and Joel and me. Your grandfather didn't give a shit."

"No wonder I always felt taken care of. I was under surveillance. Do you still have the key?"

"Yeah." He hesitated. "Do you want it back?"

"Er—no."

We studied each other. Adam smiled faintly, then turned away.

When I'd packed Brett's belongings into boxes, the bathroom looked bare, sterile. There was one toothbrush on the sink, Adam's razor, Adam's blue terry robe hanging on the back of the door. The signs of the newly widowed. In Adam's place I wasn't sure what would be more painful: reminders of Brett's presence or this underlining of his absence?

In the front room Adam was tying a stack of Brett's books with twine. "Did you want any of these?"

"Adam, you don't have to do this now."

"I want to do this now." He gave the string a final tug. "I think Brett would have liked you to have these."

"Then I'd like to have them."

I went back in the bedroom and sat down on the sleigh bed. Snapshots were spread out over the comforter, like a grim hand of solitaire. I studied a shot of Brett from the party, young and handsome in his red silk shirt. Not a care in the world. There was a snap of myself and Brett. I didn't remember it being taken, but Brett had his arm around my neck in a friendly headlock. I looked at the picture and sighed. I didn't know what I felt. I had never wanted him dead.

It took less than two hours to clear away all trace of Brett's existence; to pack away a lifetime in a few cardboard boxes.

"I'll carry these over," Adam said lifting the books when we agreed we were finished.

I guessed that Adam wanted out of the cottage. I didn't blame him. It would not be easy living with a ghost, and I suspected Brett's spirit would not go gently into that good night.

We walked across the field in silence. When we reached my cottage I opened the door and Adam exclaimed, "Christ, Kyle, you need to start locking the door."

"What's the point? Everybody in Steeple Hill has a key."

Adam preceded me in, set his load of books down and said quietly, "Has it occurred to you yet that maybe you were the target?"

"Me?"

"You could have been pinned as easily under the dock as Brett. You sun on that dock. You're down there swimming by yourself all the time. And Brett was drinking out of your glass the night of the party."

"Brett was drinking off everyone's glass." It surprised me Adam had noticed that.

"But if your heart gave out, maybe following an accidental overdose of your own heart medication, who would question it?"

"My doctor, for one," I said exasperatedly.

"Somebody jumped you in the churchyard."

I thought of the note in my Levi's pockets. "Nobody could have known I was going to the churchyard. It was spur of the moment."

"Maybe someone followed you."

At my expression he said, "I'm not trying to scare you—or, maybe I am. I want you to be careful, Kyle."

Although I wasn't crazy about his message, I liked the caring I read in Adam's eyes.

"No one has any reason to kill me." It passed through my mind that Adam could also have been pinned under the dock; he used it as much as I did, fishing and sketching.

"Maybe not. But if I were you I'd get these locks changed."

I noticed he didn't say that no one had reason to kill Brett either.

* * * * *

I offered to fix Adam dinner, to which he unwisely agreed. I was busily defrosting something that was either meatloaf or fruitcake from Christmases past when the phone rang.

The minute I picked up, Micky demanded, "Has Vince called you yet?"

"About what?"

"About the *Virgin*. He claims you stole it."

I said on a disbelieving laugh, "You're kidding."

"I'm not kidding. He thinks Adam is covering for you."

"I have no idea what you're talking about. What does Adam have to do with it? I didn't even know the painting was missing." I covered the mouthpiece and said to Adam, "Did Vince tell you he thinks I stole *Virgin in Pastel*?"

"Vince is a goddamned idiot," Adam said. "I meant to tell you earlier."

That Vince was an idiot or that I was suspected of heisting a million dollar painting?

"Micky," I said, "Adam was about to fill me in. Can I call you back?"

"Kyle, it's not a joke. Vince called the sheriff and accused you of stealing the blasted thing."

"Swell. I'll call you back."

I hung up and Adam said, "Honest to God, it slipped my mind."

That was kind of a big slip, but I guess the murder of one's lover was an equally big excuse.

"What happened? How come this is the first I've heard of the *Virgin* going missing again?"

"The night of the party," Adam said, "Vince walked out and forgot the painting. The next morning he came over to get it and Brett apparently told him that I had put it away for safe keeping. Only Brett never mentioned it to me, so I never had a chance to tell Vince I have no idea where his painting went. It wasn't there in the morning."

"It wasn't there when Joel and I cleared up," I said.

"That's what Joel says too. But Vince insists it was."

"And he thinks I took it while Joel was fetching the doctor and you were busy with Brett?"

"Yes."

I sat down at the kitchen table. "Terrific."

"Don't worry," Adam said. "If push comes to shove, Micky, Joel and I will all swear the painting was gone before you were left alone with it."

"Why doesn't this reassure me?"

"I don't know. I mean it to."

Not that I didn't appreciate my surrogate family's willingness to commit perjury for me. I laughed uncertainly. "But Adam, is the *Virgin* gone again? Was it gone before the party ended?"

"No one remembers," Adam said. "Everyone was distracted by the argument between Jenny and Vince, and then over Brett getting sick."

I tried to read his face. "What else? There's something else bugging you."

"I'm not sure that Brett didn't hide the thing for a—a joke."

"That's an expensive joke."

"I know, but it's the kind of thing that might amuse him. He liked yanking people's chains. Vince is an easy mark."

"But if Brett hid the painting, where would it be? He didn't fake getting sick that night."

"I know. I don't really think he stole the *Virgin*. On the other hand, it's hard to believe anyone else there that night did."

I raked my fingers through my hair. "Vince thinks you're shielding me?"

"He told me yesterday morning that if you didn't turn the painting over by today, he'd call the sheriffs. I'm sorry, Kyle. After Brett, I never thought of it again."

The microwave bell went off. I rose from the table, opened the door. Studying the shriveled brick, I comforted, "Don't sweat it. The food can't be any worse in jail than it is here."

CHAPTER TEN

A man in a black-hooded rain-slicker was in the churchyard shoveling out a fresh grave. Brett's grave. The cemetery was bathed in that eerie blue light that fills the wait between rainstorms. The blue shimmered on the marble statues and cast a somber hue on the woods and grass.

Beneath the spread wings and raised sword of Drake Trent's angel, the man labored, humming to himself grimly. He stopped, straightening up at the sound of my feet on the leaves. The black slicker glistened wetly. He pushed the hood back. I was looking for the hook where a hand should be. Instead I saw snowy-white hair and an Ancient Mariner beard.

"Hello, Granddad."

He jabbed the shovel in the clump of damp earth and leaned on it. "Kyle."

Aaron Lipez was in his early eighties, but still going strong. Having out-lasted his wife and only child, he would probably outlast his only grandchild as well. He not only looked like the Ancient Mariner, he apparently *was* the Ancient Mariner.

The usual silence followed our greetings because normal polite conver-sation was something Aaron Lipez didn't indulge in, and I never quite knew what to say to him anyway. He had scared the hell out of me when I was a kid. I still found him intimidating.

"Heard you were feeling poorly. You look okay."

"I'm okay."

He nodded curtly. For the first time in my life I wondered whether he might have been there for me if I'd needed him. Had he really not given a shit or had there been no point in trying to break through the tight circle formed by Cosmo and his cronies?

"This one a friend of yours?" my grandfather questioned, nodding to the empty hole and fixing his pebble-bright eyes on me.

"I knew him. He was a friend of Adam MacKinnon's."

"Faggot." My grandfather spat accurately at a beetle toddling up the mounds of earth ringing the grave.

I didn't take this as a personal affront since I had no cause to believe the old man tracked me enough to notice my sexual orientation. My grandfather's constant refrain for everything wrong on the planet was "the Jews, the fags and the liberals." The only thing the JFL was not responsible for was my mother's death. That was my father's guilt. And possibly mine.

"If you feel that way, why are you letting him be buried here?"

"He can't hurt the dead."

Just an old softie my grandpappy. I was grateful he'd granted Adam's request. He could have easily declined. The old chapel and surrounding graveyard were all that remained of my grandfather's property which had once included most of the colony and the woods beyond. The Lipezes and the Cobbs were the last of Steeple Hill's original founding families. They had been thick as thieves from the first ground-breaking pick ax blow, according to Cosmo.

A lot of money had changed hands through the years, but my grandfather steadfastly refused to sell the land where the old church stood.

"He was twenty-one," I said. "Someone murdered him."

"That's what I hear."

I wondered what else he heard. I wondered what they were saying in the village. Did he know I was a suspect?

"Do you hear why he was killed?"

"What kind of question is that?"

"You've lived here a long time. You probably know more about these people—"

"I mind my own business."

No hunting, no fishing, no trespassing, and keep off the grass. I looked up at the leaden sky.

"Granddad," I began, "All these years—did my father ever contact you?"

He knocked dirt off his shovel. "Nope." He didn't bother to glance my way.

"Would you tell me if he had?" I asked a little bitterly.

His eyes met mine briefly. "I have any reason not to?"

"Do you think my father's dead?"

He said harshly, "I hope he's dead."

I shivered as rain began to patter softly on the leaves above us. It ran down the hovering angel's face like tears.

* * * * *

I was replacing the Jeep's windshield wipers that evening when Sheriff Rankin showed up.

"I've been expecting you," I said.

"That so?"

I wiped a smudge off the hood with my shirt sleeve. "Vince Berkowitz told you I stole my father's painting. I didn't."

Rankin stroked his mustache.

"Stole might be too strong a word. The way I hear it is you might have a legal claim to that painting. Maybe you thought of holding onto it till owner-ship could be determined. What about that?"

"I don't have the painting."

"Berkowitz seems pretty convinced you do."

"Yeah, I know Brett supposedly told him I took it, but Brett was lying."

"Why would he lie about that?"

"Because he probably took it himself."

The sheriff raised his curling eyebrows. "That's a serious charge against a dead man. Tell me about this painting. Considered a masterpiece isn't it?"

"Yes."

"Why?"

"Why is it considered a masterpiece?"

"Yep."

I was nonplused. "I don't know. I'm not an art expert. It was painted at the peak of my father's career, at the height of his talent. Joel could probably explain it better: the brushwork, the composition, the use of color and light. He wrote a book about my father's painting."

"Cosmo never showed it, did he?"

"*Virgin in Pastel* was never officially exhibited, but the critics who did see it generally viewed it as his best work."

"Uh huh. Picture of a nude girl, isn't it?"

"Yes."

"What nude girl?"

"Huh?"

"Who was the model?"

"I don't know."

"Don't know or won't say?"

"I don't know. No one knows. That's part of the mystique."

"Mystique?" Rankin snorted. *We don't hold with none of that mystique crap 'round these parts!*

I tacked starboard. "The model has her back to the artist. You see only her blonde hair and her back. She's sitting on scattered flower petals. The texture of her skin and her hair and the petals…it's enchanting."

The sheriff inspected me as though I stood revealed in my true rainbow colors. "Blonde hair? That woman painter, Michaela St. Martin, she has blonde hair. Could she have been the model?"

"What does it matter who the model was?"

He shrugged his powerful shoulders. "Just interesting. How much is that painting worth?"

"I don't know. Millions, I guess."

"That's what Berkowitz says. You still claim you don't want any part of that painting?"

There was no way Marshal Dillon here was ever going to understand. I tried anyway. "The painting disappeared with Cosmo. He may have sold it or he may have given it away. I don't know. I don't know that I have any claim on it."

"That's a mighty noble attitude."

"I'd probably feel different if I were hard up for money."

"Yeah, you're pretty well set," Rankin agreed. "Your old man left you a bundle and there's money on your mother's side."

"Since you've been checking my financial records you've probably noticed I earn a decent living on my own."

The sheriff took out his tobacco. "No need to get riled, sonny boy. I'm just doing my job."

I leaned back against the rain-spotted hood of the Jeep and folded my arms. Rankin probably interpreted this as defensive body language. I felt defensive, even as I reminded myself there was nothing to worry about. My financial profile was solid citizen stuff. No huge debts, no mysterious deposits or withdrawals. I hardly even cheated on my taxes.

I asked, "Since you're so interested in that painting, did you try to find out where the dresser it was found in came from originally?"

"Yep." His mouth twitched at my surprise. "The people who sold it say they bought it a few years before at a secondhand store. They couldn't remember which one. It was old, but it wasn't an antique or a valuable piece. Cheap wood with brass lion-head pulls. Probably part of a set. Sound familiar?"

"No."

He nodded as though this was what he expected me to say. "So, getting back to this lost masterpiece, maybe you don't need the money, not that anybody minds a couple of extra million. You still might want that painting for personal reasons. 'My father's painting,' you called it. Your old man painted it. It must mean something to you."

"Not enough to steal it."

"If someone did steal it, they couldn't sell it around here. They'd have to try overseas or some place, right?"

"I guess."

He reached into his uniform pocket and pulled out a colored envelope. "Like to explain this plane ticket to France?"

* * * * *

It took me twenty minutes to explain why I had purchased a plane ticket to France. Then I headed for the Berkowitzes'.

It was almost dark by the time I walked through the broken gate. The lights were on in the cottage. The smell of frying fish drifted through the open window.

Jen opened the door to my knock and recoiled. "You shouldn't have come, Kyle. Vince will freak."

"Yeah, well, I'm a little freaked myself. Where is he, Jen?"

"He's not here," she answered with an uneasy look over her shoulder.

"Then I'll wait."

"You can't!" She sounded genuinely alarmed. "Vince thinks we're having an affair, Kyle."

I felt my jaw drop.

"Why does he think that, Jen?"

"Because I told him we were."

If she had sounded defiant I probably would have strangled her, but she said it in a small voice, her eyes shiny with tears. With her hair in braids she looked about ten. She looked like she belonged in a little house on the prairie, not in an artists' colony surrounded by thieves and murderers.

"*Why* for God's sake?"

She gestured for me to hold my voice down, and then hissed, "Because I wanted to hurt him!"

"Did you want to hurt me?"

"No, of course not. I wanted Vince to feel what I felt when I found out about him and Brett."

"Great, Jen, now you've got Vince gunning for me. He told the sheriff I stole the *Virgin*." I swatted away a couple of moths circling the porch light.

"That's not my fault!"

"Whose fault is it?"

"I don't know. Yours."

"*Mine!*"

Jen made frantic shushing motions. "Vince honestly believes you stole that painting, Kyle. He's not just saying that. He thinks that you think you've got a right to it. He's positive you took it. Brett told him you did."

I opened my mouth but no words would come.

Something else did however. Vince charged out of the back room like Sir Lancelot out to rescue Lady Faire.

"I thought I recognized your voice!"

"I want to talk to you, Vince."

"Get the hell out of my house!"

"Now, Vince!" Jenny protested.

Vince grabbed her by the wrist and dragged her away from me: seducer of women, slayer of men. "You can talk to my lawyer," he told me.

"I didn't take the damned painting."

"MY damn painting, you goddamn liar. Mine, do you hear? My wife, my painting."

"I didn't take the painting and I don't want your wife."

"Bullshit! Now get out or I'll throw you out."

I got out. I wasn't getting anywhere talking, and wrestling with Vince was going to be useless as well as humiliating.

* * * * *

I stopped by Micky's cottage on the way back. She greeted me at the door in startling purple leopard leotards.

"Wow," I said. "Cat Woman Lives."

"I was just thinking about you, kiddo."

I'd brought my bruised ego to the right place. Something soft and soothing was playing in the background: Chinese flutes and acoustic guitar. Masses of Paisley pillows were scattered across the checkerboard floor, and vanilla candles burned everywhere. It was like Betty Crocker had set up house in a Shaolin temple. The smell of vanilla and cigarettes blended with homey scents from the kitchen.

There were canvases everywhere, the overflow from Micky's studio: gigantic alien-looking flowers, yellow frogs and lime-green salamanders.

I could feel my ruffled male ego smoothing back down as Micky wafted around, serving me coffee and cake. Her cat, Macavity, wound himself around my ankles, purring hello.

"I've come to the conclusion he's gay," Micky remarked, watching the cat making up to my socks.

"Isn't everybody?" I took a muffin from the plate she offered. "Hey, pumpkin chocolate chip?"

"I used to make these for you when you were a kid. Remember?"

I bit in, licked the chocolate off my teeth. "I remember." I swallowed. "Micky, Joel said you might still have a copy of the key to my house lying around."

She stilled. "Joel said that?"

I didn't understand her expression or her tone. "He said you used to take turns playing guardian angel after my father left."

Micky relaxed. "Oh. That's true." She smiled. "You scared the hell out of me that summer, Kyle. You were so quiet. So frail. You scared Cosmo."

"Right out of town."

Her smile faded. "I didn't understand that. I don't to this day." She stooped, picked up the cat and kissed its nose. "Who's the bad boy that brought Mumsy a mouse for breakfast this morning?"

The cat meowed.

Curious, I probed, "What did you think I meant? Before, when I told you Joel said you had a key."

Micky looked innocent. Not her style.

"What did you think I was asking?"

She shrugged, but it was half-hearted. "I'm surprised Brett didn't fill you in—although I don't know how the hell he found out."

"Found out what?" I wondered if this was something I really wanted to hear. Not the stuff real detectives are made of, I guess.

Micky took a deep breath. "Cosmo gave me a key before your illness, Kyle."

I set my coffee cup on the table. "What are you getting at?"

She turned pink. I had never seen Micky blush before, but I was seeing it now. "Cosmo and I were—uh—we were lovers actually." She added hastily into my stunned silence, "This was before he married your mother. Before he came back here."

Greenwich Time. "So how could he give you a key to the cottage if you were lovers way back when?"

Micky's color deepened. "After your mother died, Cosmo was lonely. And I was lonely." She ran a hand through her long, silvery hair. "So, for a time, we were lonely together."

I stared at her. It wasn't that I was judging, so much as I was trying to make sense of it, with what I knew of both Micky and my father. It seemed so out of character for both of them.

Misreading my expression, Micky said defensively, "We didn't do anything wrong, Kyle. Cosmo never loved anyone but your mother. We comforted each other. It was...comfortable, friendly. Sex, you know."

"Yeah, I know about sex. It's just *weird*."

"It's not *that* weird."

"I don't mean it that way. I never thought about—well—"

"Damn," Micky said. "Damn, damn, damn. Somehow I knew this day would come. Frankly it's a relief to have it out. Especially once that little shit Brett started hinting around. I wanted to tell you myself." She added honestly, "If there wasn't any way out of it."

I processed this silently. Finally I asked, "Brett didn't mention how he found out?"

"No. I don't know how he knew, or why he was so interested, but he never stopped asking questions from the moment he arrived. He was at the library, the courthouse, digging away like a terrier." Micky added shortly, "Who knows? Maybe Joel told him."

Naturally, Joel would know too. It was truly unsettling to realize how little I knew about my father, about the people I regarded as my family. And though this decades-old secret was not a motive for murder, it started me wondering what other secrets Brett had uncovered.

"You have a queer look, kiddo," Micky commented.

I gave her a rueful grin. "Not so surprising, is it?"

She laughed.

CHAPTER ELEVEN

The Cobbs' car was parked outside Adam's when I finally arrived home. A formal sympathy call, I deduced. Homemade pie and homespun sentiment. I wondered how Adam was holding up. It was hard to tell; he was not a guy to bleed in public.

I let myself in the front door and stared for a moment at the mirror over the fireplace, remembering when *Virgin in Pastel* hung there. Why had Brett lied? Could he have hidden the painting before he fell ill? Perhaps he had some idea of selling it later? Or perhaps he enjoyed watching Vince sweat bullets over it.

I thought about something my father read to me a long time ago. I think it was from an essay by Giorgio de Chirico on Metaphysical Art. The example was given of walking into a room where a man sat near a birdcage. There was a canary in the birdcage and paintings on the wall and books on a bookshelf—nothing weird or unsettling about any of that because memory connected the observer to the logic of whatever he witnessed in the room.

But say one had no memory and no logic with which to view the man, the birdcage, the paintings and the books? Without memory or logic, these everyday objects might seem terrifying and astonishing—or lovely and magical. Nothing in the room would have changed; the change would be in one's self, in one's viewing of the room from a different perspective.

For a moment I felt that I hovered near some discovery; the idea was there, out of reach, like a word tingling on the tip of your tongue. Then it was gone, memory or inspiration, the impression faded, and I was left staring into a mirror.

The Cobbs stayed long after dark. After they drove off down the highway, Adam went down to the beach. I don't know how long he stayed there walking along the water's edge. It was late when I carried a couple of Brett's books upstairs and dug in for the night.

Outside the window I could hear crickets chirping; the blinds knocked against the sill, stirred by the salty night breeze. Beyond these sounds was the distant sigh of the sea.

I felt tired and depressed, jarred by the recognition that I was going to miss Brett—that I missed him already. And far from removing an obstacle in my path to Adam, Brett's death seemed to have knocked over the safety barriers. Without them in place, neither of us quite knew how to treat the other.

Flipping through Brett's copy of *Backtrack*, a newsprint clipping fell out. I turned it over and there was my own face staring up at me. It was a copy of an interview I'd done for Lambda Book Report two or three years ago. The photograph showed the spiked hair and razor stubble I'd favored back then, till my agent told me I looked like a disgruntled Boy Scout. Someone, Brett I suppose, had underlined part of a sentence: *...Bari, who still lives in* <u>Steeple Hill</u>*, California...*

I stared at the underlined "Steeple Hill" and I remembered Adam saying it had been Brett's idea to spend the summer here. I remembered Micky saying that Brett had been asking questions from the moment he arrived, that he had gone to the library, the courthouse. Why the courthouse? Records of Marriage? Death certificates? He had been looking for written proof. Proof of what?

I snapped out the light and sat behind the bars of moonlight listening to the crickets.

* * * * *

The blue woman, her mouth an open "O" but no sound coming out. Over her shoulder a crescent moon, old and tarnished. No...dipped in blood. Something else. Someone else...

My own yell of terror woke me. I found myself sitting bolt upright, my heart stuttering with fright and anger as I gulped in oxygen. I put my hands up to my face and they were shaking. I could see the white blur of them, and for some reason this alarmed me all the more.

I told myself to think of something else, but all I could think of was that Brett had been murdered, that someone had watched us and waited. And when I ran for help, that same someone had picked up a rock—

I pictured Brett lying there in the sand, helpless, thinking perhaps that rescue had come. I pictured this faceless person slipping silently through the shadows of my own home. I saw a gloved hand opening the cupboard and taking down my pills...

I don't think it was a conscious decision, but somehow I was dialing Adam's phone number.

The phone rang once. Twice. Picked up.

Adam's voice was scratchy. He cleared it, repeated, "Yes?"

"It's...me."

"What's wrong?" He sounded alert now.

I couldn't answer. What the hell was I doing?

"Kyle?"

"Nothing. I just wanted to hear your voice." I laughed. It didn't come out quite right. Embarrassing. I admitted, "Bad dreams."

"I'll come over."

My heart spread its wings like Drake Trent's angel; ready for liftoff. I said reluctantly, "No. I'm okay now. It's late."

"I'm on my way."

The phone clicked down before I could say all the things I should have. I rolled out of bed and went to the window. The light was on at Adam's, a cheery glow. A minute later I saw the verandah spot come on, saw him briefly illuminated in the grainy light as he shrugged on a sweatshirt.

I went downstairs, not bothering to turn on the lamps. I knew this place in the dark, I knew it in my sleep. I unbolted the door and was waiting on the porch as Adam jogged up the stairs.

I began nervously, "I feel like a foo—" But he put his arms around me and I bit off the rest of it.

We hugged each other. I breathed in his sleepy scent; his unshaven cheek rubbed against mine. It was like coming home. Adam's arms were strong, safe, like being held by my father, except I don't remember ever being held by my father.

Seven minutes later I was back in my nest of pillows and blankets, cradling the mug of decades-old (though I didn't like to break it to him) Ovaltine Adam had heated for me. He lay on the bed beside me, head propped on his hand, while I related my dream. To my relief he didn't laugh at any of it: the furtive knock at the window, the blue woman, the moon that turns into a blood-spattered scythe.

"You know what it's like, Adam? Did you ever see that painting by de Chirico? *Melancholy and Mystery of a Street?*"

"The one with the carnival wagon? The girl with the hoop running from the shadow?"

"Right. There's something, I don't know, sort of desolate about that painting."

"Disquieting."

"Yeah. That's it. Of familiar things being…sinister." I wasn't explaining it well. The unconscious mind digests our experiences and translates them into dreams; that's what I was trying to say.

Maybe Adam understood. He softly quoted de Chirico, "And what shall I love if not enigma?"

I sipped another mouthful of Ovaltine. The well-remembered malty taste was comforting, bringing back memories of childhood when life was simple. And safe.

"You used to sleepwalk when you were little, did you know that?"

"No."

His leg casually brushed mine as he shifted position. My body responded with an unchildlike awareness to his proximity. If I stretched out my hand I could stroke his hair; it looked black and shiny like seal fur in the muted light.

"Cosmo mentioned it once. You stopped when you were about ten."

Mildly interesting though this was, I didn't quite see the point. "So?"

"Nothing. It only occurred to me. You had a vivid imagination. Still have. A writer's imagination, I guess. I'm surprised you don't dream of Indians and cowboys. You always had your nose stuck between the pages of some damn western when you were a kid." His eyes tilted in that way I loved. "And they always had these salacious titles. *Rawhide Justice. Queen of the Purple Sage.*"

I started laughing. Adam laughed too.

"It's a wonder you don't have a thing for boots and spurs."

I stopped laughing. "How do you know?" I inquired silkily.

He held my eyes for a long moment, then reached over to take the vintage Ovaltine and set it aside.

* * * * *

"You're shaking." His voice was soft.

I laughed unsteadily, shook my head, although it was true. I was shaking.

Warm hands on bare skin. I'd forgotten how good that felt. Adam's long strong fingers caressed, smoothed, teased. I wrapped my arms around him, his body hard, thin, hot against my own, his cock pressing urgently into my inner thigh. Mine thrust blindly back. He gathered me closer still, his arms folding me tight. I rubbed my feverish face against his chest, inhaling that sexy sharp smell of male arousal. Mine, his, ours.

"All right?" He was still tender, still ready to turn it into comfort if that's what I was really after—and how funny was that?

"God, yes."

How long had it been since someone had simply touched me like this, held me? Years. Years. Oh, God, it felt good. Skin on skin felt so incredibly good.

Adam nudged my face with his, found my mouth, kissed me. A hot, sweet kiss that deepened. I moaned, opened for him, needing more. Craving more. His tongue thrust against mine. I responded with a hunger that probably startled the hell out of him. Our tongues met, dueled, parted.

His hand had slipped between our bodies; he stroked the vulnerable skin between hip and thigh, slid down to capture the tight sac, tracing with his fingernails. I broke the kiss, panting. My lips felt swollen.

"Adam…" I caught his hand with mine, shifting it to my cock, desperate for him to relieve that throbbing distended need.

"Right here," he whispered, and mercifully he was. His hand wrapped around me, working our slick, hot cocks together. His mouth covered my own again, wet and hungry. Frantic tension built inside me.

I need to do something here, I thought dizzily. *I'm being selfish.* But all I seemed able to do was writhe and shiver. Nor was there time to sort it out because, to my astonishment, I was already coming. Hard. Liquid heat splashed over Adam's hand, moistened the nestle of our bellies and thighs. Waves of relief so intense it was painful. Wet heat slipped out beneath my lashes too.

Adam's hips rocked against mine. Faster. Fiercer. The mattress springs groaned. His hands slid under, bunched into my ass, snugging me up hard against him. I ignored that painful stiffness jabbing into my belly; kissed his throat, the underside of his jaw, the hollow of his shoulder, his nipple; tasted salt and sweat.

It's real. I'm not dreaming. It felt better than any dream.

Adam bit off an exclamation and arched his body against mine. Blood-hot release spread between us, easing the friction of skin on skin.

The world steadied once more. Downstairs the clock was chiming a silvery hour.

"Three o'clock and all's well," I whispered.

Adam turned his face to me, kissed my cheek. His head jerked up.

"Are those tears?"

I dragged my arm across my wet face. "The good kind."

"Hey…" He slid an arm beneath my shoulders, cradled me against him. "Tell me."

There was no way I could put it into words.

Shakily, I said, "You had to be there." I started laughing and then, crazily, I was crying again. Adam just held me, petting me, whispering endearments, and after a few minutes I quieted.

I could imagine what Brett would have had to say about that little performance.

And on that wry thought, I fell asleep.

* * * * *

Waking up has never been easy for me. I ascend in stages like a diver suffering the bends. My college roommate used to swear he held coherent, if not intelligent, conversations with me for several minutes before I actually came to.

That morning I came gradually, peacefully back to an awareness of rain on window panes and a warm body resting against my own. I twitched my nose, tried to unglue my eyelids, swallowed a couple of times.

Lips brushed mine lightly, once, twice. A butterfly of a kiss at the corner of my mouth. I made a supreme effort and opened my eyes. Tried to focus.

Adam leaned over me, smiling. "It's alive," he murmured.

I mumbled something, holding the sheet up.

Adam pulled the sheet down. "What was that? Oil can?"

I felt at a disadvantage. Even in my less than eagle-eyed state I discerned that Adam had been up, showered, shaved, brushed his teeth. He looked good. He smelled good. He tasted minty-fresh as his mouth insisted on prizing open my own.

After a shy second or two I gave myself over to the unfamiliar pleasure of someone's tongue in my mouth before breakfast.

The warm seductive taste of him, the teasing push of his tongue against mine. I felt overwhelmed. Overwhelmed by the memory of the night before—and what it meant in the cold light of day. I felt horribly, vulnerably naked.

"Oh God, it's true," I mumbled at last when he let me up for air. "You are a morning person."

His eyes tilted. "Baby, morning was officially over fifteen minutes ago."

I sprang into sitting position. "Shit! I was supposed to see the sheriff."

"Yeah, he called." Maddeningly, he continued to sit there, calm, cool and collected.

"He called! Why didn't you wake me?"

"Because you needed to sleep."

I goggled at him. He brushed the hair out of my eyes.

"Adam," I managed at last, "I don't think you get this: we're suspects. The sheriff thinks one of us, or both of us maybe, could have killed Brett. Your spending the night here last night probably makes us look more guilty."

"I didn't invite myself." His gaze was level. Meeting it, I flushed, recollecting the intimate exploration of his hands—my adolescent response to him—his patience.

"I'm not talking fault. I'm talking you should have woke me up. You shouldn't have let the sheriff know you were here last night."

Adam's eyebrows shot up. "Now there's a guilty reaction. You think we should lie to the police?"

"Not lie." I kicked out of the tangle of sheets and blankets, groping for my Levi's. Adam sat on the bed, watching me ransack the room.

"What are you panicking for? You didn't kill Brett, did you?"

"That's not funny!"

"Calm down, Kyle."

He had a point. I stopped, took a couple of careful, deep breaths. Adam came up behind me, slipped his arms around me, pulled me back against him.

"Okay, baby?"

"Yeah." I closed my eyes, surrendering to the feel of him down the length of my body, surrendering to the memory of last night. But only for a moment. It took effort, but I pulled out of his arms.

"Adam, listen, I think we should—" I couldn't say it. After a moment Adam said it for me.

"Cool it?"

He said it gently, but there was something in his eyes. I realized he was angry with me. A first. It didn't feel too good.

"I'm thinking about how this will look to the sheriff. To anybody paying attention. Brett's not even buried."

His expression grew sardonic. "Brett was right. Appearances do count with you, don't they?"

I could feel myself getting red. It wasn't myself I was worried about. It was Adam, who I believed was Rankin's favorite suspect. How did I explain that without making it sound like *I* suspected Adam?

"Neatness counts. Appearances can be deceiving." I wasn't trying to be flippant, but it sounded that way. "Look, Adam, give me a break here. I'm making it up as I go, okay?"

After a moment he gave an odd smile and shrugged. "Sure. Whatever. When you think it's safe to come out of the woods, send a smoke signal or something."

He turned and went downstairs. I heard the front door bang shut behind him.

CHAPTER TWELVE

"**D**eliver us, O Lord, and all thy faithful in that day of terror, when the sun and moon shall be darkened, and the stars fall down from heaven."

The lonely cry of a red-tailed hawk cut across the minister's reading. I looked up from the empty grave to the empty blue sky. I looked across to Adam. In its controlled sorrow, his face was as unrevealing as any on the stone busts around us.

The evening before he had called and we spoke briefly.

"When you were clearing out the bathroom did you find Brett's anklet?"

"No." I was glad he had called, but I didn't want to talk about Brett. This however, was all Adam seemed interested in.

"The funeral home can't find it. They say it's not on the morgue's list of Brett's effects."

"Maybe he wasn't wearing it."

"Then it should be here somewhere. It's not. I've looked."

"Maybe he lost it on the beach. The clasp was weak."

Adam said finally, unconvinced, "Maybe."

His thoughts had not been with me then; they were not with me now.

The minister droned on in the breathless heat of the afternoon. I looked at Joel. He was white and perspiring in the humidity. He looked ill. Micky, next to him, appeared to be a million miles away. Back in the studio? Back in the cornfields of Kansas she had left behind forty years ago?

Brett's mourners were few. The Berkowitzes and the Cobbs, including Jack, completed the circle. Irene looked like a scarecrow in shapeless black.

Jack, as they say, cleaned up real good. He kept tugging at the tie Irene must have insisted he wear.

That would have amused Brett. This would all have amused Brett. For a moment I could almost feel him standing at my side, hear a ghostly mocking, *Hey, Kylie, want to go fuck behind the chapel? Adam always liked that...*

I risked another glance at Adam. He looked unbearably handsome and remote in a dark suit. His lashes veiled his eyes; he could have been standing here alone. In a way he was. Only he had really loved Brett—still loved him.

"...Vouchsafe to us, who are yet alive, and still have opportunity of reconciliation with Thee, the grace so as to watch over all our actions..."

Mayor Cobb cleared his throat noisily. The minister paused, his eyes leaving the page briefly, and then his voice flowed on, consigning Brett to dust and ashes and memory.

When the service was over we walked back to Adam's for a buffet of cold cuts and noodle casseroles. The baked funeral meats came courtesy of Irene who seemed to be working from the hypothesis that full stomachs left little room for grief. But no one ate much. Murder has that effect. The knowledge that one of us might have put an end to Brett cast its own pall.

The mayor gave an impromptu speech about the overall safety of life in a small town, and then popped open a beer. Miss Irene circulated a tray of homemade cookies, urging us all to eat up.

After I choked down a ham sandwich, I joined Jack Cobb out on the verandah. He was staring moodily out toward the treeline.

"Hey, Jack."

He barely turned his head. "Kyle."

"It was good of you to come to Brett's funeral."

"The old man insisted."

"You didn't really even know Brett did you?"

"No."

"And you didn't like him."

Jack gave me a direct stare like the glare of oncoming headlights. "No." After a pause he said deliberately, "Fucking faggot."

I already had it figured, but the hair on the back of my neck stood up all the same. I reached in my wallet and pulled out the battered note I'd found in Brett's bathroom drawer.

"I recognized the writing from the bill for firewood pinned on Adam's refrigerator door."

Jack stared at the note as though it were in hieroglyphics. Then he snatched at it.

I yanked my hand back, shoving the note in my pocket as I stepped out of his reach. "I don't think so," I said like somebody in a book I would never write.

"Give me that note or I'll kick your ass."

"That defeats the purpose of getting the note back, doesn't it?" Not a swerve of his single-track mind. I hooked a thumb over my shoulder pointing toward the house. I clarified, "They'll ask why we're fighting."

Jack's face twitched in pain like Frankenstein at the first volt of electricity.

"Why did you want Brett to meet you?"

"To kick his ass." *Duh!*

"Why?"

"He needed it."

It's hard to escape that kind of logic. I said, "That was me in the cemetery."

"Yeah. I noticed." He nodded his head in the direction of my cottage, by which I gathered he had deduced the rabbit's identity by the hole it bolted into.

"What did I ever do to you?"

"I don't care about you. I wanted to kick *his* ass."

I scrutinized Jack. He was twenty-seven (my age), unmarried, no steady girlfriend that I knew of, and had a fixation on Brett's ass.

"What did Brett ever do to you?"

"Came on to me."

"Ever heard of Just Say No?"

"He didn't take no for an answer."

"So you killed him?"

He seemed to find this funny. "Me?"

The screen door opened and Miss Irene stepped out on the verandah. "Did you boys want some pie?"

"I do, Auntie," Jack said. He gave me a sort of smirk and followed her back into the house.

After a bit I went back inside and shook hands with Adam.

"Thank you for coming, Kyle," he said politely, as to a stranger.

A truly improper thought went through my unruly brain. I said automatically, "Call me if there's anything I can do."

For a moment there was a gleam of irony in his baby-blues. "I'll do that."

* * * * *

My much-postponed doctor's appointment was at three. I went home, changed and headed into town.

The yellow sun blazed overhead, like a Van Gogh star. Pewter-edged clouds shape-shifted across empty blue canvas. The grassy hills rippled beneath the undulating strokes of an invisible paintbrush. The day shimmered with life and energy, and it was hard to accept that Brett was gone forever. That Brett was now just a memory.

There were living people who were less disruptive than Brett's memory.

Twenty minutes later I lay on the examining table, staring at the two pencil sketches on the wall while Dr. Hicks moved the cold cap of the stethoscope over my ribs.

"Inhale."

I sucked in. One of the sketches was of Main Street. Main Street a quarter of a century ago. Beneath a drooping American flag, old men sat outside the VFW on benches. The other sketch was of the park. More old men on benches. Interesting theme going there.

"Exhale."

I exhaled. "Who did those sketches?"

"Hmm?" Dr. Hicks glanced at me over his glasses and then looked behind himself as though to refresh his memory. "Your mother."

"My mother?" I stared at those sketches as though for the first time, as though I hadn't lain here hiding from Dr. Hicks' x-ray (literally) vision in those penciled streets for much of my life. "I didn't know my mother could draw."

"Sure she could. Kyria was a good little artist."

"Was she?" How come I never knew? "When did she do those?"

"When she was in college. She used to work here in my office on Saturdays."

There was something funny in Doctor Hicks' voice. Something neutral. Too neutral.

"You can get dressed," he told me briskly, turning away.

I unstuck myself from the tissue and leather and hopped down, reaching for my shirt. "You must have known my mother pretty well," I said, watching Dr. Hicks note something on my chart.

"Hmm? Yes. She was a nice girl. Very nice girl."

Again, too neutral. Too careful. Either Hicks hadn't liked my mother— or he'd liked her a lot. He'd kept her sketches. I thought he must have liked her a lot.

"How long did she work for you?"

Silence. A pen scratching away and then Dr. Hicks said, "Off and on, about eight years. Then Cosmo came home from New York. They got married." He shrugged, still not looking at me.

Eight years? Ma had not gone to college for eight years; something told me she had put in more than four Saturdays a month for the good doctor. Well, she had to do something during the fourteen years my old man had been sowing his wild oats. Was this one of those Turner Classic Movie moments? I sussed Hicks still found it hard to talk about her nearly thirty years later. He had never married either.

This was a new perspective on my mother. I would have liked to know more, but was it my business? Not hardly.

I finished buttoning my shirt. "Did I use to walk in my sleep?"

Dr. Hicks did look at me then. "When you were small. You outgrew it. Why? Has it started again?"

"Is that possible?" I was startled.

"I suppose it is. Do you have reason to—?"

"No. Not at all. I was surprised to hear that I ever had."

"It's not so unusual in children. It isn't dangerous, although Cosmo worried about you taking a tumble down those stairs to the beach. He used to hang a bell on your bedroom door."

"You're kidding." It didn't sound like Cosmo; he had always leaned toward the survival-of-the-fittest philosophy. I thought it over. "Why would someone sleepwalk?"

"There are different theories. Somnambulism isn't necessarily a sign of psychological distress, not in children. Even an adult can have an isolated episode of sleepwalking because of unusual stress. But if it's a recurring event it could be something more serious, the side effect of certain drugs perhaps."

"What about nightmares?"

"What about them?"

Now I had Dr. Hicks' full frowning attention.

"What could be the cause of having the same recurring nightmare?"

"A psychological disturbance perhaps. Are we discussing nightmares or night terrors?"

"What's the difference?"

"A nightmare is a bad dream. The patient generally wakes up frightened but alert. He remembers what happened in the dream. A night terror is more like a panic attack. The patient wakes up confused and terrified. He might remember nothing more than a single, vivid image. He might not remember anything. Again, it's not so unusual in children."

"But in adults?"

Dr. Hicks asked bluntly, "Is there something you want to tell me, Kyle?"

"No. No, it's for a book I'm working on."

Dr. Hicks subjected me to a microscopic gaze. "Sit down, Kyle."

I sat down. Folded up actually. That grave tone petrifies me. Always has.

"I'm scheduling you for a full series of tests at St. Andrew's next week."

"Why?" My mouth was so dry the words felt like crumbles.

"Because you haven't had a complete physical in a couple of years."

"Is my heart worse?"

Did he hesitate before answering? "I don't think there's anything to worry about. I am going to adjust your prescription."

"If there's nothing wrong, why the change in my meds?"

"There's nothing unusual about that. We've adjusted your prescription before. You've been under some strain. Had a couple of flutters this past week. Better to be safe than sorry."

"Right."

His thin mouth quirked briefly. "No need to look like that. Your blood pressure is good, heart rate normal. No need to panic."

I nodded. Heart illness isn't static. You're either getting better or getting worse.

Doctor Hicks added dryly, "And if the nightmares persist, let me know. We can prescribe for those too."

The next four days were uneventful. Life seemed to be settling back into the ruts.

Adam chased off a reporter from the *Steeple Hill Gazette* and endured two visits from Sheriff Rankin, all observed by me mowing my lawn. He made no move to contact me. I made no move toward him either, but I developed a sudden passion for yard work.

One evening while I was pruning my rose bushes I watched him on his verandah, drinking a bottle of wine, staring out at the trees; staring through the trees, I was sure, to the graveyard where Brett slept in the shadow of the stone angel's sword.

Now and then I caught a snatch of Miles Davis' *Live-Evil* on the wind off the sea. Safe behind my clipping shears, I watched and told myself that the distance I had erected between us was for Adam's protection; that the sheriff could never understand our relationship. That seemed reasonable, since I didn't understand it myself.

＊　＊　＊　＊　＊

On Monday I drove to St. Andrew's Hospital in the neighboring township of Kelsburgh to spend the morning and most of the afternoon being weighed and measured, x-rayed and scanned. I ran a couple of theoretical miles under the unimpressed gaze of a technician. They must train nurses and technicians like secret agents; you have to go code blue before they start looking interested.

I'd brought a copy of *Greenwich Time* with me, and once more I tried to understand who my father was from other people's reminiscences while taped up to the machine that counted out my heartbeats.

Joel quoted Cosmo on the subject of "Feelings."

Experience taught me it's a hell of a lot more important to have two colors in correct composition than to have a vast confusion of emotional exuberance in the guise of ecstatic fullness or poetical revelation—both overrated qualities in art. For myself, I would rather be intellectually correct than emotionally fulfilled. That's true of my art and all other aspects of my life.

I'd read Joel's bio of Cosmo when it first came out, but it seemed to me now that I had missed all the stuff between the lines. Or had not known what I was looking for. While Joel did infer he and my father had been closer than friends, there was no mention of Cosmo's relationship with Micky, or with any woman besides my mother. Joel surmised that Cosmo had a Madonna fixation on his small-town sweetheart, but that his true nature had lain elsewhere. It was stupid to find this irritating. For all I knew, Joel was right. I have no memories of my parents together.

Nearly every quote of Cosmo's related to his work.

I'm only interested in the exercise of painting. Of technique and composition. I have no wish to express emotion or personal life; I prefer to have no personal life.

Joel rambled on and on about painting, art theory and the art scene in the '50s. (Oh, the Dilemma of Being Modern!) He rambled even more about Joel. But how much was Joel and how much was a pose? I read into Joel's narrative an ambivalence I had not perceived before. References to Cosmo's boozing, fighting and fornicating struck me now as bitchy in tone. I suspected Joel's feelings for his legendary chum were a love-hate mix. The memoir ended with Cosmo's return to Steeple Hill and marriage. Not Joel's idea of Happily Ever After.

* * * * *

It was around ten o'clock that same night when Jenny showed up at my door.

"Can I stay here tonight, Kyle?" She was white and tense, but calm.

"I don't think that's a good idea, Jenny."

"I'm leaving Vince."

That threw me but I said, "I don't need more trouble with Vince."

Her eyes welled with tears. She said, "I don't have any place else to go, Kyle. Please let me stay." One tear spilled over and trickled down her cheek.

Well hell. I should have sent her to Micky or given her money for a hotel. I pushed open the screen and said, "Only for tonight, Jen."

She came inside lugging a bulging, flowered tote bag.

"I need a drink," she said.

I was thinking warm milk. Maybe the last of the dusty Ovaltine. Jen added, "Something strong."

Adam had finished off the brandy and I had never known Jen to drink beer. I decanted a bottle of red wine and brought her a glass. She downed it in three gulps, giggled and pointed at me.

"I like it when you do that. Raise one eyebrow. It's cute." She handed her glass to me.

"You're scaring the hell out of me, Jen."

She laughed again, unsteadily. "That makes two of us. Kyle, I think Vince might have killed Brett."

"What are you saying?"

"He's changed. He's different."

"That doesn't mean he killed Brett." I had to ask. "Does he still think he's gay?"

"No."

"Just a phase, huh? Why do you think he killed Brett?"

"Could I have another glass of wine?"

I didn't have to ply her with alcohol, she was willing to ply herself. I poured her another glass.

"Talk to me, Jenny."

She swallowed a mouthful of wine in a gulp, and said, "He's changed, Kyle. From the time we moved here. We quit our jobs. Well, mine wasn't much of a career, but Vince's was. We moved here year round so Vince could paint, and it's been a disaster. We're broke. I don't care, but Vince can't handle it. All he thinks about is money."

"Why doesn't he go back to his ad agency?"

"Because that would mean failure. He can't accept another failure."

"Gotcha."

"Then he found *Virgin in Pastel*. It was like a miracle."

"You found the painting, Jen."

She shrugged. "Same difference."

"You really are too good for him."

She didn't hear this. She leaned forward, saying earnestly in a little gust of Merlot breath, "But instead of things getting better, they got worse. All Vince could think about was that painting, about someone trying to take it from him. First you, then Brett."

"Brett?"

"He kept thinking of all the ways to spend the money. He put money down on a new car. A Jag. Then he started worrying about all the people who would cheat him out of it."

The Jag or the money? All of the above or none of the above?

"What about Brett?"

"Brett told Vince he was keeping the painting for you. That it was really yours. That's why Vince is so sure you have it. But that wasn't what scared me. Vince would have given Brett that painting before."

"Before what?"

"I don't know. That's just it. Something happened between them. Vince said he wanted to kill Brett, but he wouldn't say why. And then Brett said he was keeping the painting, and then Brett was dead. Vince won't talk about it."

I contemplated this and was reminded of something that had been niggling at the back of my mind for some days now.

"Jenny, the night of the party that weed killer Irene loaned me went missing. Then the bottle turned up empty a few days later. Do you know if Vince might have borrowed it?"

Vince was famous for "borrowing" stuff.

Jenny's hand shook as she set her wine glass down. "I took it."

"You? Why?"

Her expression grew defiant; a badass Pippi Longstocking. "I was going to poison Brett."

I gaped at her. When I could speak, I said, "Jenny, are you insane?"

"I didn't do it! I was so upset I didn't know what I was doing, but I knew that I couldn't do *that*. I poured the chemicals out so I wouldn't be tempted later."

She started to cry again.

Could she be covering for Vince? But Brett had not been poisoned by the weed killer.

It was a few minutes before I gathered my wits enough to ask, "Why do you think Vince killed Brett?"

"Where was he that day? He said he was painting. He wasn't painting. There was nothing wet on canvas. There was nothing new. He disappeared around lunchtime and he didn't come back till late that night. And he already knew Brett was dead. Where was he?"

I shook my head.

"Where was he, Kyle?" Jenny repeated.

* * * * *

Jen had left for the museum by the time I got back from my swim the next day.

I worked all morning, had a tuna salad sandwich and a cup of tea standing in the kitchen looking out toward Adam's, then gravitated back to the computer. Work is a great refuge for emotional cowards.

I didn't hear the front door; that's how engrossed I was. The tap on the study window had me starting up from my chair as though yanked from a dream. Vince peered through the glass, hands framing his face.

I went to the front door, but did not unlatch the screen.

"Can we talk?" he requested mildly enough.

"I don't know. Last time I tried, you told me to get a lawyer."

"I wasn't thinking straight." His mouth worked. "Where's Jenny?"

"At work."

"Are you—? Is she—?"

"I have no idea what's going on. She asked for a place to spend the night."

Vince nodded. Gulped again. "Can I talk to you, Kyle? Please?"

Ah, the magic word. I undid the screen door. Vince followed me in, dropped down on the sofa, hands between his legs prayer-style.

"I need a drink."

Kyle's Bar and Grill. I went into the kitchen, poured two fresh cups of tea and brought them out to the front room. Vince stared at the tea and laughed shortly. He took a swallow and questioned, "What did Jenny tell you?"

"Not much. She said she needed a place to stay for the night."

"Did she say she was leaving me?"

The phone rang.

I padded into the kitchen. Micky began speaking as soon as I picked up.

"The sheriff just left."

"That's always good news."

"He wanted to know if I was the model for *Virgin in Pastel*."

"Were you?"

"No. Of course not. I'm a painter, not a model. What did you tell him, Kyle? Why would he think that?"

"Not a clue."

"Did you tell him Cosmo and I were lovers?"

"No. Are you kidding? Why would I want that to get out?"

"Well thanks a lot! What a thing to say to me!"

Hypersensitivity was not normally part of Micky's makeup. I said, "I only mean I'd be the last person to spread the word about my father's private life."

"Joel," she said in dire tones. "I bet it was Joel."

"Maybe it was no one, Micky. Maybe the sheriff is investigating. It's what we pay him for."

She sounded unpersuaded as she rang off, and Joel had my sympathies if he'd betrayed her confidence.

I returned to the front room where Vince was drinking his tea. He wore such a guilty look I was sure he had been eavesdropping.

"Vince," I said, "I don't know what I can tell you. I've got to get back to work."

"Is she coming back here tonight?"

"No." I hoped not. I sipped my tea, nearly dropping the cup when Vince asked, "Are you lovers?"

"God no!"

"Then why would she come here?"

"We're friends."

"She's trying to make me jealous."

"Are you jealous?" I finished the rest of my tea and set the cup down.

"Of you?" He laughed unpleasantly. "No way."

"So what's the problem?"

Vince said nothing, simply stared at me with a fixed look.

"Vince?"

He started.

"Is there something more I can do for you?"

It seemed to take him a long time to respond.

"You can promise to keep out of it."

"No problem." I stood up too fast and had to steady myself against the sofa arm.

I waited.

Vince made no move to rise.

I said, "I don't mean to be rude, but I'm supposed to be working."

Another pause.

"What else did she tell you?"

"Nothing. She said she needed a place to spend the night. I said okay and she went to bed. Alone." The whole topic of Vince and Jenny's marriage was beginning to make me sick.

Nauseous, in fact.

"Are you okay?" Vince inquired. "You look pale."

"Excuse me," I said.

I headed for the bathroom, brushing against an end table and sending it rocking. There was something wrong with my balance. I was dizzy, cold sweat breaking out all over my body.

I slammed into the bathroom, barely making it to the toilet in time. I proceeded to lose my lunch. My breakfast followed in the next spasm.

My body was drenched; my heart thudding. Black spots floated before my eyes as I clung to the porcelain bowl. Was it my heart? Sometimes nausea accompanies an attack. *I need help*, I thought distantly. The next instant I hung over the bowl while my body did its best to reject every organ through my mouth.

When that bout ended, I slid down on the cool tile, too exhausted to move or think. I listened to my heart chugging away in my ears. I wondered if I was dying, and I decided I didn't care so long as I could lie perfectly still.

I closed my eyes.

* * * * *

"No ambulance," Joel said. "If we call an ambulance the sheriff will know, and if Kyle's tried to kill himself—"

"Kill himself? What are you talking about?"

"He didn't take this stuff by accident."

"We don't know what he took—which is why we need to get him to a doctor."

"If it's digitalis he didn't overdose accidentally."

Adam said furiously, "He didn't try to kill himself!"

"He could have," Vince said. "He fixed the tea."

"Why the hell would he kill himself?"

Into the stricken silence that followed, I mumbled, "I didn't try to kill myself."

Immediately there was commotion around me. Everyone seemed to be talking at once. I heard Joel saying urgently, "Kyle, what did you take?"

I opened my eyes. I was lying on the sofa in my front room. Joel was bending over me, repeating his question.

"Nothing." I tried to sit up. A half dozen hands pressed me back, a chorus of voices ordered me to lie still. I said, "I'm going to throw up."

Fresh commotion as I was helped into a sitting position. The couch spun once, hard, wheel of fortune style. Someone thrust an empty brass planter under my nose, and I heave-hoed some more, my insides turning out, wringing themselves dry.

Tears of aggravation and self-pity itched their way down my face and plopped into the mess in the planter.

"It's okay, Kyle," Adam said kindly from somewhere above me. I recognized his beautiful hands steadying the planter. Perfect.

"Sorry," I got out, swiping at my cheeks. I shivered back into the sofa cushions and they tucked the blankets and water bottles around me once more. I felt cold all the way through, like I'd been buried for months. As resurrections went, mine left something to be desired.

After a bit I noticed Joel bathing my face with warm scented water, making *sshh-sshh* sounds.

"Kyle, what happened?" Adam asked.

"Not now," Joel said. "Let him rest."

I blinked up at them. Vince was standing at the foot of the long sofa looking ashen, which probably made two of us. I said dreamily, "I think Vince put something in my cup."

"I didn't!" he squealed.

Adam turned his way. Whatever Vince read on his face caused him to back up. "He was like that when I found him. I swear it!"

"You said he collapsed after he drank his tea."

"I meant that Kyle already had the tea prepared. He drank it and then he was sick."

I barely heard him, my eye caught by the displacement of the Chinese Chippendale cabinet against the far wall. That hadn't been moved in years. Now white linen peeped out from behind one door like a hint of petticoat. I looked around the room. Was it my eyes or were the pictures on the wall crooked? I looked harder. The vase on the mantel was off-center. The drawers of the desk were not flush.

"What were you looking for?" I inquired.

"I don't know what you're talking about." The defense in Vince's voice could have stopped a linebacker in his cleats.

"I didn't drug myself," I said. "I didn't try to kill myself. You put something in my tea when I got up to answer the phone."

"Kyle!" Vince gave a laugh like this was preposterous, but the guilt was right there on his sweaty face.

"You fucking *lunatic*," Adam bit out. "You could have killed him." He tackled Vince as Vince dove for the door. They crashed into the china cabinet in the dining room.

"I didn't mean to," Vince cried.

Joel threw the wet cloth in the bowl of lavender water, splashing us both, and went after them.

"Knock it off, you two!"

More crashing sounds as the three of them fell against the dining room table. I heard chairs scraping, the table groaning. The chandelier tinkled musical warning. I tried to untangle myself from the blankets, gave it up and did a kind of *The Mummy Walks* stagger into the dining room.

Vince was on the floor turning puce while Adam was wordlessly, ferociously occupied in strangling him. Vince's eyes bulged, his teeth were barred—as were Joel's, who hauled ineffectually at Adam's wrists.

"Adam, you crazy bastard," Joel puffed.

Vince gurgled. His tongue stuck out.

"Adam," I yelled. I threw myself onto the huddle too.

"Adam, you're killing him!" Joel cried.

Abruptly Adam loosed Vince. We all rolled away gasping. I considered throwing up again.

"It was an accident," Vince choked out finally. He looked over at me. "An *accident.*"

I didn't have the energy to respond, all my concentration on not sliding off the tilting floor.

"Accident!" exclaimed Joel. "How could it be an accident?" He picked himself up painfully. Hobbled over to a chair.

Adam was already on his feet, facing the window that looked out over the garden. He was rubbing the back of his neck. I could see his hands shaking.

"I didn't know the sleeping pills would affect him like that. They must have interacted with his medication. I only gave him a few."

"A few! How many is a few?" I demanded.

Vince shrugged helplessly. Then he said, "Look I—I could have just left. I didn't. I got help, didn't I? I called Joel. I didn't have to do that. No one would ever have known."

Adam wheeled to face us. "You son of a bitch. You didn't have the guts for murder, that's all you're saying."

"I wasn't trying to murder him!" Vince faced me. "I wasn't trying to murder you. Kyle, this is *me*, Vince. You know me."

I sat up carefully. "What were you looking for?" I asked again.

Vince stared blankly.

"While I was puking my guts out, you were searching for something. What was it?"

Vince wiped his runny nose. "*Virgin in Pastel,*" he admitted at last.

CHAPTER THIRTEEN

After Vince had gone, Adam and Joel continued to discuss my imperson-ation of Linda Blair in *The Exorcist*, damning Vince for every kind of fool, but agreeing that he hadn't intended me any real harm. Vince's story was that he had continued to search the house after I passed out, finding nothing.

Some twinge of conscience made him look in the bathroom before he left, and apparently the sight of me sprawled on the floor breathing in stento-rian tones was gruesome enough to send him hollering for Joel. Joel had hot-footed it over, taken one look and sent for Adam. Together they had brought me round. If you could call my current torpid state "brought round."

"I think it will make things worse if you call the sheriff," Joel said to me.

I was back on the sofa, wrapped in a blanket Indian-style. I couldn't seem to get warm. "Make things worse for who?"

"For all of us. Besides, Vince is satisfied you don't have the painting."

"Hey, so long as Vince is satisfied."

"Get this down." Adam set a cup of tea on the table next to me. I looked at the tea, shuddered, glanced up at Adam. I couldn't seem to look away.

Okay. One of us needed to break eye contact.

Joel's voice was a welcome interruption. "I know you're angry, Kyle, but the last thing we need to do is to give the cops another excuse for poking around here." He seemed adamant about that.

"Joel's right," Adam said.

What were they both afraid of?

"When was the last time you remember seeing that painting?" Adam asked Joel. He sat down on the sofa next to me. So close and yet so far, as they used to say in the old romance novels. If he put his arm around me, I wouldn't have the strength to resist; I could have used a hug about then.

Joel looked irritated. "How should I know? Are you accusing *me*?"

"Somebody took the damn thing."

"You think *I*—?"

"How do I know?" Adam was uncharacteristically curt. "I didn't. Kyle didn't. You were behind the bar all night. You had access to it."

"Whose idea was it to tack it up on the wall?" Joel's voice grew shrill. "It hadn't even been appraised yet. For all we know it's a forgery."

I said, "I don't think it's a forgery."

"You don't know anything about it, Kyle. The last time you saw that painting you were a child. A very sick child."

"Are you saying you think it was a forgery?" Adam demanded.

"Who knows? It could have been. Vince was a fool to bring it that night. It wasn't insured."

"Brett wanted him to bring it," Adam said.

We were all three thinking the same thing, but Joel put it into words. "Could Brett have taken it? Rolled it up and stashed it somewhere?"

"He wouldn't have had opportunity before the power went, and there wasn't time between the power going off and his getting sick. I've thought about it," Adam said. "If the painting wasn't taken by one of us three after the party, then it had to be taken down by someone when the power went."

"Nobody could count on the power going off," I interjected.

"Right. But when the power went Brett was still on the verandah with us."

"I was also on the verandah, I'd like to remind you," Joel snapped.

"That doesn't let you out," I told him. "You, me or Adam—anyone of us could have taken the painting after the party broke up."

"If it was still there!"

"Exactly."

Joel stared at me as though I were a thankless child complete with serpent's tooth.

"I don't think you took it," I added.

"Thanks very much!"

"Joel, when the power went, you, me, Kyle and Vince were all on the verandah," Adam said patiently. "Brett went inside almost immediately but everybody else was still there. I heard Irene speak to Brett."

"Right after that Brett was sick," I said. "So he couldn't have had time."

"You could have taken it yourself, Adam," Joel pointed out.

"Yes. Or Kyle. But you had the best opportunity of getting it out of the house on the excuse of fetching the doctor."

"Did I have a canvas tucked up my sleeve when I left?" Joel demanded of me.

"Not that I could tell." I turned to Adam. "The sheriff must have questioned Dr. Hicks. Did he remember seeing the painting?"

"He didn't notice one way or another. His mind was—er—preoccupied."

Preoccupied by the sight of Adam MacKinnon locked in the arms of the boy next door.

"Swell," I muttered. I stood up, feeling a spry and active ninety-nine, and tottered into the bath. After I splashed a gallon or so of cold water over my face, I examined my dripping reflection. Red eyes, pasty complexion, chapped lips and wet hair standing on end. What's not to love? I asked myself reaching for the toothbrush.

I wondered if Joel would stay much longer and what Adam and I would say to each other once he had gone. The thought of being alone with Adam was exciting and alarming at the same time.

There's a lot about Adam you don't know, Kyle, Brett had said. No kidding. Does anyone ever really know anybody else?

I spat out the toothpaste and rinsed away the bad taste.

When I opened the bathroom door Joel was alone in the living room.

"Where's Adam?"

Joel said acidly, "Seeing a man about a dog, I believe."

"Oh."

He studied me. "Is the honeymoon over already?"

"We're just friends, Joel."

"Aren't we all, dear boy?" His smile was devoid of humor. "Well, you're a master at the art of emotional detachment. You won't suffer long."

I must have looked startled; he added, "You'd have to develop some distance to stay sane, wouldn't you?"

"I never thought about it."

"My point exactly."

I sat down and rubbed my damp hair. Joel inquired grudgingly, "Are you sure you don't need me to run you in to the doctor's?"

"I'm okay. I don't think the stuff was in my system long."

He wrinkled his nose. "It didn't appear to be."

I managed a tired grin. "Did you really think I'd tried to kill myself?"

"I suppose not. I suppose it was the heat of the moment. There was always the possibility. Brett did stand between you and Adam."

It was unexpectedly hard to meet his gaze. "Not much point killing Brett if I was going to turn around and commit suicide. Why was I committing suicide, by the way? Guilt?"

He said softly, "People don't always think things through. Sometimes they do things that they realize later they can't live with."

The humor was gone out of the situation. I didn't know if Joel was still talking about me or himself, but I said, "Thanks for racing to my rescue."

Joel grimaced. "Anytime."

I spent the rest of the afternoon searching through my father's papers. As I had told Brett, Cosmo did not keep journals, diaries or letters. Even if he had, I had to accept the fact that anyone who wanted to go through Cosmo's things had had ample opportunity during the years I was away at college, and later living in Oakland. The paper trail I was following was old and cold.

I did think it would have been nice for me personally if my father had hung on to a few mementos—and if he had not systematically eradicated my mother's existence as well. It was like not having a history.

I found a letter from the San Francisco MOMA anticipating the arrival of *Virgin in Pastel* along with several other paintings scheduled for exhibition in August of that year.

For several minutes I sat there with the yellowed paper in my hand, trying to decide if this proved anything or not. I already knew Cosmo had decided to exhibit the *Virgin*, reversing his decade-long refusal. This letter didn't prove that he hadn't changed his mind again at the last moment and taken the painting with him.

But if Cosmo had taken the painting, how had it turned up nailed to the back of an old dresser? Furthermore, why *had* he decided to exhibit *Virgin in Pastel*, after so many years of declining? Was that significant or coincidence?

Another question: *why* had Cosmo refused to show what had been considered his greatest painting? I couldn't recall another work of which he had been so protective. He had exhibited paintings of his own father, of my mother.

Granted, that had been before her death, and the subsequent destruction of these same paintings. He had painted me at age six sitting on a crate eating an apple, and sold that one to the Whitney. So I didn't think it could have been sentiment that held him back. He wasn't an emotional scrapbook kind of guy.

*　*　*　*　*

When the lights came on in Adam's cottage I found myself prowling restlessly. I went outside and checked my mail box, reading the mail on the porch in the twilight: the usual bills, circulars, a letter from a college friend and a note from my grandfather asking me to dinner Thursday evening.

Since our infrequent family get-togethers were spontaneous—either I dropped by or we ran into each other in town—I wondered why Gramps was suddenly so formal. Maybe he was getting lonely in his old age? I wasn't sure how I felt about that; I wasn't sure that it mattered how I felt. When duty calls and all that.

I phoned and left a message on his machine. Then I went back to pacing the floor.

Granted, I was no expert at relationships, but I knew the longer I waited to talk to Adam, the worse it would be. For me.

Honesty forced me to admit that while I did believe it was in Adam's best interests to keep a distance between us, I wanted that distance for my own protection—and not because I feared arrest for Brett's murder.

I strolled around the garden while the twilight deepened. The roses and peonies glimmered like phantoms swaying gently in the evening breeze. I could still see the lights of Adam's cottage winking invitingly through the tree leaves. They worked on me like a tractor beam. So much for emotional distance.

What the hell, I decided all at once, and out I headed across the field.

Adam answered the door as promptly as though he had nothing to do but wait for me to carry the white flag over.

"Howdy."

"Hey there." Adam moved aside. "Like a beer?" he asked over his shoulder as I followed him inside.

"Sure. Thanks."

He brought me a beer. There was a snap of static electricity as our fingers touched. I laughed nervously. Adam's eyes narrowed as though he didn't get the joke. He sat down across from me where he had sat the first night I had come to dinner. Fastening his pirate-blue eyes on me, he waited. No pretense that this was a casual visit or that I just happened to be in his area.

It was quiet. The other time music had been playing. I stared at the collection of Verve records gathering dust in the corner. I looked at Adam. He hadn't shaved and his hair was getting longer. Maybe that heightened the buccaneer look; I wasn't sure whether I should surrender my sword or fall on it. It appeared he was taking no prisoners. He lifted the bottle to his mouth, swallowed, eyes still holding mine.

I looked away. I felt out of my element. Unsophisticated. But I had come this far, so I said it.

"We spent one night together," I told him. "A few hours. It shouldn't have meant that much to me, but it did."

Nothing from Adam. He had always been good at listening, but right now I wished he would say something, help me out.

"I've been in love with you half my life."

"I know."

I said irritably, "Then you know what I'm trying to say."

"I don't think you know what you're trying to say." His dryness was unexpected. "We had sex. Great sex, as a matter of fact—although I guess it wasn't anything like you imagined."

I flushed, remembering breaking down in his arms. "Or like you imagined," I retorted.

"I didn't have any expectations, Kyle. No fantasy to compare it to." I started to speak, but he went on. "The next morning you couldn't get away from me fast enough. You've kept a safe distance ever since."

Epiphany. He didn't have all the answers. He was capable of misreading and misinterpreting and misunderstanding. I had the power to hurt him too, no longer a child striking harmlessly at the palms of a patient adult.

"I don't want to be a surrogate for Brett," I blurted out.

"What the hell does that mean?"

At the sharpness in his voice, I stumbled. "I—I mean that you loved Brett. I know that. I don't want to try to—I know I couldn't. It takes time to get over someone. I understand. I've waited a long time, Adam. I don't want to screw it up by moving too soon now. Timing is everything."

He followed this jumbled explanation, frowning. "Timing is everything?" He snorted. "Where do you get this crap, *Glamour* magazine?"

He set down his beer bottle and came over to sit beside me on the faded chintz couch.

"I'm lousy at relationships," I muttered, giving him a sideways look.

"You do fine, baby. I just forget…"

What? How inexperienced I was? How it felt to be the one who loved, instead of the one who was loved?

He put his arm around my shoulders like you would your little brother, and said patiently, "My feelings for Brett have nothing to do with you, Kyle. They are separate. They always have been."

I expelled a long breath. Before I had finished exhaling, Adam's mouth found mine. He kissed me long and firmly, not patiently, and not at all like you would kiss your little brother. His lips were cold and masculine, tasting of beer and Adam.

"Does that answer your question?" he asked finally, running his knuckles against the bristle on my cheek, teasing.

"Yeah."

But it didn't really.

I lay there that night, wrapped in Adam's arms, Adam's breath warm on the nape of my neck, Adam's genitals soft against my ass, spied on by the bold-face moon peering in the window. I told myself that with Adam I would be loved and cherished. I would have companionship, and I would have his strength to lean on; and there was a little kid inside me craving all these things—craving what my father had withheld. But with Adam I would also get a middle-aged mother hen nagging me to take my pills and not lift anything too heavy. What kind of healthy relationship was that? Was this the choice of an autonomous adult? Did I want a parent or a lover?

And right about then my inner child gave me the raspberry royale. Who the hell was I kidding? I was still trying to intellectualize away my gut fear that Adam didn't want *me*, he needed someone to replace Brett. Anyone. For now.

Adam needs to be needed, whispered Brett's ghost at the foot of our bed.

* * * * *

I met Mayor Cobb coming out of the Civic Center as I was pushing through the glass doors. He seemed surprised and uncomfortable when I greeted him. Perhaps he felt being seen with a murder suspect was unpolitic. If so he recovered quickly.

"Well there, young Kyle. Come to borrow the keys to the city, eh?"

"That's right."

He dropped the jolly old elf routine and asked rather kindly, "Holding up okay?"

"You bet." Instinctively I rejected the kindness and its implication that I, or anyone at the colony, had need of it because we were more suspect.

"How's MacKinnon doing?"

I shrugged noncommittally.

Mayor Cobb wore an odd expression. I wondered suddenly if the old Hon. knew what the sheriff's next move would be, and if that move would be to arrest Adam. I feared only one thing had prevented Adam's arrest so far: the theft of the *Virgin*.

Sheriff Rankin believed Brett's death and the theft of the painting were connected. Since there was no reason to suspect Adam of hijacking the *Virgin* any more than the rest of us, he had not yet been cut from the herd.

"A terrible thing. Terrible," the mayor said, shaking his head.

Thus far I had kept my mouth shut about Jack Cobb's attack on me in the cemetery. I didn't think Jack Cobb had killed Brett, but I would throw what I knew about him to the sheriff if it looked like Adam was going to be arrested. I guess I was having trouble believing that anyone I knew had killed Brett. Pretty naive, because Brett was dead, and his murder had been premeditated, which ruled out a passing psycho. So why not Jack?

The mayor spotted some solid citizens and excused himself. I headed for the Hall of Records. Our HR has been newly redone with hush-hush carpeting and Second Ice Age air conditioning. The walls are decorated with a giant mural of local flora and fauna painted by local high school kids while apparently dropping acid.

I knew the clerk, Cassie Heifetz, from my own high school days. She had been my lab partner in biology, and had Liked Me as I recalled from certain ornately folded notes passed around Home Room. So when I asked her if she remembered Brett coming in, she was helpful. Cassie remembered Brett and she remembered exactly what files he had been interested in.

"Birth records?" I echoed.

Cassie seemed gratified with my astonishment.

"Whose?"

"I don't know."

"What year?"

This Cassie could answer. Brett was interested in birth records of twenty-one years ago—the year of his own birth.

"Did he seem like he found what he was looking for?"

Cassie gnawed her lip. "I'm not sure."

"Did he seem pleased? Disappointed?"

"He seemed pleased. Pleased with himself." Cassie added, "Like he always did."

✵ ✵ ✵ ✵ ✵

A field trip to the county offices seemed in order. Steeple Hill's records were hardly complete; the church registry was probably as accurate—or possibly sticking pins in a phone book. As I sped toward home, the summer sun beating on the bare skin of my arms and the top of my head, my mind turned once more to motive. As a mystery writer I know so-called "sane" people kill for one or a combination of the usual motives: money, sex (also called love), power, revenge or protection.

Brett had no money. He borrowed from everyone, including me, so I didn't think money was a motive. Now if *Adam* had been knocked off, Brett would have been the number one suspect.

Power? I couldn't see how eliminating Brett would change anyone's position of power. It wasn't like he was next in line for inheriting a throne.

Sex? My observation was anyone who wanted Brett could have him, at least on a temporary basis. Did that give Adam a motive? I didn't think of Adam as being particularly jealous. I knew he loved Brett, but his passion seemed reserved for his art. Adam despised violence, yet I did believe he had been capable of strangling Vince the afternoon I had been poisoned. For a low-key and rational fellow, Adam's level of rage had been alarming. But this was the guy who wore T-shirts that proclaimed "Harmony." Life with Brett may not have been harmonious, but I couldn't picture Adam bashing his lover's head in to get some peace and quiet.

What about Joel? There was an uncomfortable thought. Like suspecting your favorite aunt of slipping razor blades in the brownies. Not that I believed Joel could hurt a fly. But Joel had been in love with Brett, he had suffered over Brett's relationship with Adam, and over Brett's humiliating treatment. There were two motives: sex and revenge.

Vince? Vince with his confused sexual identity. How deeply had Vince cared for Brett? Jenny said they had had a falling out. Jenny claimed she was afraid of Vince. How badly had Brett treated Vince? I could imagine a variety of cruel and denigrating scenarios.

And speaking of confused sexual identities, how about Jack Cobb?

How about Jenny who had seen Brett as a hated rival?

Or had Brett died to protect someone's guilty secret? Why else the trip to the Hall of Records? Was Brett capable of blackmail? Morally, ethically, physically t'weren't no doubt about it, but I couldn't believe that Brett, an outsider, could discover a secret about the past that none of us knew. Something so dangerous it was worth killing for?

If Brett had died because of something that happened in the past, then all bets were off. Anyone who had been in the colony ten years ago was suspect. That meant the three people dearest in the world to me were suspect. If Cosmo had been murdered, then Joel, Micky and Adam were all under suspicion, and that I could not believe.

Because I didn't want to believe it.

CHAPTER FOURTEEN

"Is something wrong?" Adam asked after dinner that night.

"Hmm? No." I refilled my glass and set the bottle of Clos du Bois on the table, avoiding Adam's gaze.

We were sitting out on the verandah, watching the sunset. In a khaki shirt with vaguely military epaulettes, he looked handsome and austere. My heart hurt every time I looked at him, like I hankered for some mineral.

"I was wondering, did you ever find Brett's anklet?"

"No." Adam's slim fingers played absently with the box of matches he had used to light the citronella candles. "He must have lost it on the beach that day."

"It meant a lot to him."

"Yes."

"Do you know why?"

I thought for a moment that he wouldn't answer, then he said, "It's the sole link he had to his past."

"What do you mean?"

"Did Brett ever tell you—no, he wouldn't." His smile was acrid. "Brett was a few hours old when he was left in a basket on the steps of a San Francisco orphanage. Real Victorian stuff."

"I didn't know."

"No. He didn't discuss it."

Adam seemed disinclined to continue.

"What about the anklet?"

"It was part of a broken necklace. It was pinned to the blanket he was wrapped in."

Real Victorian stuff was right. Maybe there was a clue in that kind of gesture. Maybe it indicated a certain mentality.

"Did Brett ever try to trace his parents?"

"Trace what? He was an abandoned baby. His birth certificate was a police report."

"But do you think Brett ever tried to find his birth parents?"

"What are you getting at, Kyle?"

After a moment of hesitation I related my conversation with Brett following the night he had faked his near-drowning.

"401K?" Adam repeated thoughtfully.

I put my glass down harder than I meant to; Adam's eyes never seemed to miss anything. "With what you've told me I think Brett must have believed one or both of his natural parents lived here in Steeple Hill." I filled Adam in on my trip to the Hall of Records and my discovery of Brett's interest in the birth records of twenty-one years before.

Adam said grimly, "And you think Brett might have tried to blackmail his father or mother if he successfully traced them?"

"I don't know."

"You think you do."

Maybe I had said too much already. I could feel Adam's tension from across the table. I finished my wine, waiting.

At last Adam said grudgingly, "It's possible. He was bitter about being abandoned, about a childhood spent in an orphanage, about serial foster parents who used and abused him."

Brett's anger made him even more dangerous than his greed. If he did try to blackmail someone it might not be for money. It might be for the pleasure of watching that someone squirm.

I reached for the wine bottle again and Adam's hand covered mine.

"Go easy, baby. You're getting smashed."

I snatched my hand away. "No I'm not." Yes, I was. I was nervous and I was drinking too much.

"You hardly touched your dinner. Are you feeling okay?"

"I'm fine," I snapped back. "Furthermore, I'm over twenty-one. If I want to get smashed—"

"Okay, don't take my head off." He spoke neutrally, even ruefully, and I reflected on his never-failing patience with Brett's moods, Brett's tantrums, Brett's rudeness. Almost nothing seemed to get to Adam. Was that because of his core of inner serenity, or because he was actually a psychopath biding his time?

Now there was a freaksome thought. Anyway, you didn't kill your significant other because he was rude. You didn't murder your SO because he humiliated you in front of others. Oh, maybe in Agatha Christie. Maybe in *People* magazine. Not in real life.

Adam went inside and came out with another bottle of Merlot. There was an uncomfortable silence while he poured himself a glass, and then refilled mine.

"How did your appointment go with Dr. Hicks today?"

"What *is* this?"

"What is what?"

"This." I gestured edgily at the wine bottle, to Adam, to the world at large. "This Big Brother routine. This *inquisition*."

I heard the angry echo of my voice in the pause that followed my words. Adam let the pause linger and then he said coolly, "If you're not ready to talk about it…"

"There's nothing to talk about." I added hostilely, "My health is *my* business."

Adam turned the glass stem between his fingers. "I see."

What was I doing? I didn't want to fight with Adam. I didn't want to push him away. Was I afraid that if he had all the facts he might want to trade me in for a newer model? A racier edition with all moving parts and batteries included?

It wasn't that my health had worsened; it was that de Chirico thing again. My perspective had changed.

Although the arrhythmia wasn't in itself life-threatening, it was a strain on my already weakened heart muscle. And while there didn't seem to be any new damage—yet—to my heart muscles and valves, my arrhythmia appeared to be worsening.

"What does that mean?" I'd asked Dr. Hicks. But I already knew what it meant. Heart failure.

Hicks had avoided a direct answer. He talked about the importance of a positive attitude. He discussed getting serious about taking my medications—and new medications: beta-blockers and calcium channel blockers and blood-thinners. He talked about catheter ablation, electrical cardioversion, pacemakers and other fun stuff. He mentioned a cardiologist in San Francisco and the possibility of surgery. I'd stopped listening. Adam had already been caretaker in one relationship. Why would he want to play that gig again? Elementary, my dear Watson. He wouldn't.

Or if he did, it would be for the wrong reasons.

I shoved aside the memory of this afternoon and my test results, propping my elbows on the table. "I found something out by accident while I was in the doctor's office. Do you know Brett's blood type?"

"AB."

Of course he knew. And if we stayed together he'd know all the names of my meds and which drugs interacted with which; he'd find all kinds of tasty low-sodium meals to cook for me; and he'd become certified in CPR.

I said shortly, "Same as me. Same as Cosmo."

Adam frowned.

"Only five percent of the population is AB."

"And your point is?"

"Don't you think that's a huge coincidence?"

"What are you getting at?"

"How many times did you comment on how much Brett and I looked alike?"

Adam sipped his wine.

"Well?" I demanded.

Adam raised his eyebrows. "Well?"

"Am I crazy?"

"You think Brett was your brother?"

I felt a weird sort of pain when he put it into words; something I wasn't ready to examine. "Half brother."

Adam studied me without expression. I leaned forward on the table nearly tipping it in my eagerness. "It's not as screwy as it sounds, Adam. You said yourself it was Brett's idea to come to Steeple Hill. I think he came here on a mission. Micky said he was constantly snooping, asking questions, hinting."

"Hinting what?"

"I'm not sure, but what was that bit about his retirement fund? What did he mean about finding out how good a friend I was?"

"Kyle, this is nuts."

"I know, I know, but maybe it isn't. I found a clipping in one of Brett's books, an old interview of mine, and he had underlined the name Steeple Hill."

I saw something flicker in Adam's eyes.

"What?"

"I don't know. Brett's fascination with Cosmo. His jealousy of you."

"Of me?"

Adam looked uncharacteristically uncomfortable. I wondered how many times I had served as a topic of discussion between him and Brett.

"I read Joel's book again," I said. "He paints a picture—"

Adam winced.

"No pun intended—of a Cosmo who got his rocks off every chance he could. Why would he be any different in Steeple Hill?"

"He was married."

"And then he wasn't. He slept with Micky."

"You think *Micky*—"

It hadn't even crossed my mind until that moment. I felt my face freezing. Brett had zeroed in on Micky for some reason. The timing would be right. Brett had been born about three years after my mother's death, putting his conception right around the time Micky admitted she and Cosmo were giving comfort and succor to each other.

Observing me, Adam said dryly, "Are you sure you want to start asking questions when you're not going to like the answers?"

* * * * *

"Tell me what you want." His breath was warm against my ear. His hands, slick with almond-scented massage oil, kneaded the muscles of my back. I groaned in pleasure. Moonlight massage. That's something you don't get living on your own.

"Tell me..." He shifted off my hips, straddled my thighs, hands working the roundness of my ass. "...what you need..."

I need you to love me. I want to spend the rest of my life with you.

"More," I whispered back. "Everything." I wriggled my hips suggestively against him. I could feel that fierce and ready hardness nudging my backside. But always under control. Always in check. Adam could probably teach me a thing or two about emotional distance.

"Yeah?" He slid his thumb down the cleft of my ass, and I bucked, biting back a laugh. "Ticklish?" I could hear the smile in his voice.

"No." It was startling in a pleasurable way, that scrape of thumbnail down exquisitely-sensitive pulpy flesh. With the edge of his thumb, he feathered the tight ring of muscle. Instinctively I spread my legs, tried to push down and capture that caress, but he just brushed back and forth in that tormenting way. "Don't tease me, Adam," I said breathlessly. "I need it—need to feel close to you."

Adam murmured something, his breath hot on the back of my neck as he bent over me. One fingertip eased inside me, and I shivered at that slow sweet piercing.

"More," I pleaded.

He pushed. A delicious shock. Involuntarily my muscles clamped around his finger. It had been a long, long time for me.

"Breathe," he suggested and rimmed me ever so delicately.

I sucked in a breath and whimpered as one finger became two. That crazy clawing ache started. "Oh, fuck..."

"That's the idea."

His fingers pushed into the oily muscle, massaging deeper. Stretching, spreading. I couldn't help it; I began to move on his fingers. Blindly, I grabbed for the pillows, shoving them under my chest, offering up my ass, as Brett would have said—and I sure as hell didn't want to think about Brett now—I reached underneath my hips and stroked myself, moaning.

Adam's fingers slipped out of my warmth and I could have wept with frustration. From a long way away a drawer slid up and closed. The snap of plastic, the breathless squirt of the oil bottle.

"What are you doing?" I groaned, although I knew exactly what he was doing, and—in some alternate universe—maybe even appreciated it.

"Patience is a virtue, baby."

And virtue was its own reward, but that would also have to be in an alternate universe because in the here and now I was ready to ignite with frustration and lust. I jumped as Adam's fingers slipped back inside, twisting, stroking...

"Now would be good," I panted, working my dick. "Now. Please..."

He worked his hand underneath my chest, palmed my nipple with unexpected roughness. It distracted me from the retreat of his fingers. The next moment I felt the head of his cock pressing into me.

I froze. This never went well for me, and as much as I wanted it, I expected it to hurt. Adam's palm circled my nipple, slid across and rubbed the other. They were amazingly sensitive. He kissed my back right between my shoulder blades; I shivered. The combination of wet mouth and sly fingers was bemusing. A kind of sensory overload. I still felt the cautious advance of that painful pressure but I couldn't concentrate on any one sensation. When he pinched my nipple I strained closer, wanting his hand to rub my breast again—and the head of his cock shoved inside.

"Jesus. You're like hot velvet." That guttural growl didn't even sound like Adam.

I whimpered, muscles spasming around that rigid thickness. Talk about blunt instrument. "I don't—I can't." I bit my lip. The last thing I wanted was for him to pull out, but there didn't seem to be room inside my skin for both of us.

"Let go, Kyle. Relax." His voice was tender as he paused, hands continuing to stroke and pet and soothe. I relaxed a fraction and he pushed the rest of the way in. Terrifying and exquisite feeling sang in every nerve; this was new. This I had never felt before.

I couldn't seem to remember any words so I made encouraging sounds.

"Now the good part," Adam promised, and he began to rock his hips against me, carefully at first, then strongly. After a helpless moment or two I humped back to meet him, falling into his rhythm. Adam's hand covered my slack one and worked my erection full and hard again. I tipped my head back and found his mouth, a frantic, slipping kiss.

"You," he said against my damp temple. "You. You."

He shifted angle, I felt him even more deeply.

"Adam," I said woundedly. My heart thundered; I wondered if it would simply give out—and not a bad way to go.

He thrust into me, again and again, lancing into some deep and secret core of delight which, penetrated, began to spill through me in rolling waves of thunder. I began to come, my seed leaking over our clasped hands. Different sensations collided and I started to laugh.

Adam's breath caught and he cried out, transfixed. I could feel reaction surging through him.

We crashed down on the bed, sticky, trembling and spent. I struggled to contain myself as tiny aftershocks continued to ripple through my nervous system. After a few moments Adam raised his head and said bewilderedly, "What the hell are you giggling about?"

"I don't know," I said shakily.

He slid an arm under me, scooping me over so that I rested against him. He stroked my hair back, kissed my forehead.

"Do you have a tattoo?" I asked him when I'd had time to catch my breath.

"Baby, I think you'd have found it for yourself by now."

Brett had lied about so many things. He had lied about when and how he and Adam had first met. Now I wondered if he had got Joel to introduce him to Adam with a deliberate plan in mind. It had been Brett's choice to come to Steeple Hill.

"This feels right," Adam said. "Being here with you like this. It feels like we've been together forever."

Forever. I closed my eyes against that unexpected pang.

"No comment?" He kissed me.

I felt fragile, exhausted and wrung out. I couldn't reassemble my defenses this fast. Maybe he felt my mouth quiver despite my attempt at a stiff upper lip. He raised his head. "Okay?"

"Yeah. Of course." I pushed away, curling onto my side and presenting him with a shoulder. "Tired."

He was silent so long I thought maybe he had fallen asleep, but then he said quietly, "Okay, baby, I won't rush you."

* * * * *

Thursday was a slow day for sleuthing. A slow day for writing too, and I was getting paid for that. I stared at the empty computer screen, the blinking cursor, and reminded myself that my boyhood idol Max Brand, a pulp magazine and early Western writer, used to average thirty pages a day of final draft; in fact, one day after breakfast he wrote an entire 27,000 word novelette. He churned out novels and short stories like there was no tomorrow—and having a serious heart condition, for Max that was a real possibility. Now here I was, facing my first bout of writer's block 230 pages into my current project. My tale of a charming IRA psychopath and his ruggedly handsome SAS counterpart didn't seem so nearly amusing these days. Real murder can make the fictional stuff uncomfortable.

Still, I struggled on improving my typing skills if nothing else, knowing in my heart most of what I was writing was destined for the delete key.

I saw Adam head out early in the Acura for parts unknown. He had not returned by the time I knocked off work and went to change for dinner with my grandfather.

* * * * *

The porch light was dark when I arrived at my grandfather's for dinner. It was past six o'clock; there were no lights on inside the house.

I knocked a couple of times on the front door.

No answer. Maybe the old man had forgotten?

I tried the door and it opened under my hand. Stepping inside, I could see the stove light in the kitchen. I walked toward it.

"Granddad?"

Silence.

I entered the kitchen, following the unpleasant smell. There was a large kettle on the stove hissing dryly, water boiled away. The burning mingled with another odor: metallic, sharp, primitive. I felt the hair on the back of my neck rise.

It looked like the set of a play. My grandfather lay on the wooden floor. Blood pooled beneath him. Blood soaked the brown-and-white plaid of his flannel shirt; a great carving knife stuck out of his chest. His hazel eyes were sunken, glazed over, his mouth ajar, his complexion gray-blue: corpse-like. He was dead and there was no mistake.

How long did I stand there not thinking, not feeling, just trying to take it in? He was dead. He had been murdered. Not complicated, but I couldn't seem to get it.

Through the open window I could hear sprinklers, and someone washing dishes next door, and the sound of birds twittering in the trees as they settled down for the night. Peaceful sounds.

Feeling a weird pressure shift in my head, I reached out to steady myself against the table. The dizziness passed. I crossed to the phone and dialed the sheriffs. Next I called Adam.

That seemed to be all I could do. Loosening my tie, I took two tablets and sat down to wait at the kitchen table, neatly laid for our never-to-be dinner.

* * * * *

Adam arrived first. I heard the front door screen bang and the sound of his footsteps crossing the parquet floors. He checked in the doorway. A muscle in his jaw moved.

"I don't understand it," I said as though we were continuing a previous conversation. "Why would anyone kill him?" This is what I had been asking myself for the past fifteen minutes.

"I don't know." Adam's voice sounded thick. "Are you all right?"

I nodded; reached for him.

For a couple of minutes we stood there simply hugging each other. Adam held me so tightly I felt like my bones were cracking.

"There's an accident on the coast road," He said against my ear. "That's why the sheriffs aren't here yet." He let go of me and looked around. "Is this exactly as you found it?"

"Yes, of course."

"You haven't touched anything?"

"No." I thought back. "I turned off the stove."

"Have you looked around at all?"

"No." With Adam there I began thinking again. "Shit. I should have. I should have—"

"Relax." He pushed me toward the doorway and the formal sitting room beyond. "Wait in there. I'll be right back."

He was back in less than five minutes. His eyes seemed to avoid mine, but what he said was prosaic enough. "Are you sure he actually lived here? The place is immaculate. If the motive was robbery—"

"It wasn't robbery." I didn't recognize that voice but since I was talking it had to be mine.

"How do you know?"

"You said the place is immaculate. He wasn't robbed. First Brett—"

Adam's tone changed. "You're not thinking this is connected with Brett?"

I jumped up. "Yes, it's connected. Of *course* it's connected. It's not a coincidence for God's sake!"

Adam's brows drew together. "Don't have a spasm, Kyle."

That was a damned irritating thing to say to someone who was a heartbeat away from having a spasm, but it did have the effect of making me stop to take a couple of much needed breaths.

"How long has he been dead?" Adam prodded.

"You're asking *me*?"

"This is what you do for a living right? Write about this stuff?"

He was probably asking in order to kickstart my mind. I tried to remember when rigor mortis set in. Four hours right? I recalled that the ME would be able to determine the time of death by taking the temp of the victim's liver. Or was it something to do with the fluid in the eyeballs?

My stomach gave a queasy roll.

"Hours, I think. The...lividity of his skin, the rigidity of his body..." My voice gave out. I stared at Adam. "He was my last relative. My last blood relation in the world."

"Don't."

I closed my eyes, nodded.

We heard the sirens.

* * * * *

This time we were separated immediately; Adam was taken into the dining room, and I was shown into my grandfather's study. I drew Rankin first. I guess that made me the #1 suspect.

"What's MacKinnon doing here?" the sheriff charged right off the bat.

"I called him."

"Why?"

"I wanted him." I noticed the deputy faithfully taking notes, and tried not to sound like the hysterical faggot he no doubt pegged me for.

"Why?"

I swallowed hard. "I don't know. I was scared, I guess."

Scratch, scratch, scratch wrote the deputy. In Rankin's eyes I sighted—as Max Brand would have said—"a cold light of suspicion, and the sight was not pleasant."

"I gather you're fucking MacKinnon these days?"

I returned politely, "Actually, he's fucking me, if it makes a difference."

"You can say that again, sonny boy," the sheriff retorted. He didn't give me time to reply, even if I'd had a reply. "What time did you get here?"

After I answered this, the questions were routine—if your routine is being interrogated by the police. I answered slowly, carefully, expecting some trick question. If there was a trick question, I didn't notice it. When I believed we had finished, we started all over again.

The clock on the mantel read ten thirty. Was Adam still being questioned? I wondered. Was he waiting for me?

A gurney bearing my grandfather's body was wheeled slowly past the open study door.

"Something you might be interested to know," Rankin said. I jerked my head back his way. "Folks around here believe your grandfather killed Cosmo Bari."

That startled me as intended. "What?"

"Killed him and buried him in the old churchyard."

"Who believes that?"

"Old-timers."

Old-timers like Doc Hicks and the Cobbs. Town Fathers. Founding families. Upstanding folks who viewed Cosmo's disappearance as no loss. My father was the resident black sheep, and Aaron Lipez was one of *them*.

I was too tired to hide my agitation.

"It's a rumor, Kyle. Gossip. No one actually accused Lipez."

"So no one ever investigated?"

"Cosmo Bari has yet to be officially reported missing, let alone the victim of a homicide."

Score one for the man in the cowboy boots.

"Why do people think my grandfather killed my father?"

"Guess they think he didn't like him much."

I must have looked as unamused as I felt.

The sheriff took out a chaw of tobacco.

"Well, sonny boy, the story is your grandfather threatened to kill your father, and that's why he took off for New York."

"But he came back and married my mother."

"That's true. Fourteen years later. But your grandfather didn't forgive your daddy. When your mother died there was some wild talk. The story I heard was your grandfather punched your daddy right there at your mother's graveside."

I sat there blinking at him stupidly, trying to fit this jagged little piece into the 3D puzzle of my past. "Why?" I asked at last.

"Blamed him, I guess. Said he broke your momma's heart."

I didn't want to ask the obvious next question, did not want to hear the answer. Sherlock would have asked. Marlowe, Poirot—hell, Miss Marple would have asked. I sealed my lips.

Rankin, seeing I did not want to play, chortled at his own private joke and dismissed me.

* * * * *

I woke with a scream echoing in my ears. My own scream.

Someone was grabbing me, hurting me. I fought back.

"Kyle! Wake up! *Kyle*—"

The darkness was a black blanket thrown over my head, but I recognized the voice, and that I was in bed.

I quit fighting.

"I'm awake. Let me go."

Adam had me pinned to the mattress. He was breathing as hard as I was. He let go of my wrists, raised himself off of me. The springs of the mattress protested. A light came on. Silky rose-colored light.

I blinked up at the ceiling, trying to orient myself, when I saw Adam's shadow come sliding across the wall as he turned back to me. Out of the corner of my eye it looked like a shadow-puppet ax falling toward me.

I flinched away throwing my arm up to ward him off.

"Kyle…" Adam sounded shocked. After a moment he reached out tentatively, as though he thought I might fight him off. "Are you okay now?" His hair was standing on end. I wasn't surprised.

I tore my gaze from the wall where I was still watching for the ax shadow, and I nodded. "Sorry." My vision focused on Adam's left eye which looked red and puffy. "Adam, did I punch you?"

He put a hand to his cheekbone as though he hadn't noticed. "You could have. You seemed to think you were fighting for your life." He sounded grim. "Was it the nightmare again?"

"I don't remember." The dream was fading fast, like always. I was so tired I felt delirious. I didn't want to think. I didn't want to remember the things that had happened that evening. Drawing the covers over me, I turned on my side.

Adam put his hand on my shoulder. "Tell me what you dreamed."

"I'm tired, Adam. I need to sleep." I pulled away from him, and burrowed down into the pillows once more.

"You can sleep in a minute. What did you see?"

I threw myself on my back, scowling. "The same thing as last time. It's always the same thing." I laid my arm across my eyes. "What is this, the third degree? Turn the light off."

He turned the light off. The darkness was soothing, like an ice pack on a headache.

I related the dream for Adam's listening entertainment. He was silent till I finished speaking.

"Did you ever talk to anyone about this dream?"

"Like a shrink?"

"Like anyone."

"No. You."

"What do you think it means?"

"Nothing." I tossed fretfully; the mattress coils squeaked as Adam avoided another collision. "It's a night terror. It doesn't mean anything."

I could see moonlight shining off the profile of the nymph lamp beside the bed. The smiling face looked evil in the shadows. I closed my eyes.

"It must mean something. Maybe the images in your dream are symbols for something?"

Like the Dali dream sequence in *Spellbound*?

I said crabbily, "I've gone my entire life without knowing what this damn dream means. Can't it wait one more night? I need to sleep."

Silence.

Peace at last, I thought, and my nerves quit sizzling.

"Have you had these dreams your entire life? When did you start having them?"

I moaned. "I don't *know*. I guess…when I went away to college."

I had always assumed the nightmares were triggered by the stress of leaving the sheltered environment I'd grown up in, combined with fears about my health and my father's desertion.

"You're sure the dreams started in college?"

After Cosmo disappeared, that's what he meant.

"Yes."

"The images in your dream are probably symbols. If you understood what the symbols in the dream meant, they might not affect you so much." The mattress dipped as he moved my way. He gathered me into his arms, his body accommodating the angles of mine, as though we had been lovers for years. He was thin but wiry; his arms surprisingly muscular. I rubbed my head against his chest. The soft hair tickled my cheek. I expelled a long breath.

Adam stroked my head, his fingers threading my hair as he thought aloud.

Held by him, stroked and petted, my muscles loosened, my body going slack and heavy. There's nothing more trusting than falling asleep in some-one's arms. I listened to Adam from a safe distance.

"Maybe this woman represents your Anima, the embodiment of what's feminine and emotional in you."

I snickered at that. Like I wasn't in touch with my feminine side?

Adam misread my amusement. "The emotional, intuitive, instinctive side of your nature," he explained.

"Got it. So why is she blue?"

"I don't know. What does this woman look like?"

I shrugged within the circle of his arms.

"Try to picture her."

A woman. Young? Old? Hard to tell, hard to see past the expression of horror that froze her face. My heart sped up in a burst of fear. I growled, "I don't know. Just…a woman."

Adam's Anima being fully integrated, he slid his hand down my back and gave my ass a reassuring squeeze. He changed direction. "The blood could refer to the blood of Christ; you know, the life of the spirit as well as the flesh."

Some kind of religious experience? I wasn't religious, why would the woman of my dreams be religious? "Maybe it's just blood, Adam."

"Is it a lot of blood? A bath of blood? That could represent baptism into maturity and manhood."

"It's a lot of blood."

"It could be the fear of castration."

"Shit—" I wriggled my hips more comfortably against his. "Where did you learn all this?"

"I read a book once. What was the other thing? She's painted blue? Blue is celestial, heavenly. It could refer to spiritual energy or intellectual understanding."

Adam used a lot of blue in his paintings. Azure skies, ultra-marine seas, robin's eggs, lupine, electricity: the memory of Adam's work centered me, tranquilized. I was starting to drowse.

"What else? A moon? Usually in a man's dream the moon represents his Anima."

"You're building quite a case for latent homosexuality," I mumbled, and buried my face in the space between his armpit and chest.

I don't know what final interpretation Adam may have drawn from my dreams, because by then I was asleep once more.

* * * * *

In the morning I went to see Joel.

I found him breakfasting on his sun porch: eggs Benedict, turkey bacon and the ever-present pot of tea.

"Sit, dear boy. Have some breakfast."

"Joel, I need to talk to you."

Ignoring my protests, Joel rose and went to get me a plate. He was wearing pajamas, white with little red and green frogs; the frogs seemed to hop and leap across Joel's slender frame as he walked inside.

I looked about myself incuriously. I knew this room as well as any in my own home. Bright sunlight poured through the glass roof upon the jungle of healthy green plants. Joel was an expert gardener, an expert cook, a connoisseur of art and tea and boys. There were several pastels of exotic adolescents in kimonos on the walls of his bedroom. I could still remember the excited, edgy feeling those pictures gave me as a youth.

Joel returned with my breakfast and poured tea from the clay Yixing pot into gleaming, white porcelain cups.

Tea is an art not a beverage with Joel. He claims there are healing, soothing properties in such whimsically named blends as Golden Water Turtle and Jasmine Pacifica. He can speak of pure varietals and tonic herbals as enthusiastically as properties of color and light, brushwork and composition.

"Now, what has you looking so troubled on this lovely morning?"

After I finished relating an account of my grandfather's murder the night before, and Joel had finished expressing shock and horror, I said, "Can I ask you something?"

"Shoot, dear boy." Joel pushed his plate away as if his appetite had gone.

"Who modeled for *Virgin in Pastel*?"

"Why, I don't know. No one knows."

"Was it Micky?"

Joel looked pained. "What a question. Why ask me? Ask Michaela."

"I have asked her. She said she wasn't."

Joel gestured as though this answered all my doubts. "Why should she lie?"

"I don't know. Who do you think was the model?"

Joel sat back, knees crossed; he had perfect posture, poised as a pin-up girl.

"I always thought the model was your mother."

"My mother didn't have blonde hair."

"Dishwater blonde, but I was thinking more of her body. Kyria was tall and slim and graceful. It could have been a composite."

"But Cosmo painted *Virgin* after she died."

"Exactly. I think he painted it from memory. I don't believe Virgin is any one woman and that's why it's so—so magical." He gave a vague flip of his hand to emphasize the magic.

Maybe this was the answer.

As the leading expert on Cosmo Bari's work and my father's closest friend, I figured if anyone knew the model for *Virgin in Pastel*, it was Joel.

Glancing around the room, I noted the telescope on its aluminum tripod aimed at Adam's verandah. I wondered if Joel ever directed that 90mm objective lens toward Adam's bedroom window. Not a cozy notion. My gaze fell on a corner table nearly swallowed by a Sprengeri asparagus fern.

Something about that table seemed familiar. Why? It was an ordinary corner table, water-marked and battered from the years. It had a mock handle: a brass lion head with a ring through its mouth.

Why was that so familiar?

"More tea?"

I covered my cup with my hand. "No."

"It's decaf."

"Thanks anyway."

Where had I recently heard about a table with a decorative handle? When was the last time I had discussed furniture with anybody?

"How about another helping of these incredible eggs, dear boy? An excellent source of protein. And breakfast is the most important meal of the day."

Jenny had been refinishing an old piece of furniture and...

"What is it?" exclaimed Joel. "What's wrong?"

I pointed to the table. I noticed abstractedly that my hand was shaking. "That's part of a set. The dresser that Jenny found *Virgin in Pastel* in, that was part of the same set."

There were a couple of reasonable explanations for this but Joel didn't offer either of them. He stared at the table. He stared at me. His mouth worked soundlessly.

"You hid the *Virgin* in that chest, didn't you?"

I was on my feet. Joel jumped up too, reaching for my arm. I yanked away.

"It's not what you think."

"What did you do, Joel? Did you kill him and steal the painting?"

Joel put his hand to his throat. "You can't think— *No*, no! I didn't kill him. I could never—"

"Don't lie to me!"

"I-I'm not. I *loved* him. I could never k-kill—"

"But you stole the painting."

Joel stared at me, tears streaming down his face. "I stole the painting," he agreed.

CHAPTER FIFTEEN

"**P**lease try to understand," Joel pleaded.

I shook my head.

"I knew it," I said. "I knew if you didn't take the damn thing, you had to have noticed it was gone. You were standing in front of it all night."

"No, no, no!" Joel gestured as though warding off the evil eye. "I didn't have anything to do with the painting disappearing from Adam's!"

"Don't lie to me!"

"I'm not! Yes, I noticed it had gone, but I didn't care. I was glad. If you didn't want it, I didn't care what happened to it. I never wanted to see that painting again."

"What are you talking about?"

"Try to understand," he repeated. "I was a different person then. Desperate. I had gambling debts—I was in hock up to my nuts. The people looking for me would have crippled me, broken my fingers one by one."

I raised my face out of my hands (which I had been using to keep my head from blowing off my shoulders). Joel had been talking without pause for almost twenty minutes. It still didn't make sense.

"I don't believe you," I said.

"But it's *truuue*, dear boy."

"Then why didn't you sell the painting?"

"I...couldn't. I *meant* to of course, but when it came down to it I kept waiting for Cos to come back."

"Why did you hide it?"

"I was afraid. He didn't come back. I thought it was because of me."

"What are you *talking* about? How did you pay off your gambling debts if you didn't sell *Virgin in Pastel*?"

"I sold everything else. I sold the brownstone, my collections. I mortgaged the cottage. It isn't a secret. And then I wrote the book. I paid my debts and I—I learned my lesson. I've never gambled since. I don't even buy Lotto tickets."

"What about the *Virgin*?" I questioned flatly.

"I hid it. At first I was waiting for Cos. I didn't know how to simply return it. Then I got scared. He didn't come back," Joel repeated.

"How hard did you hit him? Did he fall? Hit his head?"

"No, no, no! Kyle, really. It didn't faze him. He said very calmly, 'Feel better now?' Knock him down? I was the one on my knees!"

Joel's story was that the night before Cosmo left Steeple Hill, Joel had gone to him begging for money. It was not the first time Joel had been in trouble with bookies, but this time Cosmo said no. Apparently he had not put it tactfully. Joel had begged and pleaded and finally punched Cosmo in the mouth.

Cosmo had walked away into the woods, into history.

Joel, drunk and desperate, had walked into Cosmo's house and three minutes later walked out with *Virgin in Pastel*.

"Where was I?"

"Sleeping. I remember Cosmo warned me to keep my voice down. That's why we went outside."

I stood up. "That's it? That's your story?"

"It's the gospel truth, so help me."

"He just disappeared in the woods. You never saw him again? You never heard from him?"

"I swear to God that is the truth."

"And for a decade you hung on to *Virgin*?"

"I didn't know what to do with it. I was afraid. A few years ago I thought if I could slip it back into circulation no one would have to know and you could have it back. I knew it was a matter of time before it resurfaced. What I didn't realize was that Vince of all people would find it, or that he would be such an asshole, or that you wouldn't fight for the thing."

"So then you stole it back."

"No!"

"Come off it, Joel."

"Listen to me!" Joel sounded frantic. "I did not steal it back. The last thing I wanted was to get stuck with that picture again. And for what? If I was afraid to sell it before, I sure as hell wouldn't try to move it now."

That at least made sense—except that he might not have taken the painting back for monetary reasons. Joel was a collector.

"But you know who took it."

Joel shook his head. "I don't. Really I don't."

"You're covering for someone, Joel. Who?"

"You have to believe me, dear boy."

I was beginning to wonder if there was anyone I could believe.

* * * * *

I shut the front door and nearly fainted as Adam rose from the chair he had been waiting in. He had a beaut of a shiner that I would have gladly kissed and made better, but he didn't give me the chance.

"Where the hell have you been?"

"Gee Dad, we ran out of gas."

"Funny."

"Well, I'm one of those funny boys. Look, Adam—"

"No, you look, Kyle," Adam snapped out crisp as celery stalk. "People are dying. I want to know what you're up to."

"I'm not killing people if that's what you're hinting."

"Has it occurred to you that by stirring up—"

"I'm not stirring up anything! *Brett* stirred the shit up."

"THE POINT IS," Adam drowned me out, "the circle around you is getting smaller and smaller, or haven't you noticed?"

"I noticed. I'd like to keep it from getting any smaller."

"You're not a detective in one of your damn books, Kyle. You're not... Jesus Christ, you were screaming down the house last night."

Gotta admit, I didn't like being reminded of that.

"Hey, if I'm disturbing your beauty rest, I can sleep next door."

"Kyle!" Visibly Adam struggled for control. "You don't understand. What you are doing is self-destructive. It's…dangerous."

A frisson of alarm slithered down my spine. "What does that mean? Is that a threat?" My gaze fell on the book he had laid aside when I walked in. Simon's *Conquering Heart Disease.* My owner's manual. "What's this?"

He didn't speak.

"Planning to knock me off next?"

Okay, I hadn't had enough sleep, and I'd had way too many shocks in as many hours. I was scared of more things than I could name. People I had trusted all my life were turning out to be liars, thieves, possibly murderers.

"Kyle…" He breathed the word out like actors on TV do when they've been shot; kind of weak and disbelieving.

But then he fired back. "I'm not Cosmo. I'm not going to walk out on you when you need me."

My turn to figuratively stagger back and see how badly I'd been hit.

"This has nothing to do with Cosmo."

"This has everything to do with Cosmo. Everything that ever happened in this goddamn place has to do with Cosmo."

Ah, now we're getting somewhere, I thought. But I was wrong, because Adam wasn't talking about himself, he was still talking about me.

"Can't you see what this is really about? Cosmo abandoned you. You're trying to make sense of something that doesn't make sense. You want it all neatly explained so it won't hurt anymore."

"If Cosmo walked out on me, then where's the danger? What's self-destructive about wanting some answers?"

"I'll tell you what's destructive." Adam picked up the book. "According to this, alcohol will make your heart worse."

White-hot fury washed through me. "You can't let it alone, can you?"

His eyes were so dark they looked black. "Why won't you talk to me? You go to the doctor; you're obviously upset, and instead of talking to me, instead of dealing with it, you get drunk. You go to the Hall of Records, you start asking people questions like you're playing cops and robbers. What's going on? Are you trying to get yourself killed?"

"Since we're psychoanalyzing each other, let me ask you something," I said. "If Brett hadn't dragged you, would you have ever come back to Steeple Hill?"

"What the hell does that have to do with the price of turnips?"

"No," I answered my own question. "You would not have."

Adam was silent. Then he said more calmly, "You analyze this stuff too much."

"Sorry if I'm prone to thinking. It must make a change after Brett."

Anger flickered in his eyes, but his voice was level. "Kyle, I care for you. We could have something together. Something worth having. Why are you doing this?"

I didn't know what to say to that. I wanted to tell him what I feared, but I couldn't find the words. Then the opportunity was lost forever as Adam spoke.

"I thought of you as a—a—"

"Child."

"Seventeen-year-old boy. I'm not a pedophile."

"I wasn't planning on turning you over to my Guidance Counselor." I added bitterly, "Brett was younger than me."

Adam sighed. There was a wearied note in his voice that reminded me of how he used to sound with Brett sometimes. "He was an adult. You were how old when I moved here? Ten?"

"Thirteen."

"And I was how old? Twenty-something?"

"Twenty. You wore size 11 shoes and a sixteen-and-a-half-inches collar. Anything else you want to know about yourself?"

"That's my point, Kyle. You were a kid. A cute kid who followed me around like a puppy."

Oddly enough, that no longer stung. "I grew up a long time ago, Adam."

"What I want you to understand is that I would never have laid a hand on you. Ever. And not because your father and Joel and every other adult in a five-mile radius would have had my balls. I wouldn't do that to a child. I wouldn't use a child."

"No one's suggesting—"

"But then you were fifteen, and then sixteen, and you—I liked you, Kyle. A lot. You—liked me. I had to make a conscious effort not to escalate things. I had to fix it in my mind that you were off-limits." He concluded lamely, "It stuck, I guess."

"And besides, you met Brett."

A long sigh, like a final breath.

"Besides, I met Brett." Adam raked a hand through his hair. Not a lot to chat about after that. The truth will set you free. In more ways than one.

"Kyle, you're deliberately sidetracking me. Why?"

"Because I think we should clarify things."

"Here we go again." Adam's lip curled. "Let me guess, you don't think we should see each other?"

Actually my point was that he didn't have a right to rein me in—hell, I don't know if I *had* a point. Let's say I wasn't thinking too clearly. Maybe my obsession with the past was self-destructive, but right now my future didn't appear to have a happy ending in sight.

And of course once Adam said it, I figured Adam was putting into words what *he* wanted.

"There's not a lot of point, is there?"

I was still hoping he would argue. Adam said *nada*.

"I have to do this." *A man's gotta do what a man's gotta do.*

Unless another man's got a better idea?

Adam gave a small nod as though at last I made sense. He headed for the front door.

"Then don't let me keep you," he said on his way out.

* * * * *

I was afraid if I took time to reflect, I'd fall apart, so I made a beeline for Micky's and found her in her studio.

"Where's the fire, kiddo?" She shook a cigarette out of the pack of Marlboros and lit it. She inhaled deeply, studying the painting on the easel, head tilted, eyes narrowed at blue sunflowers from another planet.

"I want to ask you something."

"Ask away." Somehow she managed to rake the hand with the cig through her long hair without setting her hair on fire.

"Were you the model for *Virgin in Pastel?*"

Micky whirled, her green eyes feral. "No. I told you no. If one more person asks me that—!"

"Why was Brett blackmailing you?"

"Blackmailing me?"

If only she had sounded more indignant and less alarmed. My heart sank.

I leaned back against the wall, watching her. "He was blackmailing you then?"

"Do you think I'd put up with blackmail for five minutes?" She looked dangerous. The kind of dame Philip Marlowe might have encountered on one of his mean streets.

"No." I didn't have to think it over.

"Damn straight. I told the little prick to go right ahead and I'd sue his ass—or Adam's ass, if it came to that."

My head snapped up. "Adam? Did Adam know?"

She took an agitated puff of her cigarette. "I have no idea what Adam knew or didn't know. He brought that little snake here; it was his responsibility to keep tabs on him." Exhaling, she reminded me of a small fire-breathing dragon.

I nodded. Stared at my foot in its scuffed sneaker. This wasn't easy. I raised my head. "Brett was your son, wasn't he?"

She opened her mouth for instant denial, then shrugged. "I don't know."

"You...don't?"

Reluctantly she admitted, "He said he was. He could have been I guess, although..."

"Although what?"

"They told me the baby died. It could have been a lie."

If I said the wrong thing she was liable to clam up, but I was totally confused by now. Cautiously I tried, "The orphanage people told you your baby died?"

Micky's nose wrinkled. "Orphanage? Child Services informed me the baby died with the parents—the couple who adopted it."

It. Not exactly the maternal type, our Micky. Joel had provided most of the mothering in my life. But Micky had always been there for me, tough and tender in her own idiosyncratic way.

"You gave your baby up for adoption?"

"Bingo." She stubbed out her cigarette.

"And Brett claimed that he was your son?"

She snorted, still not meeting my gaze. "Now I know why cats eat their young."

"Yeech. They don't, do they?" She shrugged her slim shoulders. "Was Brett—was the baby—" I half swallowed the name, "Cosmo's?"

For a moment there was a sparkle in Micky's eyes that could have been anger or tears. "Yes."

My throat knotted. It was hard to get the words out. "Did he know?"

She shook her head. "I was a big girl. I dealt with it. Cos already had a kid; he wasn't in love with me. And, let's face it, I'm not exactly Brady Bunch material."

I pushed off the wall and tried to put my arm around her slim shoulders. "You were great to me, Micky. Always." After a moment she let me hug her.

"That's because I could hand you over to Cosmo when I got tired of playing with you."

Yeah, that was the funny part. Imagining Cosmo taking care of a kid. I couldn't picture him bathing, feeding, dressing a small child—tucking a little kid into bed at night. I couldn't picture it and I had been the little kid.

How long had it been since I let myself remember?

I said, "So you told Brett to publish and be damned?"

"Something like that."

"And Brett?"

"Exit stage left."

I blinked. "You didn't—?"

An unpleasant smile flickered across Micky's features.

"No, I didn't. But I could have."

When I left Micky's, I went home and went to bed. Three hours of sleep a night was definitely not what the doctor ordered. And even without the sleep deprivation, I'd had an emotionally exhausting morning. If I had bad dreams I slept too deeply to know it.

When I woke it was four o'clock in the afternoon. I lay there staring up at the shadows of wisteria on the ceiling, listening to the music floating across the meadow from Adam's cottage. I felt drained, empty. Like you do when you've been sick with a fever and the fever finally breaks.

I ran a quick internal audit. My heart thumped steadily along. Maybe a little fast, but it was a hot afternoon. Maybe the new dosage would do the trick. After all, it wasn't like the strain of the last few weeks was normal for me. Maybe...

Too soon to get my hopes up. All the same, I needed to start making plans for my future. Maybe two sets of plans depending on what my future was going to be, but somehow I didn't feel like I could move forward when the past seemed to be converging—and the intersecting point seemed to be right where I was standing.

I showered, ate a peanut butter sandwich, and sat down at the kitchen table to do a bit of mind mapping as set down by Leonardo de Vinci in his *Treatise on Painting.*

On a large sketchpad I drew a globe containing the word COSMO in the center of the page. With a different colored pencil I jotted down key words as they occurred to me in a circle around the globe. Words like Art, Lover, Father, Mystery. I connected these words to the central image.

It was a long time since I'd tried this creative approach to logic; I remembered Cosmo showing me how to map that last summer. I wondered what problems I'd thought I had back then. Or what problems Cosmo thought I'd had: the kind of trouble that could be worked out with colored pencils, a sketch pad and a few minutes to myself? A bit optimistic on his part.

Focusing on the key words I'd sketched, I started to free associate. Under "Lover" I wrote: Micky. Joel? Adam? Virgin? Not that I was certain the mystery model had been Cosmo's lover, but if she wasn't, she'd have been unique.

Under "Painting" I wrote: intellect, exhibition, Virgin. Under "Mystery" I came up with murder, disappearance, Virgin.

I drew for about thirty minutes. As I wrote "Virgin" for the third time, I examined my mind map, and I recognized a theme. In red pencil I wrote the word "Virgin." I drew connecting lines. Red lines seemed to connect the word "Virgin" to every other key word. Yet under the word "Virgin," I had to draw a big red question mark.

The summer breeze was stirring the lace curtains and I could hear the distant notes of "Bebop in Pastel." I never wanted to hear that tune again as long as I lived.

I got up and slammed shut the window.

*   *   *   *   *

It was almost closing time when I reached Cobb House. As usual the museum was nearly deserted. I found Jen in the concession shop selling post-card copies of Cosmo Bari's paintings.

I waited till she finished with her customer of the day.

"Kyle, I've been meaning to call you," she said, before I had a chance to get started, "Vince and I are getting back together."

"Congratulations."

"I know you think it's a mistake, but we do love each other."

"It's none of my business, Jen. Just because he poisoned me…"

"That was a mistake, Kyle. Vince would never deliberately hurt anyone."

"A couple of days ago you told me you thought he had killed Brett."

Jenny flinched and looked around as though the walls had ears. "Vince explained everything to me."

"Like?"

"He was in L.A. the day Brett was killed. He went for a job interview at an ad agency. He was embarrassed so he didn't want me to know. Kyle, we've put the cottage up for sale. Vince took the job in L.A. We're getting away from here." She made it sound like an escape from Alcatraz.

"Isn't this sudden?"

"We should have done it a year ago. But sometimes it takes something like this to bring people together."

"Jenny, a couple of days ago you were saying you were frightened of Vince. Now—"

She rushed in, "Because I was *hurt*. I didn't understand. Now I understand."

"What do you understand?"

"The thing that Brett did to Vince."

"What thing? Taking the painting?"

She shook her head.

"What thing?"

Out on the patio two matronly ladies were having soft drinks. Jenny looked at them and lowered her voice.

"You have to swear you'll never tell anyone. Not even Adam. Especially not Adam."

"Fine. Scout's honor."

"*Were* you a Boy Scout?"

"No. Spill it, Jenny."

"It's…horrible."

"For God's sake!"

She took a deep breath and plunged. "Vince was—curious, you know. He thought—well, he was questioning his own—his own *orientation*. He thought he had feelings for Brett."

"I know all that."

"Well he thought—*he* thought, Brett that is, thought, that they should—"

"They should *what*?"

"They went to a motel in Kelsburgh and they were, you know—"

I gestured like a traffic cop to try and speed her onwards.

"And Vince didn't want to. He changed his mind. It hurt and it was disgusting. He wanted to stop but Brett wouldn't let him. Brett forced him. Brett—Brett *raped* him." Her cheeks were scarlet, her eyes bright and indignant.

After a moment or two I closed my mouth.

"That's Vince's story," I said at last.

"It's true, Kyle. Vince *cried* when he told me."

I didn't know what to say. It was so far off the track from everything I'd imagined. I thought of that night of the bonfire; of tussling with Brett on the rocks. It sunk in on me that he had known we were half brothers even then.

"Have you told the sheriff?"

"No! Of course not! It's no one's business but ours. And you can't either. You promised!"

"Jen, don't you realize that this might give Vince a motive for killing Brett?"

She gasped. Clearly she had not realized it. "No it doesn't! That's ridiculous. Besides Vince has an alibi, and the sheriff checked it out."

One of the other volunteers came downstairs. Jenny and I guiltily moved apart. I strolled over to the far wall and studied framed black-and-white photos of Steeple Hill's glory days. A number of them were of Steeple Hill's most famous (or infamous, according to who you asked) citizen, Cosmo Bari.

I studied these relics of the '60s curiously. My father seemed to stand out in every photo, tall, dark and dramatic; the center of every crowd. There he stood accepting the keys to the city from the town fathers-past (and looking mighty satirical). There he was with Joel and other people I didn't recognize at some kind of picnic. Cosmo was not much of a picnic-er. I leaned in to better examine the picture—especially the very pretty blonde girl laughing gaily up at him.

"Who's this?" I asked Jenny as she came up behind me.

"Who?" She peered around my shoulder. She chuckled. "She was pretty wasn't she? That's Miss Irene."

"Irene Cobb?"

"Is there another Miss Irene?"

I stared at the photograph of Irene Cobb twenty-odd years before. Tall, slim with a veil of blonde hair that fell nearly to her waist. Yes, she had been pretty once, young once, and no doubt a virgin once.

CHAPTER SIXTEEN

My grandfather's house stood dark and silent in the moonlight. Though technically mine, for now I was obliged to creep in like a thief, slipping under the police tape and shinnying up the tree in the front yard. It had been several years since I'd climbed a tree—tree climbing not being recommended for heart patients.

I reached the open window on the second story and slipped inside the house.

It was hot and stuffy and dark. I pulled my flashlight out. The beam played around the room, lighting the crucifix over the bed, the photos of my grandparents on their wedding day and my mother on ponies of various shapes and sizes. I began sifting through my grandfather's dresser. As Adam had said, everything was in apple pie order.

I wasn't sure what I was looking for; finding the *Virgin* tucked between his boxers would have been convenient. Not that I wanted to believe there was a link between my grandfather and Brett's death, but to me the connection seemed inescapable. I found my grandfather's keys on the lace doily, gleaming dully in the street lamplight. I tucked them in my jeans.

Quietly, I crept downstairs.

It was an old house. Floorboards creaked beneath phantom footfalls. The beams, which had expanded in the heat of the day, now contracted in the cool night with unnerving little groans.

I tiptoed into my grandfather's study and sat down at his desk. The drawers were closed. Locked. I pulled out the key ring and slid the keys aside looking for something small enough to fit in a desk drawer.

It was not there.

I searched the desktop and found a letter opener. It was too fat for the key slot. I pulled out my Swiss army knife and went through the blades, one by one, till I found one thin enough. I used this to pry at the lock. It was so easy in books and movies. Not so easy sweating in the darkness. There was clearly some trick to it. I closed my eyes and tried to picture the locking mechanism, flipping through the memories of pages of diagrams and templates from my research.

After what seemed an eternity of blind poking there was a gratifying click and the drawer sprang open.

I sat up, shining my flashlight inside the drawer's contents. The drawer was as neat as a pin, everything in its proper tray compartment. Next to the tray was a leather journal—also locked.

I lifted the journal out and glanced up as a floorboard cracked by the door. Because I expected to see nothing it took my eyes a moment to separate the dark figure standing motionless from the other shadows.

When at last I realized what I was staring at, my heart seemed to stop. The stillness in my body matched the stillness beside the hall. I snapped off my flashlight, rising and slowly edging toward the door at the opposite end of the room.

The silent figure moved away from the doorway.

"Who are you?" I asked. "What do you want?"

It was not so much that I expected an answer as I wanted my apparition to speak. That purposeful silence was terrifying.

The figure took another step forward and tripped over one of those small tapestry footstools my unknown grandmother had been so fond of.

As he went sprawling, I bolted for the door which led into the kitchen.

The kitchen was long and narrow, the door leading to the backyard was at the opposite end. I ran for the door, unbolted it, yanked it open but there was a chain at the top and it held.

My pursuer crashed through the doorway as I scrabbled at the chain. The part of my brain that could think, noted that he was tall, and that the reason I could not see his face was because he wore a black ski mask.

Picking up one of the kitchen table chairs, he advanced on me, raising it high. There was no time to think; I had no experience, and I knew I couldn't hold up long in a fight. I grabbed the teakettle off the stove and threw it at him.

He ducked and struck at the kettle which hit the floor, spilling water. As he threw the chair at me he slipped on the water, his aim spoiled. I scrambled toward the entrance to the dining room.

The chair hit my side and I fell half on top of it, which hurt enough to galvanize me into new action. I continued anteater fashion toward the doorway, pulling out and emptying drawers as I regained my feet.

Silverware, candles, pot holders, tools clattered down on the hardwood floor. My pursuer paused, feeling among the forks and boxes of matches, to rise up, hammer in hand.

I became aware that someone was breathlessly swearing and praying, and that it was me. My assailant swung the hammer at me, and some instinct or forgotten movie memory guided me. I yanked open the dry goods cupboard door, and the hammer smashed into it with such force it wedged in the wood.

Astonishment held my attacker still for a split-second. I dived for his legs. He crashed down like a felled redwood, his head striking the edge of the table with a sickening cracking sound. He slid to the floor, and lay still, practically lined up with the chalk outline of where my grandfather's body had lain.

Putting my hand to my chest, I worked to get my breath. After a moment's struggle I could breathe again. My heart was galloping away but was relatively steady.

I got over to the phone and called the Sheriff's Department. Then I grabbed one of those long white dishcloths, and headed back to my fallen foe whose weak gurgles signified returning consciousness.

I pulled the ski mask off. Blonde hair shone brightly in the moonlight streaming through the window over the sink. For a shocked moment I thought I was seeing Brett. Then I recognized Jack Cobb.

* * * * *

"He says he didn't murder anyone," Sheriff Rankin told me over a cup of bitter coffee. "Not Hansen and not your grandpappy."

I tore my gaze away from the wanted posters on the bulletin board. We were sitting in the sheriff's station. Jack had been booked and was now sitting in a jail cell while Mayor Cobb, his gray hair sticking up like a rooster's comb, pajama shirt hanging out beneath his jacket, was signing his life away at the front desk.

"You don't believe him?"

The sheriff noncommittally slurped his coffee.

"He tried to kill me."

"He says no. Says he wanted what you found at Aaron's house."

"I didn't find anything."

"Uh huh." The sheriff eyed me with an uncomfortably keen gaze.

Getting the conversation back on track, I reminded him, "He tried to cave my head in with a hammer."

"He says he just wanted to frighten you."

"He succeeded. Does he have an alibi for Brett's murder, or for my grandfather's?"

"We're checking on that."

I thought back to the moonlit house, to his silent purposefulness, and I said, "He would have killed me if he could have."

But Rankin looked unconvinced. "You were right about one thing anyway."

"What's that?"

"Cobb admits he stole that painting of your father's. Like to tell me how you knew that?"

"A lucky guess. He was the first person to leave the party. No one could positively remember seeing the painting after the argument between Vince and myself. By then Jack had split."

Rankin studied me grimly. "That so?"

"Yep. Where is it?"

"You won't like it."

"Tell me anyway."

"Says he destroyed it. Burned it in the cellar furnace."

"Burned it?"

Rankin nodded.

I whispered, "Burned a million-dollar painting?"

"So he says."

"Does he say why?"

"Says he wanted to get back at Berkowitz."

"For what?"

"It's sorta vague," Rankin admitted. "Don't worry, we're getting a search warrant. If the painting still exists, we'll find it."

I doubted it.

*   *   *   *   *

I spent the rest of that night reading my grandfather's journal. Toward dawn I fell asleep; my dreams chaotic. I was pursued by men in black, I pursued faceless phantoms, I argued with Adam—and Adam's features melted into a black ski mask...

When I woke it was late, the hot sun streamed in. I staggered into the bathroom, relieved myself and studied my face in the mirror. I needed a shave and there was a pillow-crease running down the side of my cheek like a scar. I had to wonder if Adam didn't have a point about the self-destructiveness of my quest. And yet I couldn't stop now. I was too close. Though my grandfather's journal was not proof, his suspicions and resentments gave credence to my own wild speculation.

I knew now that the truth would bring me no happiness, but I also knew, until I had the truth I would know no peace.

The cops had come and gone by the time I reached Miss Irene's. She ushered me in, offering lemonade and fresh-baked brownies.

I sat in the Cobbs' parlor, staring at a painting Cosmo had done of an old moss-covered bridge. The bridge had been torn down, but it lived forever in my father's work. I thought of *Virgin in Pastel*'s sad fate.

As I sipped a glass of lemonade Miss Irene explained that the mayor and her nephew were seeing a lawyer, and then she flushed painfully and launched into some awkward apologies for Jack's "rude" behavior.

"I—I don't know what the silly boy could have been thinking," she said twice. The second time she said it I took her up on it.

"I do."

"You do?" she quavered.

"I think so. And I think I know why he destroyed *Virgin in Pastel*."

Miss Irene's color faded, leaving her bone white. I tried to be gentle. I said, "You were the model, weren't you, Miss Irene?"

She stared at me mutely.

"You were the model for *Virgin in Pastel*."

Her lips parted but no words came forth. Her green eyes looked stricken. Finally she nodded.

"Were you lovers? You and my father?"

She gasped as though I had struck her.

"What happened to my father, Miss Irene? What happened that night?"

"W-what night? Nothing happened. He left. Cosmo left. He left me."

"I don't believe that."

"But it's *true*," she said quite desperately. "You have to believe it. It's the truth."

"You were lovers. At least for a time."

"N-no—I was just a girl. Unmarried. I—I wouldn't have. It wouldn't have been right. It would have been *wrong*."

"Miss Irene, what can it matter now? I know you were the model for *Virgin in Pastel*. I saw your photo at the museum. At Cobb House."

"Photo? What photo?" She sounded scandalized. "What photos can you mean, Kyle?"

"Photographs of some picnic. Once I saw the resemblance, I knew." My grandfather had suspected as well.

Miss Irene stared at me like a rabbit gazing up a gunsight.

"That's why Jack stole the painting, isn't it? Somehow he recognized it. He took it and he destroyed it because he was afraid of what it meant."

"Jack wouldn't steal anything," Miss Irene disagreed feebly.

"Yes, he would. To protect you. Because he loves you. Because you're the only mother he's known. He thought the painting proved you really were his mother, and that's why he took it."

Miss Irene began to cry, a weak plaintive sound.

"But you're not his mother, are you? The rumors in high school were wrong. There was a baby, but not Jack. The baby was Brett."

At Brett's name she threw her head back and wailed. It was a shocking sound.

"My baby," she howled.

"Miss Irene," I exclaimed. I jumped to my feet and awkwardly patted her shoulder. "Don't cry. Please."

"My baby," she wept.

I poured her some lemonade.

"Here, drink this."

She shook her head. "You don't understand. You want to blame it all on Jack but it's not Jack's fault. None of it's Jack's fault. It was my fault. Mine and Cosmo's."

"Why is it anyone's fault?"

"Because it was *wrong*," Miss Irene cried. "It was immoral and wrong. I knew it, if he didn't. I tried to end it but—" She shook her head sadly. "I loved him so," she whispered.

"What happened that night, Miss Irene?"

"Nothing happened. Why do you keep saying that? I went to him and begged him not to show that painting. He had promised me." Her eyes fell from mine. Her hand went up nervously to her throat. "He promised never to show that—that thing. I reminded him of his promise, and he—he agreed."

"That doesn't sound like Cosmo," I had to say.

Miss Irene blinked her wet lashes at me. "He agreed," she repeated stubbornly. "And he went away."

"Where did he go?"

She shook her head.

"Why did he go?"

Another shake of her untidy gray head.

"Miss Irene, you're not telling me everything."

She said with unexpected dignity, "Why should I tell you everything? I have a right to my own secrets."

I guess if anyone should have understood that, it was me.

Anyway, I didn't really need her confirmation. Between my grandfather's informed suspicions and my own wild speculation, I was pretty sure of my facts.

"The night of the party," I said, "You were staring at Brett's anklet. You recognized it, didn't you?"

Some kind of internal struggle seemed to take place. "It was my necklace," she said. "The necklace he gave me. I would have known it anywhere. And he was wearing it on his foot. Like a trashy piece of jewelry. I don't believe he could have been my little boy." Tears brimmed in her faded eyes; she blinked them away. "I don't believe that."

"Who gave you the necklace?" I knew. I don't even know why I was asking.

"Cosmo." Her chin raised. "He was like that, you know. So brusque and so...hard. But now and again he could be...different. Oh, he could charm the birds out of the trees when he put his mind to it."

Out of the trees and out of their frilly little dresses and their frilly little moralities. And why the hell did I feel so bad about it? What did any of it have to do with me?

"Did you kill him? Did you kill my father?" The strained sound of my voice startled me.

But Miss Irene reacted like she'd received an electric shock. "Kyle Bari, what a heartless boy you are! You don't know anything about people!"

CHAPTER SEVENTEEN

It took the largest key from my grandfather's key ring and fitted it in the rusted padlock. After a couple of tries it turned, the chains holding the door slipped free and fell clinking to the stone steps of the graveyard chapel.

I shoved the heavy, weathered door which opened with a screech of arthritic hinges.

Despite the bright sunlight it was damp and dark, moldering as the grave inside the old church.

I switched on the flashlight and picked my way across the broken planks. As my eyes adjusted to the poor light I could make out cobwebs draped from the carved lintel posts. I stared up and felt my hair rise like porcupine quills. The vault ceiling seemed to ripple like the underbelly of a sleeping animal—hundreds of bats hung from the rafters.

"Jesus," I said softly. Although I kind of figured Jesus didn't live here anymore.

Drawn toward the chancel, magnetized as though by true north, I walked down the aisle. I set the flashlight down on the altar, propping its beam toward the apse. There, as I remembered from my childhood, was a long stone bench perhaps originally intended as a reliquary.

I set my strength to pushing aside the lid, several pounds of solid stone. As I gripped it I realized that it was actually a slab of marble, beautiful and cool beneath the layers of dirt, dust and mouse droppings.

The lid scraped over, inch by inch, until my final heave slid it clear across. It teetered, and then fell with a thump that sent the furry ceiling rippling and flapping.

A bat detached itself from the mass and swooped down, squeaking.

I grabbed the flashlight and yelled, swinging at it. Heroic stuff. The flashlight ray slid across the roof like search beams. The bat flapped away, and I lowered my arm. I was barely conscious of my victory, my attention riveted by what lay entombed in the marble case.

A skeleton lay grinning up at me in the spotlight of my torch. Time and nature had done their work. The empty sockets stared; the gaping mouth was stuffed with the remnants of a mouse nest. The print had long ago faded off the rotten tatters, but I recognized the shirt and the gold band on the bones of his left hand.

I whispered, "Father?" though he was long past hearing, long past answering. There was a split down the center of the skull, cleaving it nearly in two. My whisper echoed emptily round the church.

The band of light at the chapel entrance vanished as the door swung shut.

"This is just too bad," a familiar voice said conversationally into the darkness. "Just too darned bad."

I turned my flashlight toward the voice. There, like a convict caught in the glare of the jailbreak searchlights, stood Mayor Cobb in his khaki shorts and straw sun hat. Binoculars hung around his neck; he held a gun which was pointed at me.

Switching off the light before he could use it to target me, I knelt beside my father's tomb.

"Why?" My husky echo repeated itself over and over down the empty aisles stripped of pews.

Mayor Cobb chuckled. Maybe it was a silly question.

"Why? You know why. The bastard would have bled us dry—that's assuming he could have kept his mouth shut."

"Not Brett. Cosmo. My father."

Silence.

There was a sliver of light shining through one of the wooden slates boarding the windows. I could see the blue of stain glass, a glimpse of a wimple like the cowl of the Virgin Mary.

Like that, memory came flooding back: the knock at the window which only half woke me, sending me barefoot and still dreaming across the meadow and into the woods to see the blue woman. A stained glass face? Yes, but something else: a woman's face turning blue. A woman being choked. And voices…yelling. Arguing.

"They used to meet here," Mayor Cobb explained, as though trying to persuade me to his viewpoint. "She thought I didn't know. Hell, the whole county knew. Then it was over and she was in trouble. I told her to get rid of it. He told her to get rid of it. But no, she had to have it. Came back and bit us in the butt, didn't it?"

"Brett? She gave Brett up for adoption. But he tracked her down. And then he tried to blackmail you."

"Yup. He thought he'd hit a live one with Irene."

In books people always keep the murderers talking to stall for time. I wasn't stalling. I had to know the truth.

"Why did you kill my father?"

Even after all this time, the righteous indignation was still in his voice.

"After everything we'd been through, he was going to show that god-damn painting for all the world to see. After he promised her he wouldn't. His word was shit. I tried to tell her that, but she wouldn't listen. I followed her when she came to meet him that night. It was shameful. She was like a bitch in heat. Here I thought it was all over, and she'd learned her lesson, but at the chance of seeing him again…and here he was betraying her! I couldn't stand it. I could have choked the life out of her."

I tried to use this to glue together the broken pieces of my memory.

I said slowly, "But he stopped you? You fought?"

"The silly thing ran home crying, and I had to deal with it as usual. I offered him money. I told him what it meant to us—to her. He didn't give a damn about anyone but himself. He tried to walk away from me. Arrogant ass. I threw a punch. We fought."

"You killed him." This memory would not come, and maybe that was a blessing. There was a reason my mind had nailed down the shutters ten years ago, but it wasn't hard to guess what had happened. "You picked something up and hit him."

"The sickle left by your grandfather that day was leaning against the building. I picked it up and I—" he paused as though the memory of that was a little too real, too horrific.

"And you killed him."

"It was an accident," Mayor Cobb said automatically. "I kind of lost my temper."

"And then you dragged his body inside the church and hid it."

"He was no loss. I don't expect you to understand. Irene understood. As much as she understands anything. Aaron understood."

"My grandfather knew?"

There was nothing written in his journal, nothing at all for the month of July that year. I guess that should have tipped me off.

"He's the one who padlocked the church. Next day I came back, and it was bolted up. Windows boarded. He knew. He had to know."

"He covered for you. Why did you kill him?"

The mayor blustered, "Who says I—"

"Or did he think it was Irene?"

No comment from the mayor.

It made sense though. My grandfather had that old-fashioned chivalry reflex. He'd have sympathized with Irene as yet another woman wronged by Cosmo. He'd have covered for her.

I worked it out aloud. "But then you killed Brett, and he must have guessed. Cosmo was one thing, but your own nephew—"

"Kid, you are stupid," my elected public servant informed me. "Aaron didn't give a rat's ass about that faggot. He was afraid you'd poke your damn nose into it. He heard you were asking questions, checking county records."

If I poked my nose in, I'd be next on the mayor's hit parade. This was a man not afraid to sneak into my house and swipe my medication (probably during my morning swim). The bird watching gave Cobb the perfect excuse for wandering around the colony, but he must have had nerves of steel to tamper with the dock on the beach below Adam's cottage.

"That was a damn shame about Aaron, but I couldn't trust him not to tell you," the mayor said. He sounded like he was bent over. I could hear him moving around.

I moved as well, feeling my way through the darkness.

"This is a regular murder epidemic you've got going. You think the sheriff is going to buy it?"

"I think the sheriff is going to do his duty and arrest Adam MacKinnon any day now. He's the only one with a motive. Pervert. You people are not right in the head. Unbalanced. Hysterical."

Oh yeah, but he, the homicidal maniac, he was an up and up guy.

"So you're going to shoot me?"

"With my own gun? Heavens no! This has to seem like an accident. Or at least like it could be an accident. Anyhow, I'm going to burn this place down, raze it to ashes like I should have done years ago."

I opened my mouth to point out the obvious flaw in this plan.

There was a screech of hinges, a burst of sunlight. Mayor Cobb's shadow filled the doorway for an instant, and then the door shut once more leaving me in darkness.

Sprinting to the door, I found it locked tight. The wood was old but solid. I tried ramming my shoulder against it a couple of times but no go.

"Cobb, I already called the sheriffs!"

No answer. Maybe he couldn't hear me. Maybe he didn't believe me.

Standing back, I took a couple of deep breaths, telling myself to keep calm. From outside I could hear a dragging sound, and more alarmingly, I could smell smoke. The stench of gasoline seeped beneath the door.

There was no way this was going to look like an accident to anyone who was paying attention, but I didn't know if that was much comfort. I tried to reassure myself that someone in the colony would notice flames—fire—but would it be too late?

Stumbling and groping my way across the uneven floor, I headed for the stairs leading to the bell tower. I stepped on the first rung and it gave way.

Sweat popped out on my forehead. "Please, God…" My heart fluttered in my throat.

The second rung held.

I began to climb, coughing. Already the smoke was heavy, and the crackle of flames deafened. Crackle? This was so much louder than I could have imagined—a wall of roaring sound.

Weird to be in the center of the hearth. The church was going up like a tinderbox. I had maybe minutes. Maybe less.

The bats flew in a cloud of flapping wings around me. High and eerie, their squeaks deafened me as they swirled like a black tornado heading for the open bell tower.

The heat radiating through the walls was incredible. I scrambled up the last rungs of the ladder. As I made it to the top, the rotten floor collapsed under my foot. I grabbed for the bell rope and the old bell rang out loud and clear, booming alarm across the church yard, woods and meadow. It rang loudly enough to wake the dead.

Regaining my balance, I crawled to the side. Looked down. I had a great view of the entire colony. Mayor Cobb's Chevy was cutting a blue streak down the highway and coming to meet it from across the other end I could see the sheriff's black-and-white approaching.

So Rankin had received my message. That was good. It wouldn't take him long to put two and two together.

I had an omniscient view of Cobb's fate—and my own. No one could get to me in time now. I had one option. I could jump—I would have to—and hope I wasn't unlucky enough to break anything vital on a three-story drop.

And then like a hallucination, I heard Adam shouting my name over and over. I looked down, got a dizzying zoom of Adam, his sweaty face streaked with black. He stood in the shadow of the steeple, gesturing to me.

The boards across the stained glass windows groaned and then shrieked. Glass shattered inside the church.

"Get a ladder," I yelled.

I doubt if he understood me. I sure as hell couldn't hear him. I didn't need to hear him to know that there was no time. Already the flames were licking at my tower. The smoke billowed around us.

"Jump!" Adam gestured. "Jump and I'll break your fall."

Yeah, and we could have two broken necks instead of one. I looked desperately around to see if there was any way to climb down. The sloping roof looked like my best shot. If I could jump from the tower, land on the roof and not immediately slide off into the inferno, I would be forty feet closer to the ground, and my chances proportionally higher.

"Kyle, for Christ's sake, jump!" I could hear Adam screaming. He was too close to the building now, oblivious to the flames starting up around him. Oblivious to the falling planks and glass. His eyes streamed tears from the smoke. "Now, Kyle!"

Most people would rather die than think.

I heard my father as clearly as though he stood at my elbow. That lazy, slightly sardonic voice—as familiar as my own. That was one of his favorite sayings—and what a weird time to remember...

I stared down at the rope still wrapped around my hand and a belated thought occurred to me. Edging over to the ledge, gripping the rope tight, I let myself over the side. I thought I could ease myself down, but it didn't work like that. There was no traction for my foot and I dropped as though a scaffold had opened up beneath me, the force nearly yanking my arms from their sockets.

For a moment I dangled there while Adam yelled frantic instructions that I couldn't understand.

I squinted through my tears, and through the smoke I could see shingles peeling up on the sloping roof beneath me, and the red ribs of the building showing through.

The heat was ferocious. My skin would start to melt soon.

If I let go I was liable to fall through the crumbling roof into a barbecue. And if I didn't let go I would die of smoke inhalation and the heat. My arms shook with the strain; my heart punched furiously at the wall of my chest.

Hazily I thought, if my heart lasts through this I'm good for the duration.

Beneath me Adam was incoherent with swearing, praying and orders.

There was nothing for it. *Oh, shit,* I thought, and let go.

I landed in a half-crouch on the roof. My feet slid, stuck, and I did a kind of head-first dive off the edge, arms outstretched and mouth open in a yowl of sheer terror.

The grass rushed forward as I plummeted down.

Somehow he caught me. Sort of. We collided hard and painfully. His arms locked around me and he staggered back with a grunt, the wind knocked out of his lungs. Falling back in the shriveling grass, he sprawled there with me on top. Not moving.

After a stunned moment I rolled off him.

"Adam? Adam, are you okay?"

He nodded. I leaned over him; tears from the smoke streamed down his soot-smeared face, half concealing the black-eye I'd given him. He wheezed up at me.

"Are you okay?" I urged.

He wheezed some more, tried to get up. I grabbed his arm and we scuttled back from the intense heat of the flames now engulfing the building. Cinders blew in the air.

I watched it go in a kind of shock, starting when Adam reached to brush an ember out of my hair.

"Jesus, Kyle," he said hoarsely. "I thought you were dead." His face worked and he turned away. After a moment he wiped his face with the back of his arm. "Jesus."

Another spark landed on his shoulder. I brushed at it.

"How did you know I was in there?"

He turned toward me and I was shaken by the raw emotion carving his features. "Because I waited for you," he said. "I waited for you to come home. So that we could talk. So that we could work this out." He wiped roughly at the tears running down his face. "I saw you come home and I saw you start out across the meadow. I followed you."

Sirens shrieked in the distance; Steeple Hill's fire brigade arriving better late than never.

"You saved my life."

"No," he said. "You saved your own life. I could never have got to you in time."

A terrifying groaning seemed to split the sky above us.

I whispered, "What the—?"

We scrambled back as the bell tower slowly gave way, and the old bell crashed down, tolling one final time as it hit the ground. The trees shook. Red embers drifted down across the gravestones and statues like red snow. The bell's final reverberation echoed like a death knell.

When the sound at last died away, Sheriff Rankin's black-and-white had pulled to a stop outside the cemetery fence. The car door opened and Adam and I rose to our feet.

* * * * *

"So she did know," I said.

It was later that evening. I'd had a couple of hours sleep and was feeling weirdly calm as Sheriff Rankin explained that he had been delayed in meeting me due to a visit from Miss Irene. She had brought him Brett's anklet.

"She seems to blame herself." I wasn't sure if that was agreement or not. Rankin was smoking a pipe, the homely scent comforting in the twilight room. I glanced at Adam, who had arrived with the sheriff after giving his statement. He was staring down into his snifter of brandy.

"There are still a lot of questions," Rankin said heavily.

Mayor Cobb had been arrested and taken to jail. A forensics team was sifting through the rubble of the church.

I said, "I guess that's so." For me, the main question had been answered.

As though he felt my gaze, Adam lifted his head, and the hands cradling my own snifter were suddenly not quite steady. So maybe I wasn't quite as calm as I thought. And maybe there was still a question or two.

Rankin smoked and talked for another hour or so and then he got to his feet and offered Adam a ride back to his place.

Adam said quietly, "Kyle and I have some things to say to each other." His blue gaze challenged mine.

I shrugged and said, "Sure," as though my pulse hadn't sped up.

"Okay dokey," Rankin said in the tone of one who did not want to know. "I'll see myself out then."

The screen door opened and closed. His heavy footsteps sounded on the porch steps. The clock on the mantel tick-tocked out a few moments of crickets and then we heard the rumble of the police cruiser's engine. The crunch of tires on shell and gravel.

I looked at Adam. Waited.

He said quietly, "You've been through enough for one day. I just wanted to say…we've been friends a long time. I don't want to lose that." He set his glass down and rose.

It was so not what I was expecting. I couldn't seem to think of anything to say. I stared at him and stared—and then I nodded. Curtly.

But I must have looked as stricken as I felt because he hesitated. "I don't know what you want, Kyle. I don't know why love doesn't seem to be enough. I don't know how to reach you."

Love. There it was, out in the open. But was that what I had been waiting for: the word?

A little desperately, I said, "I don't know what's wrong with me. I don't know why I can't accept what you're offering. What you seem to be offering me."

Instead of answering he asked curiously, "Are you afraid of me?"

"No." Not of him. Of what he could do to me—of how badly he could hurt me without ever meaning to. Still, I could see why the thought crossed his mind; my voice was breathless and shaky at this moment of truth. My mouth was dry; the words came out thick and gummy. "I'm at risk for developing heart failure."

"But you've known you were at risk since you were sixteen," he said very gently.

I blinked. It was like staring at the tiny wrecked galleon in a fish bowl. Gigantic moss-covered tragedy through the glass—and nothing but painted plastic bits from above. It's all in the perspective. Adam was right. I had always known this. What had changed? I had always accepted the odds.

Now I have something to lose…

He waited for me to speak, and when I said nothing he sat down across from me again. Something eased inside me. He wasn't going to walk out the door. Not yet anyway.

His eyes were very blue in the lamplight. Very grave. I thought he was going to ask about what my tests indicated. Instead he said, "That first time I saw Brett, he was staring at one of Cosmo's paintings. And because of the shadows—because of the way the light fell—for a moment I thought he was you." His smile was derisive, but the mockery was for himself, not me. "And I had a sense of recognition. Of certainty. I thought to myself, I always knew—and then he turned. And he wasn't you."

"And the rest, as they say, is history," I said in a brittle voice that didn't sound like me at all.

"When I saw you again—when you opened the door to me this past June—it hit me all over again. That feeling of certainty. Of knowing."

I couldn't speak.

"It's not easy telling you this. It feels like a betrayal of Brett. And I did love Brett."

"But you wouldn't have left him."

"No. Brett had too many people abandon him; I couldn't have done that to him." He finished compassionately, "Because I know what it did to you."

My laugh sounded like something else. I stood up and walked to the fireplace where *Virgin in Pastel* had once hung. I could see Adam watching me in the mirror.

He said softly, "But Brett would have left me."

I turned and he was there.

* * * * *

A few days after being charged with attempted murder, Mayor Cobb made a full confession. Miss Irene was granted immunity for cooperating with the police. Cosmo's fate was a nine-day wonder, and the prices on his paintings skyrocketed once again.

A week after we buried my grandfather, we held a private memorial service for my father in the old cemetery. Wild flowers were already beginning to poke up through the blackened ruins.

I stood there holding Adam's hand, feeling surprisingly little. Joel cried. Even Micky cried. I could sense Adam watching me, waiting for it to hit me. I, too, had expected to feel more.

On the night following Cobb's attempt to kill me, Adam and I had continued to talk until dawn, and in the end we agreed on one thing: we loved each other. How far that would take us, neither of us knew. If I learned one thing that summer, it was to appreciate each day. Life is fragile and fleeting as a bubble blown on a child's plastic pipe. A walk in the woods can be the last walk you take, with words left unsaid, questions left unanswered. Not many people check out with the loose ends neatly tied up. There were enough question marks in my future to make me value the certainties.

"There's a major meteor shower going on," Adam said at breakfast a few days after we had laid Cosmo to rest. "The Perseids." He folded up the newspaper. "What do you say we zip our sleeping bags together and camp out under the stars tonight?"

He was smiling, his eyes kind and attentive, tilting up at the corners in the old way. For the first time in a long time I felt my heart lighten.

"Sure, let's give the owls something to hoot about," I agreed.

"I'll bring the hot chocolate."

"What do I bring? Marshmallows?"

He raised an exaggeratedly lustful eyebrow. "No need to get fancy. Just the standard equipment, sonny boy."

I pushed back from the table and checked. "I think it's all still here."

"It seemed to be last night."

"Maybe we should check to make sure…"

At last Adam took off to finish the final painting of his fall exhibit: a portrait of Brett and me which he was completing from sketches he had done that summer. I thought it was one of the best things he'd ever done.

I went home to work. But after a few minutes I rose and went to the bookshelves, thumbing through my father's astronomy books. I remembered him pointing out the constellations to me on clear midsummer nights; hand on my shoulder, facing me toward the stars.

"Did you know the full moon of each month has its own name?"

"What's the July moon called?"

"July's moon is the thunder moon."

He had all the answers, my father. He knew things no one else knew, and his deep voice resonated in my subconscious as the voice of supreme masculine authority. I had never really known him. Never understood him, but how I had admired him. His strength, his confidence, his utter self-sufficiency.

And how I had loved him.

A square of butcher's paper fell out from between the pages of star charts and photographs. A keepsake of the man who kept nothing.

Curiously, I unfolded the paper.

I stared at it for a long time, till the colors prismed through the tears blurring my vision. It was a child's drawing: red and yellow monster fish swimming and smiling in a navy-blue ocean. No sign of budding artistic genius there.

I turned over the yellowed paper. In my father's crisp, black hand was written, *Kyle, age 5.*

AUTHORS NOTE

Murder in Pastel *was started around the same time as* **Fatal Shadows**. *Originally it was written for my own amusement and there was no intention to publish it -- especially since I had used so many of the same themes and motifs (not to mention actual bits and pieces) of* **Fatal Shadows**. *But it remained one of my personal favorites, and I simply liked it too much not to share it.*

Initially, I self-published using the pen name "Colin Dunne." Later I sold the story to an indie publisher. Both times readers instantly recognized the Lanyon writing "voice," and it seemed best to let the novel go out of print. So I did.

But **Murder in Pastel** *belongs in the Lanyon catalog, and so I've had it re-edited and I've commissioned a wonderful cover by Johanna Ollila that brilliantly echoes Giorgio de Chirico's "Mystery and Melancholy of a Street".*

I hope you enjoy the return of one of my favorite stories.

ABOUT THE AUTHOR

A distinct voice in gay fiction, multi-award-winning author JOSH LANYON has been writing gay mystery, adventure and romance for over a decade. In addition to numerous short stories, novellas, and novels, Josh is the author of the critically acclaimed Adrien English series, including **The Hell You Say**, *winner of the 2006 USABookNews awards for GLBT Fiction. Josh is an Eppie Award winner and a four-time Lambda Literary Award finalist.*

Find other Josh Lanyon titles at **www.joshlanyon.com** *Follow Josh on* **Twitter**, **Facebook**, *and* **Goodreads**.

ALSO BY THE AUTHOR

NOVELS

The ADRIEN ENGLISH Mysteries

Fatal Shadows

A Dangerous Thing

The Hell You Say

Death of a Pirate King

The Dark Tide

Stranger Things Have Happened

The HOLMES & MORIARITY Mysteries

Somebody Killed His Editor

All She Wrote

The Boy with the Painful Tattoo

The ALL'S FAIR Series

Fair Game

Fair Play

The SHOT IN THE DARK Series

This Rough Magic

OTHER NOVELS

The Ghost Wore Yellow Socks

Mexican Heat (with Laura Baumbach)

Strange Fortune

Come Unto These Yellow Sands

Stranger on the Shore

NOVELLAS

The DANGEROUS GROUND Series

Dangerous Ground

Old Poison

Blood Heat

Dead Run

Kick Start

The I SPY Series

I Spy Something Bloody

I Spy Something Wicked

I Spy Something Christmas

The IN A DARK WOOD Series

In a Dark Wood

The Parting Glass

The DARK HORSE Series

The Dark Horse

The White Knight

The DOYLE & SPAIN Series

Snowball in Hell

The HAUNTED HEART Series

Haunted Heart: Winter

The XOXO FILES Series

Mummy Dearest